WAYNE STINNETT

RISING CHARITY

A JESSE MCDERMITT NOVEL

Caribbean Adventure Series

Volume 14

2019

Copyright © 2019
Published by DOWN ISLAND PRESS, LLC, 2019
Beaufort, SC

Library of Congress cataloging-in-publication Data

Stinnett, Wayne
Rising Charity/Wayne Stinnett
p. cm. – (A Jesse McDermitt novel)

ISBN-13: 978-1-7322360-4-2 (Down Island Press)
ISBN-10: 1-7322360-4-6

Cover photograph by Goran Jakus Photography
Graphics by Wicked Good Book Covers
Edited by The Write Touch
Final Proofreading by Donna Rich
Interior Design by Ampersand Book Designs

This is a work of fiction. Names, characters, and incidents are either the product of the author's imagination or are used fictitiously. Any resemblance to actual persons, living or dead, businesses, companies, events, or locales is entirely coincidental. Most of the locations herein are also fictional or are used fictitiously. However, I take great pains to depict the location and description of the many well-known islands, locales, beaches, reefs, bars, and restaurants throughout the Florida Keys and the Caribbean, to the best of my ability.

FOREWORD

I had a whole lot of fun writing this book. Parts of it were co-written with Kimberli Bindschatel, and her characters appear here and as do mine in her new book, *Operation: Dolphin Spirit*. The fun part was that we both write in first person. That choice of narrative technique illustrates how two people can see, hear, or feel the same thing, yet have two completely distinct interpretations. We kept the action and dialogue exactly the same in both versions, but Jesse and Kimberli's character, Poppy McVie, don't always see things the same way.

Great appreciation goes to my pre-editing team for helping to hammer out the logistics and details to get everything just right. Thank you to Dan Horn, Dana Vilhen, Tom Crisp, Ron Ramey, Katy McKnight, Charles Hofbauer, Drew Mutch, Mike Ramsey, Debbie Kocol, Marc Lowe, Glenn Hibbert, Torrey Neill, and my special gratitude to Gary Cox, who gets a big nod of thanks for the basic plot of this and many stories to come. You've given Jesse direction again, cobber.

As always, I must thank my wife, Greta, for all her help and support. The weekends and evenings during which I'd been lost in Jesse's story, or off to writer's conferences and book signings have been many. The two of us wouldn't be where we are today if we weren't, we. They say two halves make a whole, but in our case, Greta and I become more than a whole.

A man without a family to work and strive for has nothing. Our kids, Nikki, Laura, Richard, and Jordan have been very supportive in my new writing career. Going into 2019, my sixth year as an author, I can honestly say that none of what I've accomplished so far would have come to pass if not for them. There wouldn't have been any reason for it all.

I hope you enjoy this story. It's been a while, I know. The last one was published nearly six months ago. I promise the next one will come sooner. If you read Nick Sullivan's novel, *Deep Shadow*, you may recall a familiar and salty character who plucked the hero and heroine from the sea at the end. He called himself Stretch Buchanan, and he was aboard an old steel-hulled Seaton trawler called *Floridablanca*. Stretch is the name Jesse has used a few times, to keep his identity secret. Well, that was a future Jesse in Nick's book. And in Rising Charity, you'll see the building of the framework needed to put Stretch off the coast of Saba in time to pull Boone and Emily from the water.

If you'd like to receive my twice-monthly newsletter for specials, book recommendations, and updates on coming books, please sign up on my website:

WWW.WAYNESTINNETT.COM

Charity Styles Series
Merciless Charity
Ruthless Charity
Reckless Charity
Enduring Charity

Jesse McDermitt Series
Fallen Out
Fallen Palm
Fallen Hunter
Fallen Pride
Fallen Mangrove
Fallen King
Fallen Honor
Fallen Tide
Fallen Angel
Fallen Hero
Rising Storm
Rising Fury
Rising Force

THE GASPAR'S REVENGE SHIP'S STORE IS OPEN.

There, you can purchase all kinds
of swag related to my books.

WWW.GASPARS-REVENGE.COM

DEDICATION

This story is dedicated to the folks at Lady's Island Marina, where I have my office, my boat, and many friends. Remember, whenever I'm around, anything you say or do is fodder for fiction.

"You know, as a writer—I'm more of a listener than a writer, cuz if I hear something, I *will* write it down."

– Jimmy Buffett

MAPS

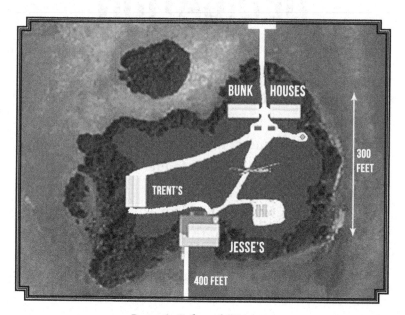

Jesse's Island Home

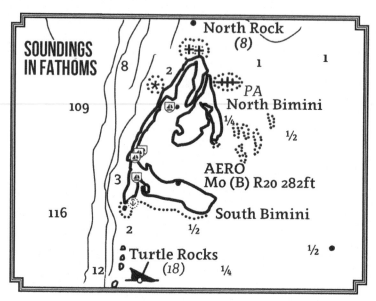

Bimini, The Bahamas

CHAPTER
ONE

On a nearly barren promontory jutting out into Monterey Bay stands the oldest continuously active lighthouse on the west coast. Point Pinos Lighthouse rises above the rocky shoreline at the southern end of the bay and has been guiding mariners to safe harbor for more than 150 years.

Unlike many lighthouses, the Point Pinos light rises only slightly above the roof of the tender's home, which was built around it. The high headland itself lifts the house well above the Pacific Ocean and Monterey Bay. Its piercing light can be seen for fifteen nautical miles out at sea, conditions permitting.

But on that early spring morning on the coast of California, conditions weren't so permitting. The sky was gray with broken clouds scudding in off the ocean from a storm building to the north. The air was a brisk 60 degrees and seemed to be charged by the approaching gale. Though the wind blew steady at fifteen knots, an occasional gust would rattle the windows of the old lighthouse. To the west, out over the Pacific, the horizon was shrouded in mist.

Inland, just a couple hundred yards from the lighthouse, were the unnaturally green fields of Pacific Grove Golf Links and El Carmelo Cemetery. The color of the verdant sloping hills was a sharp contrast to the muted browns, grays, and greens of the uneven natural landscape.

Two men were watching through binoculars from the observation deck of the lighthouse. They'd arrived before dawn. And they weren't looking out to sea.

One of the men was tall and ruggedly built, his tanned features and graying hair a match to the natural terrain he was observing. The other man, slight and balding, appeared as if he'd be more at home on the golf course.

The two men were gazing in the direction of the links and graves. The early morning players were strolling the greens in groups, breaking up in search of their balls and the opportunity to take another swing.

Occasionally a car pulled off or on to the road near the gate to the cemetery.

"How sure are you that she'll be here?"

"I'm not," the taller man replied in a gravelly voice. "You asked where I thought she might be, and this is my best guess."

"And you haven't had contact with her in over a year?"

The tall man shifted his weight as he continued to stare through powerful binoculars. "Correct."

"So, how do you know she'll be here?"

Lowering the binos, the rugged-looking man looked down at his companion. "Like I said, I don't know. What I do know, Bremmer, is human nature. She was an only child, abandoned by her mother when she was very young and orphaned before reaching adulthood. I know she sailed into the Pacific a year ago last January. She has no family and few friends to speak of, and today marks ten years since she lost her father." He shrugged his broad shoulders. "She could be in Hong Kong for all I know. Or she might be standing right behind me. Do not take this woman's abilities lightly."

"I've read her jacket."

Travis Stockwell raised his binos again, peering toward the cemetery. "Not all her training and exploits were written in her record book. I know, I sent her."

Charlie Bremmer dressed in a gray business suit, sans the tie, looked out toward the links. "You keep alluding to that but never mention specifics. Our agency wants to know more."

"Not from me, you don't. I doubt she'll even want to be a part of your organization." Stockwell lowered his glasses and looked at the balding man. "By the way, your organization could use a better name."

"Yeah, well, that's not for me to decide," Bremmer replied, looking up at the former Airborne officer. "We're counting on you to persuade her, Colonel. You, as well as a few other people, have said she's the only person who can find McDermitt."

"What others?"

"I've spoken with two of the men in your old team," Bremmer said.

Stockwell already knew that. "Yeah, Deuce called me right after you met with him. Without McDermitt, you won't get him, and without him, his team's out of reach. McDermitt's another one who won't want to be found. What do you want with him, anyway?"

"It's not just you and Livingston who are of the opinion that he's the absolute best at infiltration."

"Yeah," Stockwell said. "There's that. He could be standing behind her, standing behind me, and neither of us would know it. But last I heard, he slipped off the deep end."

"And nobody's heard from him in over a year?"

"Have you ever been to old South Florida, Bremmer?"

"I *am* the AIC in our Miami office."

"Fishermen settled the Keys more than a century before anyone even thought about draining the swamps to build a trading post and call it Miami. The people of the Keys are tough and resilient; that's why they're called Conchs. And they look after one another. He's been back there now and again, I'm sure. But nobody on those bony rocks will say anything about it to an outsider. He's one of them."

"That was the gist of what Livingston said," Bremmer replied, looking through the binos once more. "We want him to be one of us."

"Deuce and I have talked," Stockwell said, lowering his binoculars, and turning toward the man. "None of us have agreed to anything yet. And those two? Her and McDermitt? It'll take a helluva lot more than money to win them over."

"We're counting on that," Bremmer said. He paused, leaning forward until his binoculars almost touched the glass surrounding the lighthouse's observation deck. "Is that her?"

"Yeah," Stockwell said. He'd already seen her.

The woman arrived on a small scooter, wearing jeans, a blue flannel shirt, and boots. She had a small pack on her back and parked 100 feet from where Stockwell knew her father was buried.

She climbed off her scooter and stood, looking all around. She was tall and lean, with her hair piled beneath a faded blue cap, but a few blond locks fell on either side of her face.

"She's beautiful," Bremmer said.

"She's also a cold-blooded killer, Bremmer. If you screw this up, neither of us might ever leave here. Shut up and let me do the talking."

"This is—"

"It's my meet," Stockwell said, putting away his field glasses, and glaring at the man. "She was my asset. And I think a part of her saw me as a friend. Now, let's go."

Exiting the front of the lightkeeper's house, the two men got into a white Suburban with dark-tinted glass. Though the cemetery was only 200 yards from the light-house, the rugged landscape made it faster and easier to take the road around the point. Fast and easy didn't relieve the anxiety Stockwell felt. But he knew he'd feel even more anxious out in the open.

Bremmer pulled into a parking spot just past the cemetery entrance and shut off the engine. "I hate cemeteries. Depressing use of land."

As he reached for the door handle, Stockwell stopped him with a hand on his arm. "Sit tight, Bremmer."

A narrow lane turned off the entrance road and ran parallel to the main road. Stockwell could see the scooter, leaning on its stand, but the woman was nowhere in sight.

Stockwell put both hands on his knees. "Roll down the windows and keep your hands on the wheel."

"What—"

"Just do it, Bremmer. She was expecting us."

"I don't see her."

"Me neither," Stockwell said, his eyes searching among all the headstones. "And with this lady, that's damned unnerving."

"You said she was your asset."

"I told you I haven't had any contact with her in a year," Stockwell replied. "And at that time, she suspected I might be trying to kill her. So not seeing her has me a little on edge. Best thing to do is sit tight and let her make the next move."

"You need to be a bit more forthcoming, Colonel."

Stockwell's eyes saw movement far to the left. But it was just a crow on a low tree branch, flapping its wings. "Yeah, well, in my business that shit'll get you killed."

For ten minutes, the two men sat silently in the car, looking beyond the weathered picket fence in the direction of the scooter. The only movement either man saw were occasional crows flying from tree to tree. The engine ticked as the metal cooled. An old man walked by on the road, carrying a bag.

There was the slightest sound of crunching stone outside his window, and Stockwell froze. Before he could even turn his head toward the passenger-side mirror, the long barrel of a suppressed pistol was placed against the side of his head.

"What do you want?" Charity Styles asked, her voice calm and deadly serious.

Stockwell didn't flinch. He kept both hands on his knees, and prayed Bremmer kept his on the wheel.

"Jesse's missing."

"No, the man knows exactly where he is. But you don't."

"We're just here to talk," Bremmer said. Stockwell winced slightly.

"Shut up, whoever you are," Charity hissed. "Or the next thing you *won't* feel is a nine-millimeter jacketed round exiting Stockwell's skull and entering yours."

Neither man said anything.

Charity pressed the muzzle of the suppressed handgun harder against the side of Stockwell's head. "With all due respect, Colonel, I asked you what you wanted."

Though he'd spent 30 years in service to his country in some of the most dangerous places in the world, Stockwell had only felt fear a handful of times in his career. This was one of them. In every dangerous encounter he'd had, he knew he had his soldiers around him. Now he had only Bremmer, and the woman with the gun was one of the most dangerous people he'd ever worked with. What made her truly frightening were the violent demons locked in her mind.

"We want you to find Jesse."

"Why?"

"So the man beside me can ask you and him for help."

"Unlock the back door."

Bremmer moved his left hand very slowly and pushed the button. The doors unlocked.

"Both of you," Charity ordered. "Left hand only—disarm and toss them in the back."

"I'm unarmed," Bremmer said.

"That makes you a dumbass, mister."

Slowly, Stockwell pulled his jacket open with his left hand. Even more slowly, he lifted his Colt with two fingers and moved it over his head, so Charity could see it the whole way. Releasing it, the Colt fell to the floor behind him.

"And the backup on your ankle, if you don't mind, Colonel."

Stockwell complied, and in an instant, Charity opened the back door and slid in. Stockwell didn't have to see that she'd picked up his Colt; he heard the cock of the hammer.

"You won't be offended if I don't take you at your word," she said, reaching over Bremmer's left shoulder, and holding Stockwell's pistol against the man's chest with her left hand. "Hope you're not ticklish. If you move even the slightest, you will die."

Stockwell noticed that his Colt needed only change a few degrees of angle to be pointing at him. Charity used her right hand to search under Bremmer's jacket and all around his waistband. Stockwell knew full well that she was equally adept at offhand shooting and was more than familiar with a Colt 1911. He also knew that there was a round in the chamber. As did she.

Satisfied, Charity sat back in the middle of the backseat. "How did you know where I was?"

"Your father died ten years ago," Stockwell said, quietly. "He was all you had. I took a guess. I apologize for intruding."

"You got a lot of balls interrupting me. I saw you in the lighthouse."

"We were going to wait here until you were through," Stockwell said. "We really do need your help. You know the man's true worth better than anyone. Even Deuce."

"Who's this guy?"

"Charlie Bremmer," Stockwell replied. "He can tell you who he works for."

"Well?" Charity asked, bumping the back of the other man's seat.

9

"I'm the associate-in-charge in the Miami recruiting office for Armstrong Research. I oversee the Mobile Operational Readiness Division of the company, working together with the expeditionary division."

"Say what?" Charity asked.

Travis grinned slightly.

"Armstrong Research—"

"I heard you the first time. Quite a mouthful."

"I get that a lot," Bremmer said. "We're working on it."

"And just what does this word-vomit organization want with me and Jesse?"

"I can only talk to him about that," Bremmer said, with a gulp.

"So, give Jesse a call," Charity said, slumping back in her seat. "That's what I do."

"We don't know how to reach Captain McDermitt."

"We just want to talk," Stockwell said. "Hear Armstrong out, that's all."

Charity leaned forward again and glared at Stockwell. "And how is this Armstrong *Whatever-it-is* different from what we did before?"

"For one thing," Travis began, "It seems to be privately funded. No government oversights."

"And nobody gets killed," Bremmer added.

"Seems to be?" Charity asked, ignoring Bremmer.

Someone always gets killed.

"A few others have been approached besides me." Travis turned his head toward Bremmer. "But so far they haven't been real forthcoming with enough information for me to make any decision. I was asked to find you, both because they wanted to talk to you and also so you could help find Jesse. They're also interested in Deuce and a few other people you probably never met. But Deuce and I aren't going to decide without Jesse's input."

Charity sat back in her seat. Stockwell and Bremmer slowly turned their heads. Though she looked relaxed and fully composed, it hadn't escaped Stockwell's attention that the suppressed weapon in her right hand, and his Colt in her left, were both leveled at the middle of their backs. And Bremmer had been right. She was even more beautiful than when he'd last seen her.

"Your time off seems to have agreed with you," Travis said.

"All of us?" she asked. "Working together again? Doing what, exactly?"

"For security reasons, I can't say much right now," Bremmer began, "I will tell you this. Our organization is on the good side. We're well-funded. And our intent is to thwart evil without hurting anyone."

"Big words, Bremmer," Charity said, scowling at him. "And well-rehearsed, I'm sure. But do you think I care about money, Bremmer? I have more than I can spend in two lifetimes."

"No, I don't think you care at all about material things," he replied confidently. "That's one of the reasons most of you were chosen. That and your individual skills."

"What individual skills would those be?"

"In your case," Bremmer said, "and yes, we do want you on board also, your notoriety as one of the best Olympic and long-distance swimmers of modern times. In Captain McDermitt's case, his reputation as a charter boat captain and his ability to see things others miss."

"You're tipping your hand," Charity said. "And you have nothing. Anyone who knows Jesse knows he never really liked chartering tourists."

"Yet he was once very successful at it," Bremmer said. "We're looking for a crew to operate, and supply logistics to, a small fleet of remarkable research vessels."

"Research?"

Bremmer actually smiled. "The full scope of our plans will be unveiled to very few, very closely vetted, former operatives who believe in justice and self-determination."

"More big words," Charity said. "But that's not enough to get me back into the fold. Nor Jesse, considering his current state."

Stockwell turned in his seat. "What current state?"

"Mostly drinking," she replied honestly. "And hanging around with the wrong people. But hey, the man's finally having fun. Whatever he thinks of as fun, anyway."

Bremmer's finger tapped the wheel as he studied Charity in the mirror. "That may present a problem," he said. "At any rate, I can tell you one more thing. Our goal is to collapse the plans of those who would oppose liberty and civility, whether it's socially, economically, or environmentally, in such a way that they won't be taken seriously by anyone again."

"Collapse the plans?"

"Outsmart them and make them look like fools," Stockwell said. "I asked the same question."

"The meeting will be at an as-yet-to-be-determined location," Bremmer said. "On the water, at the precise time of the vernal equinox. The coordinates will be delivered to Mister Livingston's office by private courier two days before the meet."

CHAPTER TWO

The flight was only going to last 30 minutes, so Charity relaxed and looked around the empty cabin. This was the last leg of a four-part journey during which she'd not been in control. For the last three years, anywhere she'd traveled, she'd been at the helm, or sharing the task.

She'd felt trapped on the previous three flights, a part of her mind urging her to get out, or at least get to the flight deck. But since 9/11, the pilots were separated from the passengers by a bulletproof door, locked from the inside.

The first flight, she'd ridden in first class, surrounded by business people texting on cell phones, typing on tablets, or reading into voice recorders during the short hop from Monterey to LA. She flew first class again from there to Miami. But her seat was at the back row of the first-class cabin, separated from an excited family by only the thickness of her slightly wider seat and a curtain that the flight attendants left open. Apparently, the family was with a group of tourists, chattering away, ignoring the crying babies as they flew across the country.

The third leg to Nassau was on a smaller plane, no first class. Most of the people were tired anyway and on their way to their final destination. Charity remembered seeing quite a few of them on the flight out of LAX. Spotting someone she'd seen before always bothered her, made her nervous.

At the airport in Nassau, she kept stopping and glancing behind her, to check if anyone she recognized was following her to the Bahamas Air concourse. The gate was empty, but her flight wasn't for more than an hour. When she asked at the desk if the plane would be on time, the ticket agent told her to wait just a moment before disappearing through the door leading down to the tarmac.

The plane Charity was scheduled on wasn't due to leave for an hour. But the ticket agent had caught the crew of the earlier flight just in time, changed Charity's ticket to the flight about to take off, and escorted her down. She'd boarded as the pilot was starting the engines. With all the seats available, she sat in the back, on the starboard side of the aircraft.

Through the forward windows, she could spot Exuma Sound's deep blue waters beckoning her, out on the edge of the horizon.

Great Exuma was barely visible, as if about to slide into the Sound from the far side. Puffy white clouds stretched the length of the bank of islands.

The Tongue of the Ocean lay below the right wing, stretching out to the west. Charity stared down at the cobalt waters. The submerged banks encircling nearly all of the abyss had once been dry land, surrounding an inland sea.

It was because of those shallow banks encompassing the 6000-foot-deep sea that the navy had chosen the TOTO as a location to conduct sonar and guidance tests. They worked closely with civilian researchers from the Atlantic Undersea Test and Evaluation Center on Andros Island. The larger northern part of Andros was just visible, where the deep blue waters of the TOTO faded to green just inside the barrier reef. Ahead, far across those deep waters, lay southern Andros, now obscured by clouds.

It had taken Charity two days to get *Wind Dancer* buttoned up and secured at Monterey Bay Boat Works. That was another reason she'd gone to Monterey. That and to pay respects to her father.

She'd called the yard a week before arriving to arrange for a list of long-overdue service items to be taken care of. Work that needed to be performed with *Dancer* out of the water.

The yard owner had been a long-time friend of Charity's father and had helped keep *his* old Alden sloop in top shape for all of Charity's childhood and adolescence. He'd been ecstatic hearing from her after ten years. He'd been full of questions, but Charity had told him that she was on a sat-phone, and George became all business.

It'd been nearly two years, two oceans, and 20,000 miles since *Dancer* was out of the water and the bottom needed to be cleaned, scraped, caulked, and repainted. George had beamed when she'd idled up to his dock in a boat that looked very much like her dad's.

When she'd learned that his business was slow and the yard faltering, she added a lot of extra work to the order. She left him with $20,000 in cash to order whatever he deemed necessary and told him she could send more if that wasn't enough, since she planned to be gone for at least two or three weeks.

Leaving George to haul *Dancer* out, she'd rented a scooter and gone to a nearby hotel, paying for a room for two nights. Once she'd showered, Charity had called to check on flights to the Bahamas and then gone to bed.

She'd agreed to meet with Stockwell and Bremmer again the day after the incident at the cemetery. Over the last year-and-a-half she'd talked to McDermitt at least twice a month and he'd finally convinced her that neither Stockwell nor anyone else was a threat to her. Jesse trusted the man and she trusted Jesse. Still, seeing Stockwell again had brought back the dark storm clouds in her mind.

Charity had been late to the second meeting, and she was tired. Packing for a week away wasn't much work for her. She'd only packed a few things and would buy more if she had to. But she'd worked since before dawn, walking George through the boat, explaining everything she wanted done. Then she'd pitched in and helped his shipwrights with the prep work until it was time to go.

She'd insisted that the second meeting be in a busy public place, a bar called *Sandbar and Grill* on the municipal wharf.

Neither Stockwell or Bremmer mentioned her tardiness, though she'd been more than 30 minutes late. In the noisy bar, Bremmer had described his organization a little more, calling it a self-funded vigilante group, committed to non-violence except as a last resort. He'd told her that the founders had a combined net worth that was greater than a few industrialized countries and had pooled their considerable resources to form an alliance aimed at correcting injustices around the world. Bremmer had admitted that he'd never met any of them in person, except Mr. Armstrong, and Bremmer's counterpart in the expeditionary side of the company.

She'd liked the organization's mission, providing what Bremmer had told her was true, and had finally agreed to go to McDermitt and talk to him. She'd been bumming around the South Pacific and Australia for the last year without purpose. This might be something she could sink her teeth into.

With the meeting in just a little over a week, there was no way she could sail there, and she really did need to have the work done on her boat. When she'd asked about transportation, Bremmer had immediately produced an AmEx black card with her alias embossed on it. She was duly impressed, having one just like it. He'd also given her a business card, with just the word *Logistics* and a phone number on it.

"Call that number," Bremmer had told her. "Whoever answers, and it's rarely the same person, give them the name on your AmEx card, what you need, and where and when you need it. Give them 24 hours and it'll be there. Less notice than that, and you might have to improvise. Never call for the same thing twice. One call per request."

Bremmer had instructed her to go to wherever in the world Jesse McDermitt was, by any means she chose, and try to convince him to meet. He'd assured her that what would be discussed at this meeting would pique both her and Jesse's interest.

Now, on final approach to Dead Man's Cay Airport on Long Island, Charity looked out the window. Just below the plane's starboard wing, submerged canyons between Dollar Cay and Sandy Cay looked like miniature rivers and tributaries of indigo ink, carving through the surrounding shallower waters dotted here and there with gold sandbars. The canyons were carved by water draining from the relatively flat sea floor into the abyssal depths to the south and east. Anchored on the edge of the easternmost cleft lay a Formosa ketch.

Charity smiled, remembering the many nights aboard the boat with Victor. Jesse had been reluctant to accept it, but *Salty Dog* was now his home and had been for some time. Charity's late boyfriend, Victor Pitt, had been murdered in Nassau, leaving the boat to her.

When the plane touched down, Charity gathered up her backpack and shoulder bag from the seat across the aisle. She smiled at the pilots and thanked them for the ride. Both men smiled back.

Hurrying through the small, nearly vacant, terminal building, Charity found a lone car waiting outside. The driver, an older black man, was leaning against the fender holding a sign, *Gabriella Fleming*. He pushed away from the car quickly as she approached.

Okay, that's pretty good, she thought.

She strode toward the man, her right hand resting on her open purse out of habit. She was unarmed. "Hello, I'm Gabby Fleming."

"Yes, ma'am," the driver said. He was middle-aged, with ebony skin stretched tight over a lean face. "I am to take you north, but dey didn't give me a destination. Do you know it?"

"I will when I see it," she said, opening the back door, and getting into the car.

If it's there, Charity thought, closing the door.

Getting a car to meet her at the airport was one thing but arranging a 24-foot center-console boat to be waiting with the keys in it was another story altogether.

The old car smelled of marijuana. Charity wondered if the driver worked for Armstrong or was just a hired local. It reminded her of the day she'd first seen Vic. He'd just exited a taxi and she was on her way to meet Stockwell on Grand Cayman Island. That taxi had smelled the same.

Within minutes, they were leaving the airport. Turning north on Queen's Highway, they passed through a few small townships. Then, after several miles, the clear waters of New Found Harbour appeared on the left side of the road.

"Right up there," Charity said. "See that boat anchored near shore? The center-console with the red T-top? Just pull over there."

When she tried to pay the man, he told her he'd already been paid. She gave him a nice tip, just the same. Charity threw her backpack over her shoulder and waited for the car to turn around. When it disappeared around a curve, she crossed the road and moved quickly down a rocky path to a small beach. There, she kept walking out into the water toward the sleek-looking Contender. It was anchored in three feet of water and there didn't seem to be anyone aboard. Charity hadn't expected there to be.

"Okay," she said aloud, "now I'm duly impressed."

Lifting her duffle, she tossed it over the low transom, then flipped the stern boarding ladder down and climbed aboard. Charity dumped her pack and purse on the left seat and searched the console. She found the key in a small glove box below the helm.

The engine, a 300-horsepower Yamaha, fired up instantly, then settled into a quiet burble. She let it run for a few minutes, while she secured the boarding ladder and familiarized herself with the instruments. Clicking through the digital gauge, she noticed that the engine only had 31 hours on it. Not brand-new, but probably this year's model.

The combination chart plotter and depth sounder showed that she had just a foot of water under the keel. Farther from the beach, the water deepened to ten feet with a few small patch reefs, but mostly a flat, sandy bottom.

Zooming out, she found the place where Jesse was anchored. The lines showing depth were tightly packed, indicating a steep drop off. Not deep, but very sudden. The four-mile jaunt would be easy. The beginning of the fissure in the sea bottom was just east of two small islands to the southwest of where she was now. They were too far away to see but should come into view within a mile or two. Then she'd only need to stay in the dark blue water the rest of the way. A simple run. There was no need to figure out how to program a destination.

After quickly hauling up the anchor, Charity moved to the helm and turned the boat seaward. When the water was deep enough, she brought it up on plane and turned southwest. Zooming the GPS so she could watch for patch reefs and shallows, she soon realized it was unnecessary. The water was so clear, she could see the dark shapes of the reefs far ahead of the boat.

When she passed beyond the two small islands and turned south, Charity saw *Salty Dog* lying at anchor, its tiny inflatable dinghy floating alongside. She steered a course along the edge of the deep-water drop off and slowed to idle speed as she neared the ketch.

She'd called Jesse the day before leaving Monterey and had asked if she could meet with him. He'd seemed reluctant at first, which was unlike him, but finally told her where she could find him.

"Ahoy *Salty Dog!*" she shouted, when her boat was twenty or so yards away.

Shifting to neutral, Charity waited.

There was no answer. Charity called out again, wishing she had a hand-held VHF at least. Again, Jesse didn't respond. Worried, she put the Yamaha in gear and idled toward the much larger vessel.

"Jesse!" Charity shouted, as her bow came alongside the ketch. "Are you okay? It's Charity."

Still no answer. She idled forward along the port side, then shifted to neutral. Hurriedly, she tied off two fenders to the starboard cleats, to keep the boats from bumping into one another, then came alongside and tied off to the big ketch's deck cleats.

Gaining the *Dog's* deck, she moved quickly around to the starboard side of the cockpit. The companionway hatch was open and inviting, just as she remembered.

Knowing that Jesse had a large dog named Finn, she moved cautiously and shouted down into the cabin, "Mc-Dermitt! It's me."

Nothing. It was unlike Jesse to leave anything unsecured. She was worried the new lifestyle he seemed to be a part of might have taken its toll and he was sick or injured. Or someone had surprised him.

Charity turned to the helm and opened the cabinet on the starboard side of the pedestal. She reached inside and pushed up against the underside of the cabinet top and the false bottom she knew was there. It clicked and lowered on its hinge, dropping something heavy into her hand.

Removing the cloth-wrapped bundle, she unfolded the oily rag and found a nine-millimeter Sig Sauer. She pulled the slide back slightly. There was a round in the chamber. The gun was clean and well-oiled.

At least he hadn't been neglecting the important things, she thought.

Climbing quickly down the steps to the pilothouse, she noticed that everything was in order, just as it had been when Vic owned the boat. She turned right and went aft, opening the engine room door and peering inside. It was clean and orderly too. Jesse had installed a new air compressor, its long hoses hanging from the overhead next to a deck hatch that hadn't been there when the boat was Victor's.

With the Sig up and leading the way, she continued aft. The master stateroom was empty, the bunk unmade. Aside from that, everything looked fine. No sign of a struggle.

Going forward again, Charity checked the lower salon, the forward head, and the office that Vic had converted from the original guest v-berth. The boat was deserted.

Up on deck, Charity looked all around. There wasn't anyone in sight. She noticed that the boarding ladder was hanging on the starboard side. She hadn't seen it when she'd first arrived. Had Jesse gone swimming or diving?

Taking a deck chair from the forward storage box, she set it up on the stern and sat down to wait.

She'd told Jesse that she'd be arriving that afternoon, but hadn't given him a precise time, since she didn't know it when they'd talked. And even if she had, she was at least an hour earlier than she'd planned.

The dinghy was there, so he'd probably just gone for a swim. But where was the dog?

Over the last year, Jesse had changed. Their weekly calls, via the two sat-phones he'd bought just for the two of them, had grown less frequent. When she'd called him before leaving California, it was the first time they'd talked in nearly a month. Most of the times she'd called him, he'd sounded drunk. A couple of times, she'd heard people laughing and talking in the background. On more than one occasion, it had sounded like she'd interrupted a frat party. It was obvious that he'd begun hanging out with a younger, more boisterous crowd.

Charity had enjoyed a few wild times in the past year herself. After sailing to French Polynesia, she'd reunited one of her passengers with her family. It had been an awkward time, and Charity had felt completely out of place. Moana had only been ten years old when she'd been taken from her island by a pair of men on a large sailboat. Charity had returned the girl at the physical age of 24. Her baby brothers were now grown men, and her parents prematurely aged. Intellectually, Moana had still been a ten-year-old.

A week later, in the Marshall Islands, she and her other passenger, Fiona Russo, had gone to a local navy bar for drinks. Things got out of hand with a few drunken sailors, who thought that any single American woman in a bar on the island of Kwajalein was fair game.

Russo had always dreamed of visiting Australia, so they had. After provisioning in Samoa, the two women had crossed the southern Pacific for another 3000 miles, with stops in Fiji and New Caledonia, before finally sailing into Sydney Harbor.

Somewhere along the way, Fiona had finally made peace with her past, burying it forever. In Sydney, Charity had treated her friend to a shopping spree, buying far too many clothes for both of them, and not just sailing garb. They'd been invited to a party aboard a neighboring yacht, owned by a very rich Aussie businessman.

Fiona and Charity had dressed for the party on the elegant yacht. It was mostly attended by other wealthy business people and their spouses, but there were quite a few single people as well. Young men of means treated them both the way Charity had been telling

Fiona women should be treated. With the respect that all people deserved.

They'd sailed up the coast all the way to Brisbane, stopping along the way many times. In each new marina, there was no shortage of men who were eager to be seen with the two American women sailing the antique sloop.

After two months in Brisbane, Fiona had decided she liked it there. She'd found a job, met a very respectable young man, and fallen in love. Charity had used her contacts to check the man out. Humble beginnings, old money earned honestly and handed down from generation to generation without drama.

Parting company with a tearful goodbye, Charity had sailed back to Sydney. There, she'd dated a succession of men, and had even brought a few back to her boat, just to satisfy her own needs. But there was no spark, no fire. So, one day she decided it was time for the ultimate challenge.

Plotting a course from Australia to California had been no easy task. It was over 6,500 nautical miles away. The shortest leg, Samoa to Oahu, had taken eighteen straight days of sailing, day and night. She'd stopped at several ports, saving her energy for the long ocean crossings.

The journey across the Pacific had taken her three months. She and *Dancer* had sailed into San Francisco Bay exhausted and beat up. That had been just over a month before she'd gone to her father's grave.

Hearing the blow of a dolphin, Charity glanced toward the sound. It wasn't a dolphin at all. A big yellow dog was swimming silently and effortlessly alongside a man wearing long fins. They were swimming straight toward the boat, about 100 yards away. The man arched his back and disappeared below the surface. She could just make out his shadow gliding across the bottom, the dog continuing to swim above him. The man stayed under a long time, Charity guessed more than a minute, and closed the distance by half. Then he surfaced and blew the water from his snorkel with a whoosh, sounding much like a dolphin.

Charity stood. Finn saw her and started barking. Jesse stopped and raised his head.

CHAPTER THREE

The shadow below me moved with effortless precision. The gin-clear water hid nothing, and the approaching shadow frightened small fish into hiding. The sun was high over a cloudless sky and it felt warm on my shoulders. The water was cooler, about 78 degrees. But I was only in it for an hour at a time and working every muscle during that hour, so hypothermia wasn't an issue.

I'd stopped counting kicks long ago. Now, my brain measured time the way the fish and dolphins do, by the angle of the sun. I knew how long I had left on this swim, almost to the minute. When I surfaced, the slow, measured breaths I took through the snorkel rising above the back of my head were neither forced, nor labored.

To my left, the sandy bottom was four feet deep and extended toward shore at a slight incline. To my right, the sand gave way to a ragged limestone cliff, dropping into water that was measured in fathoms.

A dolphin appeared suddenly from the deep. An Atlantic bottlenose dolphin. It didn't seem surprised or threatened by my appearance. It simply swam along lazily at my relatively slow pace, about ten feet away. He could easily quadruple my speed and disappear.

I slowly rose toward the surface for a breath of air. Incredibly, the dolphin did the same. We each exhaled, took a single breath, and dove beneath the waves once more.

I couldn't help it. I smiled.

The dolphin continued to swim slowly along next to me, as if studying me. Its lung capacity was far greater than mine. I had to surface two or three times to its one. And it probably wasn't even trying. After several minutes, the dolphin disappeared over the ledge and was gone. Probably headed off to tell his friends about the crazy human he'd encountered swimming in the middle of the ocean.

I continued swimming and thinking. An hour each way to the island with my body on auto-pilot allowed my mind to wander.

When Charity had called me, I'd been tempted to ignore the phone's alert. If it was important, she'd follow it with a text. But a part of me was glad I'd taken the call. I knew that she'd been all the way to Australia and had only recently returned to the States. She'd sounded sort of cryptic and didn't say exactly what it was that she wanted to meet with me about, only that she didn't want to talk about it on the phone. Not even our secure satellite phones. That alone told me it was important.

If her travel plans weren't delayed, she'd arrive in an hour. More than enough time for my swim.

The truth was, I'd been living life way too large for over a year, just wandering aimlessly around the Bahamas and northern Caribbean. I'd been as far as the Windward Islands and indulged in things that I'd once thought poisonous to my body. I'd involved myself in matters that were none of my business and enticed more than one woman onto my boat.

Waking up two months ago with a massive hangover, only to find my boat had been ransacked, was the final wake-up call. She hadn't gotten away with much, just some electronics and a few hundred in cash that she'd found in my pants pocket. She'd had an accomplice, I'm sure.

I'd stumbled up on deck with Finn that morning. The bright tropical sun had burned into my eyes like lasers. She'd even stolen my sunglasses. But the hiding spots on my boat had been untouched.

Throwing off the lines, I'd sailed day and night to reach Conch Harbor on the lee side of Long Key. The deep cuts and blue hole were the perfect place to get my neglected body back into shape.

There was something coming. Deep in my gut, I knew there had to be something out there that a boat bum and washed-up old Jarhead could do besides greeting customers at Walmart. I had no idea what it was, but I felt certain I'd recognize it when the time came. Chance favors the prepared mind. And a prepared mind needed a prepared body.

For the last six weeks, I'd eaten from the sea, run on the loose powdery sand, swum laps around the islands, and free dived in the deep, clear water. If another boat dropped anchor nearby, I moved. Having people around would be a disruption I didn't want.

Overcoming the deep dive into debauchery and self-indulgence wasn't easy. And when Charity called, I didn't think I was completely ready for normal people again. Admittedly, coming to grips with the fact that Savannah had had a life after our affair ten years ago had taken the wind out of my sails.

The feeling was a kind of a throwback to my youth. I'd learned that no part of the world was there just for my amusement. At least, no part of *that* world. I'd countered it by trying to find a life for myself.

Any life.

The life I'd blindly stumbled into was one of drunken beach parties, dope, and cavorting with younger and younger women. I'd financed dozens of crazy parties and become the rich and experienced older guy that all the young ladies wanted to hang out with.

I was nearing fifty and the years had taken a toll. But not nearly the price I'd paid in the last year. Call it a mid-life crisis or whatever, but I knew I had to make some changes, both mentally and physically. At that age, men in corporate America were just hitting their stride, wielding great power. There were still a lot of things I could do, a lot of things I wanted to do. I just wasn't sure of my direction. I would have to force my way into the modern 21st century lifestyle of my own peers.

Slowly wasting away on my island hadn't been the answer. Nor had gallivanting around the Caribbean, looking for bigger opponents to knock down and younger women to *bed* down. I felt my life had really had purpose during my time as an active-duty Marine. But after the terrorist attacks of 9/11, when I'd only been retired two years, the Corps had said I was too old to re-enlist. Another period that had purpose was the four years I'd spent working and training with Deuce Livingston's team of snake-eating counterterrorist operatives. I just had to find a new objective in life.

Swimming allowed me to think. It took a while to rebuild the endurance, but every day for the last week, I'd made this five-mile swim to a tiny island at the west end of this little chain. There, I'd run ten laps around the little island, perhaps four miles, then put the fins on and swum back to the boat. Each day, I was back aboard a little sooner.

I'd eaten fish, lobster, crab, chitons, coconut, wild mango, and almonds. I'd dumped what little booze was left on the boat and drunk only water. It had taken a year of laziness to add what I guessed was a good ten pounds of fat around my middle, weight gained from all kinds of over-indulgence.

It had become a challenge to get lobster from deeper and deeper water. Soon, I was taking the dingy out to the canyons that fringed the drop into the deep waters of Exuma Sound, making free dives to 100 feet and occasionally bringing up dinner. I'd passed 120 a few times and could now stay submerged for nearly two full minutes.

The pounds slowly melted away. I'd always considered swimming and running the ultimate exercises. Weight lifting built a powerful but bulky body. For endurance, you wanted long, sinewy muscle and high lung capacity.

I'd used Finn's clippers to cut my hair short, as close as I could get it on my own to a regulation high-and-tight. I shaved daily until I ran out of blades. Then I'd honed my favorite filet knife to a razor's edge. In the mirror, I'd been able to see the change. And for the most part, my mind was clear. Memories faded in and out, like watching a movie of someone else's life.

All these thoughts flowed into and through my consciousness, as my body plowed through the water on auto-pilot. With my new, extra-long fins, I could now maintain what would be idle speed for some boats and could do it for miles on end. While idle speed doesn't sound like much on a boat, swimming ten nautical miles in just over two hours is pretty damned fast. Of course, I was using fins. I'd bought a pair of Cressi fins with interchangeable blades. The 30-inch attachments transformed me into a dolphin, transmitting the power from my legs to the water far better than any I'd used in the past. The added resistance pushed my thigh muscles to capacity with every kick.

Six weeks of constant training, exercising, and pushing my body beyond its limits had me in possibly the best physical condition of my life. But not without aches and pains. At my age, that was unavoidable.

Pain is weakness leaving the body. That was the constant mantra in Marine Corps PT. But time took a toll on joints. The calcium found in almonds helped and I doubled up on them, stripping two trees of their nuts in a month.

Swimming across the deep canyon, I raised my head and blew my snorkel clear. *Salty Dog* rested easily at anchor and I turned toward her and dove again. With slow, measured kicks of the 30-inch-long fins, I moved effortlessly across the sandy bottom, covering 50 yards before surfacing for air.

Finn had taken to waiting for me on the beach at the entrance to the anchorage and I spotted his shadow, now moving toward my own. He could probably swim for hours if I let him. But on the long swims, I'd made him wait on the boat. In the last week, he'd decided on his own to go ashore to explore, while he waited to join me on the last leg.

I surfaced next to him and blew the water from my snorkel.

"Wanna race to the boat?" I asked him, as he swam toward me.

Turning instantly, Finn poured on the coal. He loved a good race, and I made sure that when I did beat him, which was rarely, it wasn't by much. Dogs needed positive reinforcement, too.

I put my snorkel back in my mouth, dove, and easily caught up to him. Underwater, I went for distance, not speed, taking long, fluid kicks with the fins, while streamlining my body to its fullest.

From below, Finn's graceful technique was easily observed. His front paws never came out of the water, nor even close to the surface. Most dogs aren't efficient swimmers because they're not very buoyant. They use most of their energy to keep their head above water. Their paws frantically beat the surface, in what looks like near panic. But Labs have webbing between the toes of their very large paws, and a dense underfur that traps air to make them more buoyant. From below, he looked like one of those Tennessee Walkers, head up, and opposing legs taking long strides.

When I surfaced next to Finn, he was barking. Stopping, I saw someone standing near the boarding ladder on my boat. Charity.

I waved, then dove and followed the bottom toward the large shadow *Salty Dog* cast, easily outdistancing Finn now. He knew Charity, but not well. And I didn't want him clawing up the side of the boat trying to get at someone he might consider an intruder. Coming up next to the ladder, I quickly pulled my fins off and handed them up.

"Sorry for boarding without permission," Charity said. "I called out and didn't get an answer, so I got worried."

Quickly climbing the ladder, I stepped up onto the deck next to her. She'd changed a little since I'd last seen her. For the better. If anything, she looked healthier, more tanned, and leaner. But the real change was in her eyes. She'd always had a far-off gaze, as if she were looking right through you. Now her eyes were a clear, bright blue, and focused on mine.

I gripped her shoulders. "Damn, it's good to see an old friend again. I'd hug you, but I'm dripping wet."

She stepped forward, putting her arms around my waist, and squeezing tightly. I cradled her head against my chest for a moment and held her close. Charity and I had a history together and shared a deep, emotional attachment. I felt closer to her than I ever had with either of my wives or even my old friend, Rusty Thurman.

Years ago, Charity and I had spent several weeks together, alone on my boat, *Gaspar's Revenge*. She was an amazingly beautiful woman, but we'd never been physically intimate, since she still contended with psychological issues stemming from her captivity and torture at the hands of Taliban fighters. But we'd shared our darkest secrets during those few weeks.

In the end, we'd both laughingly agreed that the world would probably implode if our collective hunger was unleashed at the same time in a physical way. The truth was, I knew that no man could match her passion, and I'd kill myself trying to do it. But I'd been on a pretty steady diet of one-night stands, some of which lasted for many days, and now it'd been nearly two months since I'd held a woman. I didn't even know the last one's name.

Finn climbed up the ladder and proceeded to shake the water from his coat, sending droplets and mist flying in all directions.

I pushed Charity back and looked into her eyes. "You look like a million bucks."

Her eyes drifted down to my body. "And you look priceless! I was expecting to find a drunk old fool."

Lifting the port bench seat, I grabbed a towel and dried off. "If you'd come here a couple of months ago, that's what you would have found."

I pulled on a faded T-shirt that once had either the *Gaspar's Revenge* or *Rusty Anchor* logo on it. I only had a few changes of clothes on board. The salt and sun were hard on them.

She eyed me sharply. "What changed?"

"I did," I replied, extending a hand toward the cockpit and the shade the Bimini top offered. "I just decided it was time to get back to the business of living."

"I'm sorry about Savannah," she said, stepping beneath the Bimini, and moving around to the other side of the fold-up table in front of the helm.

I'd told Charity about finding Savannah in Cane Garden Bay, just a few days after it happened. After that, neither of us spoke of her again. Sitting down across from Charity, I studied her face for some indication of why she'd flown all the way across the country and then some. Her expression was one of relief—I guess for not finding me dead or dying.

"Nice ride," I said, indicating the sleek center-console tied off to the port side. "Where'd you get it?"

"A perk from a company I'm thinking of hooking up with," she replied. "I guess you're wondering why I called to meet with you."

It didn't matter what she needed help with, I was ready, willing, and hopefully able, and I told her as much.

"I don't need anything," she said. "Except maybe something to do, a job or whatever. And I think I may have found it."

"A job?"

"Not a nine-to-five," she said. "Neither of us fits that mold. But I think it might be something that would give me direction again."

"You could have told me that over the phone." I reached into a cooler and took out two water bottles, offering her one. "It's RO," I explained. "I had the last store-bought water two weeks ago. What sorta job?"

Charity accepted the bottle and took a drink. "Reverse osmosis water from seawater like this is probably better than spring water." She turned her head slightly, gazing out over the water for a moment. When she looked back, I could see fiery conviction in her eyes. "They're putting together a new team."

"Who is? Deuce?"

"I've been told that he was asked to join. As was Colonel Stockwell."

Stockwell? I thought.

"I was under the impression that you didn't trust him," I said, watching her eyes. I grinned. "Those convinced against their will, are of the same opinion still."

She grinned back. "You're a poet and don't know it."

"A *Papism*. Funny how things he used to say come back to me."

Charity knew that I'd been raised by my grandparents from the age of eight, and I'd explained to her how I looked at life through the eyes of a previous generation. She knew who Pap was; one of the Greatest Generation. A Marine Veteran from World War II.

"You convinced me Stockwell was okay," she said. "Or don't you remember our conversations this past year?"

It was my turn to look down at the deck. "It's been kind of a blur."

"Yeah, weed will do that," she said, not taking it easy on me. "What the hell were you thinking?"

"I wasn't thinking," I replied. "For thirteen months after Tortola, I unplugged my brain and just did whatever felt good."

"From the fragments of conversation I heard in the background during some of our calls, it seemed like you did *whoever* felt good."

"Yeah, I'm not real proud of that either."

Charity was the only one who could talk like that to me. Even Rusty knew where the line was. She and I had no boundaries. She put it aside and went on to tell me about Stockwell meeting her in California just last week. He'd been asked to find her, so she could find me.

"Me? I thought this was about a job offer *you* had."

"It's a big organization, Jesse. Well-funded, too. They're creating a group of operatives that sounds like it could rival all of DHS combined."

"What department will it fall under?" I asked. "State or Defense?"

"Private research," she replied.

"Research?" I asked, completely puzzled.

"They do legitimate research," she began. "Nobody has been completely read-in yet, but it seems the founders, particularly a man named Jack Armstrong, have long-established roots in ocean engineering and research. And they're all filthy rich."

"I have a pretty good nest egg."

"Not like this, Jesse. Armstrong makes as much in a single month as you and I are worth combined."

I pushed my hair back to wring the water out, forgetting that I'd cut it all off. "I just don't see Stockwell getting involved in any kind of research project."

Charity's eyes danced. "That's not all they do."

Charity went into operational mode, recounting word-for-word what Stockwell and a man named Charlie Bremmer had told her at their second meeting. Over the next hour, with the sun drifting westward toward the horizon, she explained all she'd learned about Armstrong Research.

"I get why they want door-kickers," I said. "And I think I can still kick 'em down as well as the next guy, but the reasons stated for wanting me and you don't make sense."

"Yeah, I didn't get that either. And Bremmer wouldn't elaborate. What's Olympic swimming and running a charter business have to do with correcting injustices preserving self-determination?"

"No clue," I said. But my curiosity was piqued. "And the meeting time and place? What the hell's that about?"

"The equinox isn't just a day," she said. "But a specific time of day."

"I know," I said. "I was born on that day, just a few minutes after spring began. And a precise place and time in the middle of the ocean?"

Charity grinned. "I asked him that same question. He said it was so slower boats could rendezvous on time. Arrival at a preset location at a precise time, no earlier and no later, he said would be the first test."

"I haven't taken a test in decades," I said. But I was interested. "Are you going to the meeting?"

"I think I'll wait and see what Deuce does."

"He hasn't even decided if he'll attend?" I asked. "It's next Saturday."

Charity smiled again. "He's waiting to see if you're going."

CHAPTER FOUR

We had a lot to do and a short time in which to do it. I'd already decided before she arrived that whatever Charity needed help with, I was in. Our conversation dovetailed perfectly with my need to find myself a purpose again. But I had no idea it would be anything of the magnitude she told me. I did have one major concern, though. I knew that in some parts of the world, going in with a non-lethal directive to overthrow some despot could easily get you killed.

But if they were looking for operatives like Deuce, a former SEAL team commander who was as straight-laced as they came, then Armstrong must know that violence was possible and he wanted the best people to thwart it. Charity and I were a little different. Sure, I'd been a Marine sniper and Charity an undercover assassin, but both of us now lived completely off the grid. Hell, I'd been somewhat unplugged for over a decade.

I wanted to get back in the game. I needed it. My old friend Tank used to call it *the jazz*—that feeling of doing something that is good and right, while at the same time unleashing one's own inner demon against those who would do evil. Not to sound biblical or anything, but the struggle between good and evil was very real. Somewhere in the world, that struggle meant life or death for someone at any given time. *Real* struggle, not just sleeping around and smoking dope.

Sailing straight through, Charity and I estimated that we could reach the Keys in less than three days, weather permitting. Leaving *Salty Dog* here was out of the question. Charity asked about my friend on Andros Island. It was half the distance and Charity kept her helicopter there. With the meeting in just seven days, it would be advantageous to get together with the others and find out all we could about the people and organization we were going to meet.

I called Henry Patterson and asked if I could dock *Salty Dog* at his cove for a week or two. Henry was pushing 90 but was still an active charter skipper. He owned a sweet little hole-in-the-limestone-wall marina and mini-resort. It was on the north end of Andros and minutes by boat to the TOTO. He and my grandfather had been close. They'd served together, fighting the Japanese in the Pacific, and later lived just a few miles apart until Pap died. Kind of like me and Rusty.

And Henry didn't ask questions.

Charity called the airport on Andros and asked them to have her bird prepped and ready when we arrived Tuesday morning. We'd leave early tomorrow, sail through the night in watches, and arrive at Henry's place Monday afternoon, where we could rest up before flying home.

Home, I thought. My home for the last year had been wherever I found myself.

Together we called Deuce and set up a meeting with him, Tony, Chyrel, and Julie for Tuesday morning. Chyrel Koshinski was his computer genius. She could run circles around the best computer hackers on the planet. Deuce sounded excited, but with a new son, I felt his wife, who is also my goddaughter, might be a little annoyed by the plan. We'd work that out after hearing what Armstrong Research wanted with us.

With the immediate planning done, Charity helped me make the *Dog* ready to sail in the last couple of hours of daylight.

"Where are you staying?" I asked her, once we finished.

"Here on *Salty Dog* if you don't mind."

"What about your boat?"

"Not mine," she reminded me, stepping over to the side deck and down into the boat. She tossed her bags up, then untied the lines. "I'll anchor it here and send word to the owner where it is in the morning."

Before she shoved away, she quickly pulled her shirt off and wiggled out of her shorts, tossing them on the side deck with her bag. She wore a red one-piece, scooped low in the back, with high-cut thighs that greatly accentuated her already impossibly long legs. As I watched, she moved the boat about 100 yards away from *Salty Dog* and dropped the hook in ten feet of water.

Finn and I both watched as Charity dove off the little boat's swim platform, entering the water with very little splash. She dolphin-kicked a good twenty yards as she slowly rose to the surface. It'd been ten years since she'd competed with America's swim team in the Sydney Olympics and won a bronze medal. But I couldn't tell. Though not swimming for speed, just taking slow measured strokes, her form was flawless. She glided through the water back toward my boat as if born to the sea.

"She's good," I told Finn, rubbing his neck.

Finn watched her swim with what looked like envy and excitement. Maybe he was thinking that he might have a new swim buddy.

I handed Charity a towel as she climbed up the ladder. I'd moved back around to the port side. She accepted it and rung her hair out before patting her body dry.

"You still have an Olympian's style."

"Ha!" she exclaimed. "Kids today will swim circles around me. How are you without those gorilla fins?"

The gauntlet was thrown. In most physical contests, men had a distinct advantage over women, being taller, heavier, and generally stronger. However, most of that advantage disappeared in the water. Add to that the fact that Charity was already a trained competitive swimmer when she was just twelve years old, and it was likely few men would be her match in the water. Her training in Israel, in the hand-to-hand, war-fighting technique of Krav Maga, made few men on land a match for her, either.

"Race you to that beach," I said, pointing to a coconut palm leaning out over a wide expanse of powdery white sand. "First one to touch the base of the palm wins."

"What's the bet?" she asked playfully.

"I have a good supply of lobster tails; the loser cooks dinner."

"You're on," she said, stepping back over to the side deck.

We dove in together and started swimming for the shore. A splash behind us told me that Finn was joining the race.

Sorry, bud, I thought, as I reached long for top speed. *She doesn't need any positive reinforcement.*

This wasn't a long-distance swim, but a sprint. Charity had an early lead, so I dug deep to close the gap. When I came alongside her about halfway to the beach, our speeds were nearly matched. Then she began to slowly pull away, increasing her lead with every stroke. My strength and weight advantages were useless. But being taller, I'd be able to stand and start running sooner. I swam as hard as I could so as not to lose any more ground and focused on the timing of my sprint.

The water became shallow very fast once we were about twenty yards from dry land. The instant my hand touched bottom, I rose. Charity was just coming up when I took my first stride. I had her.

Yeah, I'm competitive. So is Charity. Losing to someone of her ability would be no blow to my ego. She'd already beat me to the beach, but my advantages were on land. Then, her amazingly long legs stripped that away. She beat me to the tree by half a step.

Charity fell onto her side on the sand, laughing. I dropped to my knees next to her, breathing hard, and laughing with her.

"At least you haven't ignored that training," she said, breathlessly.

"Losing to you is no insult," I said. "A close second suits me just fine."

Finn trotted up the beach and once more showered us. We both laughed some more. I hadn't heard Charity laugh very often. It was good.

"What is this island?" she asked, sitting up.

Wet sand clung to her side and outer thigh. The contrast of the nearly white sand brought out the rich, golden tone of her skin.

"It's called Dollar Cay," I replied, then pointed out beyond *Salty Dog*. "That next island is Sandy Cay."

"It's beautiful here," she said. "I don't know how Victor and I missed it."

"There are thousands of places just as empty," I said. "Care to take the Dollar tour?"

She grinned, and we got to our feet. Finn led the way, as was his nature, trotting off with his nose to the ground.

As we walked along the shoreline, Charity stepped out into the water and knelt to rinse the sand off. I cupped my hands and poured water onto her back to assist her efforts. The water made her tanned skin shine.

Her hair was longer than I'd ever seen it—her wet locks streamed down her toned back almost to where it disappeared into her bathing suit.

Together, we walked around the tiny island and I pointed out the bare coconut and almond trees growing back beyond the mangroves.

"I've been here a few weeks," I said. "I'm afraid I've eaten just about everything that's available on Dollar."

"No, you haven't," Charity said, turning inland through clumps of sea grass. She worked her way toward a bush with large pink flowers. "What about hibiscus?"

"It's a flower," I said, following after her.

"And the petals make a great salad." She picked a couple dozen of them and turned to me. "Hold these."

She transferred the pink hibiscus flowers into my hands, then walked past the bush to a grove of saw palmetto. There, she found a sprout with only a few fronds sticking up out of the sand. She pushed the fronds down with her bare feet and gripped the center unopened frond with both hands. She pulled hard on it, the long muscles of her exposed back flexing, until the frond broke free from deep inside the plant. Laying it on the ground, she did the same thing with several more palmetto shoots.

"Heart of palm and hibiscus," she said, picking up the small bundle.

We made our way back to the beach. "How are we supposed to swim?" I asked, holding up two fists full of flowers. "We don't have anything to put these in."

"Back float," she said, walking straight out into the water. Turning, Charity smiled. "Not as fast, but the better swimmer has already been established."

Back aboard *Salty Dog*, I got my small grill from the lazarette and mounted it on the side rail. I kept a close eye on Charity. If it bothered her being on Victor's old boat, she didn't let it show.

We ate with our fingers, twisting and pulling small chunks of meat from the lobster tails. I had to admit, the flowers and palm chunks tasted good, though a little on the sweet side. Charity had cut the palm into tiny pieces, sprinkling them over the flower petals and shaking a little coconut oil over them.

After cleaning up the galley, we sat in deck chairs on the stern as the sun began its final glide toward the sea.

"You don't ever get tired of doing this?" she asked, stretching her legs out on the deck. "Watching the sunset, I mean."

"Never two alike," I replied. "The backdrop can be the same, day after day, but the sky is always different, and the sun is never in exactly the same position. Plus, the company you're in changes."

"I mean your daily ritual of stopping to watch."

I looked over at Charity's profile. The muted orange glow that brightened the color of everything at this time of day seemed to have found its match in her skin and hair. Through dark sunglasses, she looked straight ahead toward the setting sun, the low angle of the light accentuated her high cheekbones and full lips.

I'd always thought Charity beautiful, but I don't remember a time when she'd looked so lovely, self-assured, and composed. Like a princess on a throne of gold and emeralds. Had she finally found peace with her inner demons?

I returned my gaze to the west. The point where Sol was falling would be very near the equator in these last seven days of winter. In a few more days. this magnificent, life-giving orb would shine more on the northern hemisphere and another winter would be over.

"Evening is the time I think back on what I've accomplished," I said, as the sun reached the sea. "To consider all the decisions I made and ask myself if they were good choices. Sometimes I fail, but I never lose. I can only win or learn."

Charity touched my elbow. I looked over and she smiled. "Maybe some of our doubts will be removed on your birthday. But tomorrow we have to sail the full length of the Tongue of the Ocean."

"Yargh," I growled in my most piratical voice.

CHAPTER
FIVE

The crossing hadn't been an easy one. After sailing through some less-than-perfect seas the following day, the night had calmed, and we'd sailed on into darkness, uneventfully. Through the night, we took shifts at the helm. I'd awakened Charity just after midnight and slept quite well, knowing she was piloting. Monday morning, the foul weather had returned. I had to restrict Finn below deck all afternoon, and both Charity and I had vested up and tied off to the jack line.

The TOTO could be like a giant washing machine at times. It was surrounded by shallows, save a small opening to the North Atlantic at the north end of the east side. Storm-whipped waves could build quite high in the vast expanse of very deep water. They bounced off the surrounding banks to come at you from any and every point on the compass.

We'd arrived at Henry's sheltered cove under a torrential rain. His little resort was being renovated and he was without water and electricity at the docks. Charity and I both needed a shower and some rest. Henry'd offered us a cabana with two beds; he was otherwise full up with a dozen adventure tourists who wanted to see the real Bahamas, away from the tourist spots. We'd accepted his offer and, being exhausted from the 36 hours of mostly rough sailing, turned in early.

The following morning, Henry took us to the airport, where Charity kept her helicopter. It was a Bell UH-1 Iroquois but was probably more well known by its nickname. Especially among Vietnam Vets. The Huey had already been fueled up and made ready. We'd lifted off with bad weather once more approaching from the east.

On a northwest heading, the Huey easily outran the storm, which rained down on Henry and his adventuring guests in typical Bahamas fashion.

Finn was in the back. I'd put his life vest on, and he was tied to the aft bulkhead with a short tether, looped at the end. He had enough lead to stand and move around between the seats a few feet, but not enough to reach the flight deck. Ten minutes after takeoff, his head lay on crossed forelegs, napping.

Charity's voice came over my headset. "What's wrong? You seem a little tense."

"For more than a year, I've been traveling at the speed of mud," I offered. "I haven't even been in a car in all that time."

"Wanna take the stick for a while? Maybe it'll get your mind up to speed, no pun intended."

"My aircraft," I said, taking the cyclic in hand.

"Your aircraft," Charity responded, releasing the primary on her side.

Flying a helicopter on the off-hand side is a bit of a challenge. Unlike an airplane, the pilot's seat in a chopper is on the right, like many power boats. There are two hand controls in a helo. The collective, with the throttle control, is to the left of both seats, and controls lift and engine speed. The cyclic controls direction, and most people being right-handed, prefer their dominant hand on the cyclic, leaving their left hand free to flip switches or turn knobs, many of which are on the console between the seats. So, early on, chopper pilots in dual-control aircraft started using the right-hand seat, in order to have their right hand on the cyclic.

But we were already at the altitude and course we wanted, so I didn't need to bother with any of the dash switches. I concentrated on just keeping us level and maintaining forward air speed. I'd always preferred being the one in control and didn't much like riding shotgun.

Charity was right. Taking control did seem to relieve the stress brought on by high-speed travel, even if we were a mile up in the air. I looked at the air speed indicator. We were traveling at 120 knots, with a tailwind. So maybe a buck-thirty over the water below us. Roughly twenty times faster than my usual mode of transportation this past year.

I was also nervous about returning to civilization. I'd been home a few times in the last year, but never for long; a day once, and a couple of days on two other occasions. I was worried about how I'd be accepted and how I would now view said civilization.

Living completely off the grid for a year, anchored in faraway coves and shelters, my mind and body had become accustomed to the slower pace. The sun rose, I enjoyed the day and whatever company I happened to find myself in, and then the sun went down. If I was alone, I enjoyed just being alive to witness it. Only in the last month had I even begun to keep track of what day it was.

As Charity started our descent toward Marathon Airport, I could just see my island off in the distance to the northwest. The long string of islands that stretched out to the north and west of Big Pine Key disappeared at the horizon, where my island was located.

She put us down softly on the tarmac and shut down the turbine. I helped her with the post-flight and tie-down.

"Crap," I said, opening the side door to let Finn out.

Charity reached past me and grabbed her pack. "What's wrong?"

"I don't have a leash," I replied, looking toward the terminal and busy highway just beyond it.

Reaching past me again, Charity unhooked the short cargo tether Finn had been tied to. "Try this," she offered, handing it to me.

I slipped the bitter end through the loop, then dropped the makeshift leash and choker over Finn's head. He just looked at me, his head cocked to the side. He'd only worn a leash a few times. The last time I'd seen his, was on *Gaspar's Revenge*. Most of the places we visited, friendly dogs were welcome, and if not, we just didn't go there.

Together, Charity and I walked toward the small terminal and the inevitable encounter with Customs and Border Protection. We each carried nothing more than a backpack, and Finn walked at my side, ignoring the rope dangling from his neck. I did notice that he made eye contact with every person we encountered, and his nose was constantly twitching.

To my surprise, the agent moved us through quickly. Charity used her alias passport, Gabriella Fleming. It was also the name of the CEO of the magazine whose name was stenciled on the side of the chopper, *Tropical Luxury*. She played the part well. Since the bird was American and we were American, the agent glanced quickly at our passports, took only a cursory look inside our backpacks and we were on our way.

"Let's walk," I said, turning away from the single cab waiting in front of the terminal. "Deuce won't be here for a couple more hours."

After covering the short distance to the Overseas Highway, we turned right. It was high tourist season and cars were speeding down the highway toward Key West and the end of the road. Finn ambled along on the grass beside the sidewalk, away from traffic, with his nose to the ground. He seemed unaffected by the rush but looked back every few steps to check.

"Why'd you want to meet Deuce at the *Rusty Anchor*?" Charity asked. "Instead of at his office?"

"Rusty'd probably like to see Julie a little more often," I replied. Deuce was married to Rusty's daughter. Then I grinned at her. "And I haven't had Rufus's cooking in several months."

The three-mile walk helped work the kinks out, after having been crunched up in the cramped cockpit for two hours. The sky was a brilliant blue, and the air crisp and dry. A slight breeze at our backs cooled our skin wherever the sun found it.

We waited for a break in traffic, then trotted across the four-lane highway. Everyone's apparent need to move fast and the lack of courtesy annoyed me. Cars zoomed past, most of the drivers unaware of the place we were heading to. We reached the other side and stepped into the shade provided by dense tropical growth, which seemed to swallow the crushed shell driveway leading to the *Rusty Anchor*. Immediately, the air seemed cooler, and the scent of frangipani and jasmine filled my nostrils. Since Finn knew where he was, I slipped the tether off his head.

"Stay close," I told him. He trotted a few steps ahead of us.

"Who tends this jungle?" Charity asked.

The sounds from the road diminished with every step we took beneath the over-arching canopy of banyan and ancient gumbo limbo trees. Now, I felt as if I'd come home. I'd visited Rusty's bar many times while both of us were in the Corps. His dad ran the place then, but I'd continued to visit whenever I could after Rusty got out. A few years later, his dad passed and Rusty, being an only child, naturally took it over.

He and I had ridden the same bus from Jacksonville to Parris Island more than 30 years ago, served in the same unit a couple of times, and had remained the closest of friends ever since.

"Rufus and Jimmy, for the most part," I said. "About 70 years ago, this was mostly mangroves and stagnant water. When Rusty's dad dredged the canal after World War II, he dumped the dredgings into the marsh, enlarging the dry area of his property quite a bit, but destroying a lot of mangroves. Can't do that now, they're protected. The bigger native trees flourished, and the mangroves never returned. Rusty dredged the canal again about five years ago and that's when Jimmy and Rufus started planting ornamental native species. They've been landscaping this area like a botanical garden since then."

"It's really beautiful," Charity said, glancing back through the dappled sunlight at all the flowering plants. She closed her eyes. "And the fragrance is intoxicating."

"Back there," I said, pointing. "At the edge of the property. See that massive mahogany tree? Its branches keep the mangroves, gumbo limbos, and buttonwoods at bay. That's where the confederate and night-blooming jasmine grow.

Charity looked over at me. "How come he doesn't advertise the *Rusty Anchor*?"

"Rusty's dad always saw the place as a local's hangout in the '60s and '70s. His dad took it over from his grandpa, who owned it during Prohibition. A low profile was a necessity for a rum runner."

"There's a little bit of old piratical blood in his veins," she said. "Yours, too."

"I think Rusty kinda hangs on to that legacy."

It occurred to me that, not unlike the tourists whizzing past on Useless One, she'd probably never walked down this no-named shell road.

"One thing's clear," she said, as we rounded the last bend to the shell parking lot. "It's no accident if you wind up in there."

The *Anchor* sat far back from the highway, and the foliage masked the traffic noise, calling to mind a simpler time, when people in the area traveled only by boat. Before Flagler's Folly, the Overseas Railway, which is now the Overseas Highway. There was no sign out by the road, indicating it was there. Only a weathered old mailbox, leaning on a post. Known to most locals, it was a sort of gathering place during turmoil, and a hangout for fishermen and divers. Only in the last year had word gotten out that the *Rusty Anchor* was home to some of the best food in the Middle Keys.

"You're right about that," I said, pulling the door open. "Unless you know where the *Anchor* is, it's hard to find.

"Dammit," Rusty growled, when I stepped inside. "I thought I locked that door. "Now I got a big ole wharf rat in here."

"A hungry wharf rat," I said, grinning.

Rusty came out from behind the bar, where he'd no doubt been regaling the two women sitting there with tales of big fish and bigger storms.

"How've ya been, you old mud dog?" he asked, grabbing me in a tight bear hug. "Damned good to see ya."

"You remember Charity, don't you?" I asked, stepping back.

He pumped her hand vigorously. "Sure do." Then nodding toward me, he asked, "What're you doing sliding around with this old boat bum?"

Charity smiled. "I sometimes wonder that myself."

Rusty grinned at me and waved his hand toward the bar. "Somebody I want you to meet."

The two women sitting there were watching us. The nearest one looked to be in her early forties, maybe, of average height, fit-looking, attractive, with shoulder-length brown hair. Her companion had long, wavy, dark auburn hair, which I remembered. I'd Googled her when Eric Stone had first told me about her and Rusty last year on Tortola. I'd found the semi-nude pictures of her from back in the eighties. She wore her hair the same as she had back then. She was a beautiful, big, curvy woman, perfectly proportioned. Both women had the perpetual tan of people who live in the tropics and spend a lot of time outdoors.

"Sidney, these are my friends, Jesse McDermitt and Charity Styles," Rusty said. Then he turned to me. "Jesse, meet my lady, Sidney Carter, and her sister, Terri Jaworski."

The redhead stood and came toward us in bare feet. She was much taller than Rusty, even taller than Charity, who was close to six feet. She was dressed in casual Keys attire; baggy shorts and a stylish tank top. Her face was pretty, without the trace of a line that would bely an age I knew to be the same as mine and Rusty's, or within a year or two. She still had the same million-watt smile of the model who'd adorned the inside of many young Marines' wall lockers, warm, open, and eager.

"Rusty's told me all about you, Jesse," Sidney Carter said, stepping past my hand, and throwing her arms around me in a tight hug. She was all woman, and then some, but at the moment her arms felt like boa constrictors.

Stepping back from her embrace, I smiled a bit awkwardly. "Um, pleased to meet you."

Rusty made for the cooler behind the bar. "Hell, bro, you drop in unannounced only three times in the last year and disappear the next day. That ain't even enough time to talk about the weather. You wanna beer?"

"Just water," I said.

Charity said she'd have the same.

"Let's go over there to the back table," Rusty said, leading the way after passing out drinks. "Won't be anyone here for another hour or so."

"Is Rufus here?"

Rusty stepped over to the door, opened it, and shouted for the old Jamaican. When he appeared, Rufus's smile was wide and toothy, with a tiny gap between his front teeth.

"Cap'n Jesse! And Miss Charity? How wonderful! Ah, di two of yuh look better dan when I and I saw yuh last time. Yuh've been to sea, I can tell dat."

I shook hands with the old Rastafarian. "I've been all over *El Caribe*, Rufus, even visited your homeland, but I just couldn't wait any longer for your blackened fish sandwich. Got anything good?"

"Ah, yes," he replied. "Dink was just here. He left me wit six big cobia filets and say he gwon come back dis evening and eat two."

"Dink still hasn't learned to cook?"

"Why should he?" Rufus said with a shrug. "He much better at catchin' dem. Besides, dat bwoi is just dangerous around a cook fire."

There was some truth in that statement. Dink was a backcountry charter captain, taking solo anglers into the shallows in his skiff to test their skills against bonefish, pompano, and snook. On the boat, he was as nimble as a ballerina, but once ashore he had the grace of an ox. Perpetual sea legs.

"Blackened cobia sounds great," I said, pulling chairs out for Charity and Terri. Charity took the one closest to where I intended to sit, with my back to the wall, and ordered the same. "Anyone else eating?"

Rusty and Sidney sat across from us. Rusty smiled nervously, the top of his head and face reddening. "We ate a little while ago," he said, "Truth is, I'm damned glad you're here. Where's your sailboat?"

Sidney turned to Rusty. "I thought you said he owned a charter fishing boat."

"They're both his," Rusty said.

Sidney giggled. "Then I guess that makes you a *transvesselite*, Jesse."

I laughed. "I'll have to remember that one. Glad to be home," I said to Rusty, who was watching Jimmy Saunders cross the yard towards the back door. "What's up?"

Jimmy came in from the back and stopped just inside the entry. A slow grin crossed his face. "Seen Finn out back, man. You home to stay?"

I stood and shook hands with my friend and part-time first mate, Jimmy Saunders. He was living on my island now, along with Angie Trent, his girlfriend. Angie's father, Carl Trent, had taken care of my island before him, along with his wife Charlie and their two kids. Jimmy and Angie had volunteered to take over when Carl announced that they were going to move to Louisiana.

"Not exactly," I replied. "At least not right now. I'll be here off-and-on for the week. But my boat's in the Bahamas. Charity and I flew in."

"You're gonna take my spot then?" he asked, an unmistakable look of relief on his face. Then he turned to Rusty. "That's good, right? 'Cause I don't wanna get all dressed up anyway."

"What're you talking about?" I asked, looking from him to Rusty.

"Sidney and me are gettin' hitched," Rusty blurted out.

Rusty had been a widower for nearly 25 years. His wife Juliet had died giving birth to their only child. Since that day, the only girl in the man's life had been his daughter, Julie, now married to Deuce and living up island. To my knowledge, he'd done nothing but work hard to give her a better future, sacrificing any social life during that whole time.

"You're getting married?" I asked.

"Saturday," Sidney said, taking Rusty's hand in her own. "Not next Saturday, but the one after. He proposed last night, and since everyone we love is right here on this rock, or within a few day's sail, we figured we didn't need a lot of planning."

"So, you'll take my place, man?" Jimmy said hopefully. "It really oughta be you anyway."

"If you're gonna be here," Rusty said, somewhat sheepishly. "I'd sure be happy to have you stand up with me again."

I had been Rusty's best man when he and Juliet married, and he'd stood with me when I married Sandy, the mother of my two daughters.

"A week from Saturday?"

"Just before sunset," Rusty said, perking up. "Then we're gonna raise the roof on this place."

I glanced over at Charity. "Think that meeting will go into something requiring a whole week?"

"I seriously doubt it," she replied. "It's more like a meet-and-greet, from what I was told. To see if they like us and we like them. I know I won't be rushing into anything."

I grinned over at my old friend. "Then I'll be happy to relieve Jimmy from the burden of having to put shoes on his feet."

Rufus came through the back door with a tray holding two plates.

"Y'all eat," Sidney said, rising with her sister. "We'll talk more about it later, when the kids get here."

"You mean you haven't told Julie?"

"I think she's gonna be pleased," Rusty said, standing. "Her and Sid hit it off right away. They even kayaked around Key Vaca a couple months ago, fishing." He leaned in closer. "You're gonna like her too, bro. Oh, and the shoes? Always optional. Keeping it Keys casual."

CHAPTER SIX

The sandwich was everything I remembered; an explosion of flavors in my mouth. Charity grinned around a bite, nodding her head, and rolling her eyes. We both ate quickly.

When we'd finished our lunch, I took the plates out back and left them on the counter of Rufus's outdoor kitchen, giving him a thumbs up. He and Jimmy seemed to be in deep debate over something. Finn was playing in the water, down past where my plane was parked and tied down.

Inside, Charity had moved to the bar, leaving a spot between her and Terri. I took the empty stool, nodding to both women.

"So, what is it you do, Jesse?" Terri asked.

Rusty's eyes came up quickly.

"I'm retired. Sort of."

"How do you *sort of* retire?"

"I retired from the military," I said. "I have my pension and a little money coming in from various sources. For the last year, I've just been sailing the Caribbean."

Terri's face brightened. She had the same smile as her sister. "That sounds incredibly exciting. I work in a law office in Miami and don't get much of a chance to do anything exciting." She sipped at her drink, looking over the rim of her glass at me and Charity. "The two of you are sailing together then?"

"We flew in together," Charity said. "We left Jesse's boat over in the Bahamas for a little while."

Glancing over at Charity, I winked a thanks. Not that Terri wasn't attractive. She was. But right now, I didn't need the drama of a Miami woman in my life. Not even for flirtatious chit-chat.

Just then, the front door opened. and Julie came bounding in, rushing behind the bar to greet her father. Then she danced back around to hug me and Charity. Deuce followed, carrying a small bundle wrapped in a blue blanket.

"Hey," Deuce said, smiling. "You're here already."

I met him halfway across the room and shook his hand. "We had a tail wind."

"Jesse, meet my boy Trey," Deuce said, beaming.

The baby he held cradled in one hand had his dad's and grandfather's features, no doubt. Russell Livingston Sr. had been Rusty's and my platoon sergeant many years ago in Japan. Russell Livingston III was sound asleep.

"He's what? Six months old now?" I asked.

"Yeah," Deuce replied. "About a week ago."

Tony and Chyrel came next. Tony was carrying a large, zippered bag, which appeared to hold supplies for the baby. Or the balloons on the side meant something else completely. For him, it'd be a great way to smuggle explosives. A computer bag was slung over Chyrel's shoulder, as usual. We hugged, shook hands, and exchanged greetings and introductions.

"Here," Julie said, reaching for the baby, "let me take him so y'all can get to work."

Charity and I led the others to the same table in the corner. Deuce let Chyrel take the seat against the wall, where she opened her laptop and powered it on, out of view of anyone else. Charity and I sat on either side of her. The only empty chair of the six that encircled the round table was the one closest to the bar. The four of us shifted the remaining seats closer, so we could see Chyrel's screen if necessary.

Chyrel looked questioningly at Deuce, who nodded. "I haven't been able to find out a whole lot about Armstrong Research," Chyrel began, speaking softly with her homey, Alabama accent. "Jack Armstrong was a very private man before he lost his wife and son. Now, he's become an icon in the business world for how to stay in the game and stay below the radar at the same time."

"Lost his wife and son?" Charity asked, before I could.

"He'd had an office in the World Trade Center," she replied. "The wife helped out in the daycare, a few floors below his office. Armstrong was on a business trip when the attack happened, and he hasn't been seen publicly since then. But his businesses have all flourished. He's still running things, apparently, and doing a good job of it."

"What kind of businesses?"

"He has a hand in a lot of things," Tony replied. "A lot of stock trading. Computer research, manufacturing, oil and oil exploration, a shipyard in New Jersey, and another in Taiwan."

"Armstrong's expeditionary division is made up of a fleet of research vessels," Deuce added. "They vary from long-range boats of about 50 or 60 feet, to a huge long-range research ship measuring nearly 200 feet, fully capable of crossing the Pacific."

"So, he's a legit businessman," I said. "A bit reclusive maybe. And he does some sort of ocean research on the side?"

"Remember I said his businesses flourished after 9/11?" Chyrel said. "Maybe a little too much. A lot of businesses took a nose-dive during that time. But Armstrong Research always seemed to be flush with cash to buy up assets and other businesses."

"Where's the money coming from?" I asked, knowing that Chyrel always followed the money.

"Oh, it's barely noticeable," she replied. "He was a multi-billionaire before he lost his family and is even richer today."

"The question still stands."

"If I had to guess," Deuce said, "and my guess is based on what Chyrel showed me, he receives quite a bit in federally-funded research grants."

"And by quite a bit," Tony added, "Deuce means well into nine figures a year for going on five years now."

"Hundreds of millions?" Charity asked. "They told me they were privately funded."

"That's just it," Chyrel said. "They are privately funded. The grant money comes from the Departments of Energy and Interior mostly. The research work Armstrong does? It's totally legit and the government gets their money's worth. But it pales in comparison to the vast fortunes of the board of directors. They're all in Forbes list of wealthiest people in the world."

Tony chuckled. "But remember, this is the same government that pays hundreds of dollars for a screwdriver."

"Those screwdrivers helped fund some of our ops, Tony," Deuce reminded the former SEAL petty officer.

Chyrel glanced at her screen and continued. "A lot of the money, for the last few years now, has gone toward purchasing and maintaining a fleet of so-called research vessels. Captains and some crews stay on, and for the most part, they continue doing what they were doing before, but with lots of upgrades to their equipment. He's building what has begun to look like a private navy."

"I had Chyrel dig into a few of the captains' backgrounds," Deuce said. "Nearly all of them are prior service, many from the spec-ops community. Same with a lot of the crew members, too."

"You said, 'for the most part these research vessels continue doing what they did before,'" I commented. "Just what does that mean?"

Tony grinned. "Kinda like you were with DHS. Running charters during the week and hauling us around when we needed you."

"But in his case," Chyrel said, "fifty times as much."

"He's buying up charter businesses?" Charity asked.

"If the information Chyrel gathered is accurate," Deuce said, getting a disapproving look from the ex-CIA analyst, "he has the manpower and wherewithal to take over a number of countries, if he wanted to."

"Mercenaries?" I asked.

"Not in the true sense of the word," Chyrel explained. "I ran the dates of some of their legitimate research projects through my computer, trying to find a link to anything else happening in the areas they were working in. Around the time of many of their projects, certain unscrupulous developers, or just outright despots in general, had suffered huge failures, putting many out of business, and ridiculing others to the point that nobody wanted to do business with them."

"Outsmart them and make them look like fools," Charity said. "That's what Stockwell told me."

"How so?" I asked.

Chyrel switched to another screen. "Well, did you hear about the company in Brazil that was working on a new method of conservation forestry about a year ago?"

"Afraid not," I said.

"Well, the environmentalists seemed to love them, and the company really was managing the timber in a way approved by conservationists. But it was a front for a slavery operation. They worked deep in the rain forest. Young girls and boys from indigenous tribes along the Amazon began to disappear. Armstrong sent their big research ship down there, working on a joint project between the Brazilian environmental ministry and our own Department of Interior. It was to be a six-month study of pollution in the Amazon River. During that time, the president of the forestry company was caught on film with a very underaged boy and forced to publicly resign."

"Is that what they want us for?" Charity asked. "To spy on bad guys and take pictures?"

"That was just the short version of what happened," Deuce said. "Long story, the forestry CEO and the whole board of directors fell into a sting operation that not only foiled their slavery ring but exposed their poor business practices. Most went to prison or were facing it. That led to the apparent suicide of at least three of them. A few remain broke and destitute, living in the slums of São Paulo."

Deuce looked from me to Charity and back. "Chyrel found five similar projects that Armstrong Research was probably involved in. And there are likely a lot more."

"What's the reach of this company?" I asked. "I mean, what are the limits of their operations?"

"Worldwide," Tony said. "They have major offices here in the States, on both coasts, as well as one in the Med and another in Japan. Their primary research ship, *Ambrosia*, can sail anywhere in the world, even Antarctica."

Deuce looked across at Charity. "What else did this Bremmer guy tell you?"

"Just that the full scope of their plans would be unveiled to very few, very closely vetted, former operatives who believe in justice and self-determination."

"Big words," Tony said.

"Those were his exact words?" I asked. Charity nodded and I looked around at the others. "If they're recruiting just us, why the 'very few' part? I think we can assume we won't be the only possible recruits at this meeting. Think about that a minute. We three, maybe a couple more, plus the fifty Chyrel mentioned? Plus their crew? What if they're all like us?"

"And there's something about that ship," Chyrel said.

I looked over at her. "What's that?"

"They either have two of them, or it's capable of great speed. It turned up again in the Azores, just five days after their work in the Amazon concluded."

"No way," I said, surprised. "That's gotta be— what— 2500 miles?

"2800 nautical miles," Chyrel corrected me.

"That's 600 miles a day," I said, astonished.

"Probably more than that on the second through fourth days," Deuce said. "Day one would have been getting out of the Amazon. There are a few ships that can attain that speed, mostly military, but there are also a few very high-end luxury yachts that can reach 40 or 50 knots."

"Those things use massive turbine engines," I said. "And running at that speed for any prolonged period would eat up a whole lot of fuel."

"Did I mention that Armstrong was in the oil and ship-building businesses?" Tony said. "They have a fleet of more than 40 tankers. He specializes in moving refined fuel, not crude."

It boggled my mind. A 200-foot ship that could run for days at 30 knots was incredible. But throw in a few strategically placed tankers, and *Ambrosia's* range was unlimited. "I wanna see this ship."

"The three of us," Deuce said, pointing at me and Charity. "We're the only ones who can attend this meeting on Saturday. But—"

"Who else do you plan to bring along?" Charity asked. Like me, she knew that Deuce always had a backup plan and redundancies.

Always have a backup plan, I thought. Even though Armstrong and his associates seemed legit, and even though Colonel Stockwell was involved, we didn't know the people we'd be meeting.

"I want Chyrel on the boat, with Andrew, Tony, and Paul as backup," Deuce replied. "I'm sure we won't be talking across the gunwale, probably all on one boat or the other. That means anchored or someone dropping the invitees off."

Everyone nodded, and Deuce continued. "If we like what we hear, I'm prepared to throw all our resources behind it. Are you two in?"

"We didn't fly all the way here for Rufus's fish sandwich," I said. "Though it is worth the trip."

Charity nodded.

"It's settled then," Deuce said. "Why don't you two come up to the office Tuesday on *Gaspar's Revenge*? We'll stage it at a marina just down from the office. By then, Chyrel may have something more."

CHAPTER SEVEN

We stayed around the *Anchor* for a couple of hours, getting caught up. Oddly, nobody mentioned either my or Charity's absence over the last year. Nor did we volunteer any details.

The sun slowly started its downward arc toward the mangroves and casuarinas aglow with early spring foliage on the other side of the canal,

Deuce and Julie needed to get back up island to get Trey to bed. Rusty had told his little family about the coming marriage and asked Julie if she would come down later in the week. She'd promised to return every day, to help Sidney and Terri plan it. As a bonus treat, Rusty would babysit his grandson.

Charity, Finn, and I rode back to my island on Angie's skiff, with Jimmy at the helm. The ride took less than an hour, as Jimmy took the scenic route west of Howe Key. The familiar sights and sounds of the backcountry tranquilized my mind as the sun fell lower toward the horizon.

As we idled past the mangroves, we watched a heron and a small flock of ibis stalking along the shoreline, looking for small fish to eat in the shadows. Up in the branches, half a dozen frigate birds roosted. With wings spread wide and his red throat pouch inflated, a male croaked a mating call, vibrating his whole body to emit a sound a little like that of a bull alligator's.

"I'd forgotten how pretty it was here," Charity said.

"Yeah, me too."

"Never could figure out why you'd ever want to leave this place."

We were sitting on the forward casting deck. Charity knew why I'd left. To chase after a woman I barely knew. Behind the wind screen of the little center-console, all Jimmy could hear was the burbling engine behind him.

Charity grinned at my discomfort. "You could have any number of women, but I guess you already proved that to yourself. The cruising community is small, and they talk a lot."

Ouch.

I shrugged. "Probably learned a lot more than I wanted."

"But did you find out the one thing you most wanted to learn?" she asked, her blue eyes fixing on mine.

Looking deep into Charity's eyes, I nodded. "Yeah, I did."

Standing, I moved back along the starboard side to the console, one hand on the post of the T-top.

"How's the *Revenge*, Jimmy?" I asked.

"Been keeping up with the maintenance," he replied. "Take her out once a week to fill a few folks' freezers and shake off the cobwebs. But, man, every now and then those engines need to be run hot and long, or they start to get old and cranky. I don't wanna do that, man. Not my boat."

"You want to take her out on the Gulf tomorrow?" I asked. "Let her breathe a little?"

"Hell yeah, man!" he said enthusiastically—or at least with what qualified as enthusiasm in Jimmy's world.

Charity joined us, standing on the opposite side of the boat, as Jimmy easily threaded through the many cuts and channels, only a handful of them marked.

The cuts were a little different, I noticed. The backcountry of the Middle Keys wasn't just a cluster of islands. It was a living and *moving* watery habitat. Since it was made up primarily of skinny water, few visitors ever came out there. There were places in the backcountry that rarely saw a human visitor and were reminiscent of the primordial ooze that life evolved from.

The islands themselves made up a very small part of the ecosystem. The water was where nearly all life in the backcountry began or ended. There were birds that never rested on land, and fish that never swam out beyond the one-or two-foot shallows.

Tides and storms changed the contour of the shallows constantly. Sandbars were cut through or washed away entirely, just by the force of the ever-changing tide, and new sandbars covered up old cuts. There was far more life *below* the surface than above it; the cataclysmic event that moved a sandbar could be triggered by something as simple as a crab or ray burrowing in shifting sand.

Finally, we made it to the natural, sweeping channel between Howe Key and Water Key. Half a mile ahead, I could just make out the low dock at the south end of my island. Only the gray-green metal roof was visible above the trees. Finn barked, and his tail began to beat against the inside of the hull. He knew he was home.

I'd been thinking for years that those trees needed to be trimmed. But in truth, the view through them from my deck wasn't all that diminished. Sure, it'd be nice to have an unobstructed view, but from the water, the house was nearly invisible now.

We tied up at the dock and carried our things up to the deck. Instead of following us, Finn immediately splashed through the shallows and disappeared into the trees, headed toward the island's interior.

"Angie isn't here right now," Jimmy said. "I gotta run back and pick her up. She gets off work in an hour."

"Why don't you each use a different boat?" I asked. "There are plenty available."

My question triggered another one in my brain. I collected boats, each for a different job or purpose. For the backcountry, I had a nice little Maverick that could practically skip across a puddle. I'd bought it to chase permit and bonefish. The *Revenge* was for offshore, as was the smaller Winter center-console, *El Cazador*. The old Grady-White I'd picked up in Beaufort, South Carolina was the most utilitarian. It could haul a good bit of weight, was comfortable in moderate seas, and could get almost as far into the skinny water as the Maverick. Different boats for different jobs. I made a mental note to see if Chyrel could give me a list of the boats in Armstrong Research's fleet and their home ports.

"*No problemo, hermano,*" Jimmy said. "I like driving her around. And it gets me off the island twice a day."

"You're welcome to use any of them," I told him. I'd also told him the same thing a year ago, when he signed on as caretaker.

"Her little Whaler's a great boat," he said, by way of reply. "I'm gonna head back to *Dockside* now. She gets grumpy if I'm late. Need me to bring anything back?"

"Is there any beef on the island?" Charity asked. "I could really go for a steak."

"No," Jimmy said. "Sorry. But I can pick some up, and Angie and I will be back just after sunset."

"Use my card," I said. "You still have it, right?"

"Will do, man," he shouted, as he retraced his steps down to the dock.

I turned to Charity. "I have no idea what condition the bunkhouses are in. Kim has probably transformed the other half of yours into her house."

"She lives here full-time? I thought she was still in school."

"She is," I replied. "Up in Gainesville." I had more news for Charity about my youngest daughter, though. "But she's getting married next year, and she and her fiancé wanted a place of their own here."

"That deputy?"

"Marty Phillips," I confirmed, nodding. I dropped my backpack at the door to my little stilt house. "They plan to get married when she graduates."

Charity paused at the steps going down from the back deck. "She's graduating so soon? I thought she was only in her sophomore year."

"She changed majors," I said, pulling open the door. "She's studying criminology now. She plans to finish her associate degree studies next year. Then she wants to go to through FDLE training here in Marathon. I'm hoping after her law-enforcement training, she'll go on to law school, but she and Marty plan to join Fish and Wildlife." I shrugged. "She's an adult now."

"I see," Charity said, heading down the steps. I stood there a moment and watched her cross the yard toward the two bunkhouses on the north end of the island.

Finn came running toward her from between the buildings, dancing around her and barking out a list of all the things he'd missed since he'd been gone. At least, that's what I imagined he was trying to tell her.

Charity tossed her hair over her shoulder and looked back to see me watching her before she smiled and continued walking.

Inside my house, I immediately opened the windows on either side of the living room. The air inside had probably been trapped there for a year. The times I'd returned, I hadn't come back to the island.

Next, I dropped my pack in my bedroom. Everything was exactly as I'd left it. The blanket on the bed remained slightly disheveled where I'd sat on it the day I'd decided to leave. The drawer to the nightstand still sat open, from when I'd removed my Sig to take with me.

Sitting back down in the same spot, I reached to remove the Sig and its holster from under my T-shirt and realized it wasn't there. Though I was surrounded by familiar things, I felt like a stranger in someone else's home. The aft cabin on *Salty Dog* had been my bunk for over a year—except for when I'd slept in whatever beach, hammock, or young woman's cabin I happened to pass out in.

"Full circle," I told myself, closing the drawer. Finn stuck his head through the doorway, then sat in the opening, his tail swishing back and forth on the deck. "Glad to be home?" I asked.

He barked in the affirmative.

"Jesse," Charity called. "Can I come in?"

I strode to the bedroom door. She stood in the entry to the house, the bright light from the setting sun streaming over her shoulder.

"Yeah, sure," I said, crossing my tiny combination living room, galley, dining room, and workshop. "Anything wrong?"

"The fridge in the office is empty. Got any water?"

"I don't know," I replied, approaching the small re-frigerator in the corner of the galley. I discovered that, aside from a six-pack of Red Stripe, it was empty. "No water. Care for a beer?"

She stepped inside. "Why not?"

I took two out and opened them with the bottle opener hanging on the front by a magnet. "I'm sure Jimmy has plenty of water."

"Glad to be home?"

After opening the window over the sink, I gestured with my chin toward the table and chairs in the corner. Charity took a seat.

"I don't really know," I replied honestly. "Been a lot of miles under my keel since I was last in this house."

"You haven't been back here in all that time?"

"I came back to Marathon a few times," I said, taking a seat in the chair opposite hers. "But I didn't stay long enough to come up here. Kim was up in Gainesville, and I really only stopped into the *Anchor* to sign some papers over at the bank."

"You haven't seen her or Eve in a year?"

"Flew them all out to where I was a couple of times," I replied. "Once in Dominica, and again in Mexico."

"Planning to stay?"

"I don't know that either. What about you?"

"My boat's in California," Charity replied. "I'm having some work done on her. But yeah, I think I might come back here. Maybe not *here* here, but South Florida some-where."

"I guess that anything I'm planning," I began, while staring out the window, "depends on what happens next Saturday."

Charity reached across the table and touched my hand. "I think we're both looking for some sort of ultimate cause, a lofty principle to live by once again. But not necessarily some*one*."

I lifted my beer, breaking the contact of her hand on my arm, and took a swig. It was my first beer in over a month. "Tide's high. You bring your bathing suit?"

She smiled. "I could really use a swim to burn off this nervous energy."

"What are you nervous about?" I asked, on my feet once more and heading toward the door.

She followed me but paused in the doorway. "Same thing as you, probably. The unknown. What tomorrow, or Saturday, might bring." Walking toward the back steps, she called out over her shoulder, "Meet you on the pier in ten minutes."

I watched her until she disappeared, then went into my bedroom to change.

We swam north across the flats, to a little sandbar I know on the edge of the Gulf. No competition this time, since the bar was a mile away. It was just a nice long swim to unwind. Finn swam along with us and we adjusted our speed to his, side-stroking at times so we could talk.

We walked around on the sandbar, looking for anything of interest, while Finn dug up and ate clams. The water to the north deepened quickly, and I'd found all sorts of odd things on the bar in the past. But the wind today was out of the east. It took a north wind to bring anything ashore.

Charity did find a shell that she liked. It was very small, mostly white, but with a little brown fringe around the opening. She asked me to put it in my pocket to bring back, since she had opted for a tiny, lime-green bikini for this swim.

On the return, we took a different, shallower route, mostly walking in water up to our waists, so we could continue talking. The tide was falling quickly, leaving occasional shallow tidal pools. We discussed places we'd been and people we'd met in the time since we'd last seen each other.

Finn took an even longer way, following the shallows and sandbars around the west side of the lagoon, rather than swimming against the current. But occasionally the flats we were strolling on rose up to where he could half-walk along with us, stopping to shower us several times.

Charity looked off toward the now-setting sun. "What are you looking for, Jesse?"

"Not sure," I replied, as we sloshed through knee-deep water. Finn was off on a sandbar again, nose to the ground. "I don't really need money or a job—you know that."

"Nor I," she said. "I never told you, but Vic and I took down this big-time money launderer in the Virgin Islands two years ago. It was off the books. His goons killed a couple of locals and he needed to be stopped. We came away with a pile of cash and gave a lot to the locals he'd hurt."

"I'm sure he deserved what he got," I said, looking over at her expectantly.

The fading sun highlighted her hair and gave a warm glow to her tanned skin. She was deep in thought, or so it appeared. I waited.

"Cruising is fun, but there has to be more challenge to life than just having fun," she finally said.

It was my turn for introspection. "A challenge?" I said, more to myself. "Yeah, I guess that's what I'm looking for."

"You didn't find it a challenge to bed down one young girl after another?"

"It wasn't like that," I said.

"Come on, Jesse. I've heard quite a few people talk about you over this past year."

"Okay, a few. But most nights it was just me and Finn. Nobody else around for miles."

She looked over at me, her white sunglasses perched on top of her head and strands of golden hair blowing across her face. "I'm just busting your chops."

"Rightly so," I admitted. "I've been an idiot."

"Did you get it all out of your system?"

I grinned back at her. "Yeah, I think I learned something about myself in the process."

"Yeah? What's that?"

"I don't *need* a woman in my life. It's nice now and then, having a warm body to hold, but eventually people become boring."

"No argument from me," she said. "And what about the girl? Savannah's daughter?"

When I glanced over at her again, she seemed truly concerned. "On the day I saw them pull into Cane Garden Bay, Florence left a nearly empty water bottle on their boat. When they went off with the rich guy, Savannah's dog knocked it into the water."

"And being a good steward of the sea," she said, elbowing me in the ribs, "you went over and picked it up. Come on. Give."

We sloshed through more water, which deepened as we neared the pier.

"I held onto it for three months," I finally confessed. "Last summer, I gave it to Chyrel, to see if she could send it to a lab or something and get a DNA match from any saliva in the bottle."

"And?"

"There's a 99.97 percent certainty that Florence is my biological daughter."

Neither of us said anything as we walked across the waist-deep water just before the pier. Even at low tide, I could dock a boat there, but the surrounding shallows meant only the smaller boats. I sometimes tied my plane off to this pier, but mostly this part of my island had been where Carl and Charlie's kids had played.

"What have you done with this information?" Charity finally asked.

"Nothing. Savannah claims she doesn't know who the father is."

"I got the feeling," Charity said, "when I met her last year in the Bahamas, that she did know."

"Either way, she doesn't want me to know," I said, reaching the ladder at the end of the pier. "But I met with my attorney and added Florence to my will."

Finn went up his ramp, shook himself off, and ran toward the bunkhouses. I climbed up the ladder first, and grabbed some clean towels from the towel locker, offering Charity one as she stepped up. Her hair was dripping down her back, and her wet bikini clung to her body. The cooler air brought goosebumps to her exposed flesh and caused her nipples to poke through the fabric of her tiny swimsuit.

I remembered the sexual tension that had hung between us the night we'd seen each other showering. Thankfully, she wrapped the towel around her body under her arms and knotted it in front. Together, we sat on the side of the pier to watch the sunset.

Charity continued our conversation. "That's one way to handle it."

"I'm open to suggestions."

"Don't be a wimp," she said. "Tell her you know. That is, if you want to be a part of the girl's life."

That stung a little. "I'd be her dad if Savannah asked."

"That's exactly what you should tell Savannah. Any idea what happened to her after Tortola? Do you know who the guy was?"

"Yeah, I found out who he is. Some hot-shot business lawyer out of Charleston, not far from where Savannah's from. Name's Mark Walker."

"And you haven't kept tabs on Savannah's whereabouts?"

"No."

The sun slowly became one with the ocean just off the tip of Racoon Key. We sat in silence, watching Mother Nature's display. It was already darkening, but the sun was still a fiery orange ball that could easily be observed directly. Just as the last of the orb disappeared, I closed my eyes briefly and made a silent wish.

There was no green flash.

In the distance, off to the southeast, I heard an outboard, a boat moving at planing speed.

"That's probably Jimmy and Angie," I said, rising, and offering her a hand. She took it and stood in front of me.

"We're good, right?" she asked.

"Why wouldn't we be?"

"How long have we known each other?"

"Over four years," I said.

"And we've spent quite a few nights alone together." Then she grinned. "Not to mention we've seen each other naked."

I felt my face flush, the memory of the night she'd stayed on the island flashing through my mind again. She'd chosen the outdoor shower at the same time I was stepping into my indoor shower. My bathroom light had illuminated both of us through the adjoining window.

"Let's try to avoid that tonight," I said, laughing.

"I don't know," she said, turning to walk slowly toward the foot of the pier. "I've been three months crossing the Pacific alone, and another week tracking you down."

CHAPTER  EIGHT

The purpling sky outside my window told me it was pre-dawn. In years past, it had been the attack hour—the time when the enemy was less active and vulnerable. Today was quiet, though, the only sound a gentle lapping of waves on the eastern shore. Lying alone in my bunk, I thought back to my days in the Corps.

During my time, I'd worked and trained with some of the smartest and most capable people America had ever produced. But now, to a man, we'd all become obsolete. Today's warriors were better equipped, better trained, bigger, faster, and deadlier than any force in the history of the world. By a long margin.

Leaving it all behind had been difficult. A camaraderie existed between those who trained and fought together; a bond that the civilian world never knew and couldn't possibly understand. Moving out of that world and into the average life of a civilian was a major change, and I'd never much liked change. I guess that's why the Corps' regimented lifestyle had been so comfortable for me.

After twenty years of eating, sleeping, working, training, and occasionally fighting alongside others like myself, adjusting to a different lifestyle was like removing a mask. On the day I retired, I'd worn the mask of the warrior for the better part of my life. It had become a part of me, molding to my face like a second skin.

The Marine Corps didn't issue emotions and feelings. Out of necessity, that extra baggage a person brought with them was sometimes forced into a deep-freeze, leaving only the Marine Machine, with a heart like Arctic ice.

Problems often arose when warriors returned to their wives and families. They were required to remove their warrior masks, hang up the mantles, and melt those frozen blocks of emotions and feelings that had lain dormant during deployment. But not all of them could; not all those frozen emotions were easily thawed. What happened on the battlefield stayed on the battlefield.

If you did this often enough, the donning and doffing of the warrior mask, the repeated thawing and refreezing of little frozen cubes of emotion and feeling, they began to leave behind a rocky residue that just never melted. The calcified remnants of emotions encircled the memories of the battlefield, locking them away tightly for all time, while those repressed feelings were pushed deep into the old warrior's mind and heart, unseen by the outside world. But that constant peeling and replacing of the mask could leave rough, visible lines in the face, hard eyes, and a jagged soul.

It'd taken me more than five years to learn how to simply enjoy the predawn hours without anticipating an attack.

I padded barefoot to the little galley. The only light was a shaft of blue-gray from the window and a tiny red glow from the coffeemaker. I poured myself a mug of joe and stepped out into the cool darkness, Finn following right behind me. He quickly trotted down the back steps as I took a seat at the rough-hewn table in the corner, overlooking the island's interior.

My house blocked the larger part of the eastern sky. Sunrise was still a good half-hour away and the only light visible was from the stars. Thousands and thousands of them were spread across the northern and western skies. The Milky Way, the visible part of our own galaxy, stretched across the sky like a hazy veil.

I'd thought Rusty a really deep thinker when he first told me that the stars were timeless and predictable. Maybe he was, but I heard the same words in a Jimmy Buffett song several months ago. I liked the song, which was on one of the CDs Victor had left behind, and I played it over and over. Who knows? Maybe Jimmy got the line from Rusty. He used to live in the Keys back in the day. And Rusty knew everyone in the Keys.

I heard the click of a door latch and looked over in the direction of the sound. I recognized Charity's confident stride in the starlight, as she moved silently toward my house. Knowing she'd want coffee and didn't have any in the office, I went inside to get her some, leaving the door open behind me.

"You forgot to get water from Jimmy," I said, meeting her at the table and handing her the mug.

"Thanks. What's on the agenda for today?" She took a seat opposite me.

I shrugged and joined her. "I thought I'd give the *Revenge* a thorough looking-over before we take her out later."

"Didn't Jimmy say he'd been on top of that?"

"Yeah, but I've been away a long time."

She grinned over her mug.

"What?"

"You're a speed junky," she said. "You get your jollies tinkering with powerful engines and you need your fix." She grinned again, wrapping both hands around her mug. "Admitting it is the first step."

"And you didn't get a charge from flying your Huey?"

"Oh, I'm definitely a junky," she replied. "Can I give you a hand?"

We finished our coffee and then went down below my house. My quarters were completely off the grid. Everything up there ran on a pair of twelve-volt batteries, charged by a solar array on the roof, and a small wind turbine mounted above the rainwater cistern. The stove and fridge were propane-powered boat appliances I'd picked up years ago and managed to keep working. But below the house, everything was wired into the main power source on the island, a big diesel generator charging a large bank of deep-cycle marine batteries.

I flicked a switch just inside the doorway and bright LED lights instantly illuminated the walkway around the dock area, as well as the water and the boats tied up to the docks. The house was 50 by 20 feet, with a fifteen-foot wide deck around three sides. The dock area was under all of it, 65 feet wide by 50 feet deep, with giant doors on spring-loaded hinges. The space was separated by a middle catwalk with nearly 30 feet of berthing room on both sides for boats up to 48 feet in total length.

The *Revenge* filled nearly the first quarter of the berthing area, towering over the other boats. The arrays on her roof cleared the subfloor of the house by only a foot on the highest high tide. Her hull was a cobalt blue, the bow flaring out in typical Carolina fashion. The deck and cabin were gleaming white under the bright lights, chrome rails sparkling like brand new.

"I'd forgotten how beautiful it was," Charity said, walking along the narrow catwalk that surrounded the dock area on three sides.

Following her, I trailed my hand along the *Revenge's* fiberglass gunwale. "Yeah, me too."

"What's that?" she asked, pointing to the far side of the dock area.

"You remember Carl and Charlie, who used to take care of things here?" She nodded as we walked around to the little wooden boat on the far side, and I continued. "He and I built Knot L-8 a few winters ago."

"Ha!" she proclaimed, reading the name on the stern. "Knot with a K, and an L with the number eight: *not late*. Nice word play. I didn't know you were a boat builder."

"My grandfather was," I said, admiring the lines of the custom-built barrel-backed runabout. "I picked up a few pointers when I was a kid. Even helped him build a few before I joined the Corps."

"Let me guess," she said, stepping around to the side and gazing down into the twin seating cockpits. "With a name like that, and you being you, I bet it's got a small turbo-diesel?"

Reaching past her, I raised and turned the latch for the engine cover. It glided up slowly, hydraulic arms hissing.

Charity laughed, holding one hand to her flat belly and the other to her mouth. She had a very nice laugh. "Dammit, Jesse! You really are a speed junky."

"Remember Doc Talbot?"

"Bob?" she asked. "How are he and his wife doing?"

"On their second kid now," I replied. "I'd been leaning toward diesel, and Carl thought we should go with a big-block Chevy engine. Doc suggested custom-built motorcycle engines."

"Is it as fast as it looks?"

"Faster," I said. "Somewhere north of 60 knots. Combined power is over 300 horses, with half the weight of a single outboard."

"We've got to take it out."

I'd never seen Charity so animated about anything. "Sure. Maybe this evening. But right now, I want to make sure all the bugs are worked out of the systems on the *Revenge*."

"Let's get to it, then." She squeezed past me on the narrow catwalk, holding my hips from behind and raking my back with her breasts. Then she stepped down into the cockpit of the big Rampage fishing machine.

Over the next two hours, we examined all the electronic systems, stopping only to refill our coffee mugs and watch the sun come up over Harbor Channel. We checked the fluids, and from the log, I saw that Jimmy had just changed the oil last month.

Charity had some knowledge of the systems my boat employed and a good overall working knowledge of all things mechanical or electronic.

While inspecting the engines, she kept glancing up at the top of the bulkhead. "What's in there?" she finally asked.

"In where?" I asked, knowing full well what she meant.

"It's only noticeable because I knew you'd have one," she replied, nodding her head toward the spot. "You've got a stash spot there."

"Inside it, there's a Ma Deuce."

She dropped onto an upturned bucket. "You really are paranoid, aren't you? A .50-caliber machine gun?"

"It's come in handy a couple of times."

Jimmy joined us, announcing that Angie would have breakfast ready soon. We worked and then ate, and then worked some more. Eventually, I was satisfied that Jimmy had taken care of my boat just as well as I would have. He took no offense at the thoroughness of my inspection.

By clicking the fob on the starboard engine key chain, I opened the big door in front of us. Then I started the engines, Jimmy tossed off the lines, and we slowly idled out from beneath the house as Jimmy climbed up to take the second seat beside me. The girls were talking on the forward bench seat in front of the helm, and Finn stood spread-legged on the foredeck as we glided the short distance to the main channel.

I turned left into Harbor Channel and bumped the throttles up a notch, following the deep blue water. The big diesels responded with a low, throaty growl as we headed toward the light on Harbor Key and the open Gulf of Mexico beyond.

Truth be told, I did like to go fast. Or I used to. The last year aboard *Salty Dog*, with her much slower speed, had taken some getting used to. But I'd grown to love the tranquility of the hull quietly pushing through the water and the gentle push when cresting a wave.

Now, though, it was time for some speed.

Nearing the mouth of the natural channel, I called to Finn, telling him to get back down to the cockpit. He seemed to understand and climbed down to his usual spot in the corner, curling up and ignoring the small vest I made him wear when we were sailing. He'd never fallen overboard, but in the big Formosa, turning around to pick him up could take time. Even a dog as big as Finn could become invisible very quickly. The *Revenge* was far nimbler, but at higher speed, just as dangerous.

I pushed the throttles halfway and the engines roared. The big props instantly displaced water from beneath us. The stern dropped, and the bow rose a few degrees as the powerful Caterpillar engines pushed the big boat up on top of the water. In seconds, we were beyond Harbor Key and headed due north at 30 knots.

Jimmy was busy with the electronics, checking the radar and sonar equipment, moving each through their ranges, checking for full functionality.

"Everything looks good, man," he said after we'd traveled several miles. His voice was only slightly above conversational tone. "No surface craft for ten miles and no underwater obstructions."

The previous owner of *Gaspar's Revenge* had been a tournament fisherman out of Texas, and a bigger speed junky than me. He'd spent a fortune tweaking the engines beyond their standard 1015 horsepower to well over 1300. He'd supercharged the already turbocharged engines. The superchargers didn't kick in except at high demand, nearly wide-open throttle. The combination was like opening a bottle of nitrous-oxide on a hot rod.

"Watch the boost gauges," I said, reaching for the throttles once more.

As I slowly moved the throttles forward, the boat responded like a finely tuned sports car. At 40 knots, a double click from far below and the low whine of the superchargers told me the clutches were engaging correctly. I slowed a little and heard them disengage.

"Boost was nominal," Jimmy said. "Everything looks good."

I pushed the throttles back up. At 50 knots, the superchargers were screaming like banshees, but the sound was falling behind us. I held the compass on due north, which would eventually take us to the Ten Thousand Islands in Southwest Florida.

"Boost is steady!" Jimmy shouted, scanning the gauges. "About 30 percent with no fluctuation. Oil pressure's right on the money. The starboard engine's running a little hotter than the port side, but still well within the safe zone."

"Let's keep an eye on that," I said, pushing the throttles to the stops, while turning the wheel slightly to port.

The big boat accelerated, leaning into the turn like a greyhound as we flew across the calm, late-morning waters of the Gulf. I didn't need Jimmy to tell me the superchargers were at full boost. The sound resembled whatever nightmarish creature could swoop through Hell devouring banshees left and right.

I straightened her up as we reached northwest, and watched the speed indicator on the GPS, comparing it to the boat's knot-meter. We were moving with a slight current and what little wind blew was now at our backs.

The knot-meter read 53 knots, and the GPS's digital display was ticking back and forth between 54 and 55, which would account for the just-over-a-knot-and-a-half of current.

"Incredible!" Jimmy shouted, as I pulled the throttles back until the superchargers dropped out.

I had to agree. The *Revenge* was a fine boat with as solid a hull as you could find. But she was not designed for sustained speeds of more than 40 knots, and at 55, we were teetering on the edge of compromised stability. It was good to know the speed was there if you needed it, though.

We spent the rest of the morning just running the old girl through her paces, making sure all systems were functioning properly. The disparity in engine temperatures was nagging, but less than ten degrees, and as Jimmy had said, well within the norm. The big eighteen-liter Cats just never got hot. We both decided to stop and check it out anyway.

With the boat drifting, Jimmy and I climbed down into the engine room, checking the water-intake strainers. We found only a few bits of frayed plastic and sargassum, so we went on to check that all the valves were fully opened. Finally, I dove over the starboard side to check the bronze raw-water intake ports.

A large piece of heavy white plastic, perforated by water suction at the slots in the bronze openings, was fouled inside the port, ragged and barely hanging on. I removed it and surfaced beside the swim platform.

"What is it?" Jimmy asked.

"Dunno," I said, handing it up to him.

Jimmy unwadded the plastic, turning it in his hands to examine the writing. "Bentonite?"

"What's that?" I asked, climbing up onto the platform.

"It's mined out west, man," he replied. "Northern Rockies mostly. It's used to make drilling mud to line the shaft and keep contaminants out before the casing goes in."

"Is there anything you *don't* know?"

Jimmy shrugged. "Just naturally curious, man."

I grabbed a towel and dried off before we went back up to the bridge. The GPS indicated that we were 50 miles out in the Gulf, and just west of the Particularly Sensitive Sea Area boundary in 60 feet of water. I brought the *Revenge* up to trolling speed, turning toward the southeast. Jimmy reported that both engines were now operating at the same temperature.

"Let's catch some fish then," I told him.

Jimmy actually slid down the ladder, bracing the handrails under his upper arms, and was on the deck in seconds. I'd forgotten what a competent first mate he was. With no wasted movement, he rigged a pair of green-skirted deep-running lures and had both lines in the water, rods in the two outboard holders in record time. Charity and Angie joined him and within minutes, the bite was on.

Charity was first in the chair, fighting what looked like a 50-or 60-pound yellowfin tuna. As Jimmy reeled in the other line to keep them from tangling, he hooked a small amberjack, which quickly found its way into the fish box, as Charity fought with the bigger fish. Finn barked at the flopping jack until Jimmy closed the box, then began dancing around the cockpit, watching Charity. It was just one of the odd things he did when he came out fishing with us. He'd bark constantly at any fish brought aboard, then stop as soon as the fish box closed.

Angie and Jimmy were urging Charity on. Jimmy occasionally gave both me and Charity instructions, as I did my best to keep the fish astern.

Charity's long, slender arms belied her strength. With her feet planted on the chair's foot brace, she put her whole body into the fight, tanned skin stretching over taut muscle.

Over the next two hours, we each took a turn in the chair, adding another yellowfin, two wahoos, and four big bull dolphins to the box. Some people reacted with surprise or revulsion when we talked dolphin fishing, thinking we were hunting Flipper or something. Even when you explained that they were two different things, one a fish and the other a mammal, some folks still didn't get it. So, to landlubbers, we usually used the now-more-common Pacific term, mahi-mahi. Off Texas and Mexico, they were called dorado. Whatever your choice, it was still one of the best tasting and best fighting, most aerobatic fish in the sea.

Satisfied that all systems were working not just normally, but very well, I called the turnaround, somewhere 40 miles north of Key West. Turning due south, I decided to return to my island along the backbone of the backcountry.

When we sighted the tops of buildings on Key West, I turned toward the east, angling closer to the islands of the backcountry. I slowed to a speed just fast enough to stay on top of the water as we followed the ten-foot line on the chart plotter, running just a few hundred yards off the outer mangroves and small sand beaches. Just off Johnston Key Channel, I spotted something closer in to the shore and slowed.

"What's that?" I asked.

Both women rose and looked out over the starboard bow. Jimmy went down the ladder, knowing that whatever it was, I'd turn to investigate.

"Looks like a lot of trash?" Angie said.

"Or clothes," Charity added. "Bed sheets maybe."

Jimmy grabbed the boat hook as I turned toward a large blob of floating whiteness. Closer, I could see that there was more than just the blob. All along the mangrove abutment of Barracuda and Johnston Keys I could see swaths of white tangled in the roots.

I slowed further, shifting in and out of gear as we neared the edge of the floating debris. Jimmy reached out with the boat hook and snagged a piece, hauling it aboard. It resembled the plastic that had earlier fouled the raw-water intake.

Jimmy turned and held it up over his head. "Benton-ite bags!" he shouted up to me. "Must be thousands of them."

Reversing the engines, I slowly backed away from the roiling mess of thick, empty bags, tapping the GPS screen to drop a waypoint marker.

"No way we can clean all that up," I called down to Jimmy. "We'll have to call it in to the Coasties as a hazard to navigation. Maybe they can alert one of the environmental groups to send some boats out here."

Later that evening, after washing down the boat and eating a dinner of tuna and fresh mango, the four of us sat around the firepit off to the east of the bunkhouses. I'd found the heavy metal fire ring when I'd first bought the island. Some long-ago camper had probably left it; the thing sure didn't float out here. The fire I'd built in that ring had saved me from being hauled away by the Florida state bird—the mosquito.

"Funny thing about those bags," Jimmy said. "They didn't look like they'd ever been used."

"How can you tell?" I asked.

"The openings were raw, man, never heat-sealed. See, once a bag's filled, they use a heat bar to melt the plastic together at the open end."

"Just naturally curious, huh?"

"He does it all the time," Angie said. "Looks up one thing on the internet, which leads him to some-thing else, and something else. Watch out if he gets to YouTube. And he remembers everything."

This surprised me. Jimmy had been known for a long time to be a regular pot smoker. I was too, for almost a year. The times I'd been high, I often forgot to breathe.

"You said that stuff was mined out west?" Charity said. "Anywhere else?"

"Depends on the type," Jimmy said. "Those bags were marked *sodium bentonite*. That's only mined in the western part of the U.S. and in a small area in Turkey."

"What is it, exactly?" I asked.

Jimmy shrugged. "For lack of a simpler term, man, it's a clay made of weathered volcanic ash. In this case, sodium ash."

"Is that dangerous to sea life?"

"Not that I know of," Jimmy replied. "It's just clay, man. But it wouldn't take much of it to muck up the water."

"So maybe the bags are made here in Florida?" Charity asked. "Or one of the other Gulf states?"

"Wouldn't make sense, *mi amiga*," Jimmy replied. "If it's gonna be used for a specific purpose, and that purpose was only in one area, they'd wanna buy them from somewhere local. And like I said, there's really only a handful of places you can sell them too."

"Could be," I said, reaching into the cooler and taking out a bottle of water. "But the western states are mostly agricultural and livestock. Not a lot of industrial plants to make plastic bags out there. Seems to me, you could truck the bags in for a couple hundred years and it'd still be cheaper than building a factory."

Angie stretched her feet toward the fire. "I wonder if maybe they were accidentally dumped from a shipping container or something. Plastic lasts forever in the ocean."

"It might be jetsam," Charity added. "Not flotsam at all."

Some might confuse the two terms and use them interchangeably or even together. But Charity was right. Those bags might have been intentionally jettisoned, and not accidentally floated off a freighter in a storm or accident. Either way, the problem was the same; plastic floating in the water.

"It happens," Jimmy said. "Somebody orders too much of something and it's so cheap to buy they just throw away what they don't use rather than warehouse it. Warehouse space might've been at a premium."

"Really?" I asked. "Just dump it in the ocean?"

"Absolutely, *hermano*," Jimmy said. "The ocean is the last big trash dump. Anything dumped in some creek up in Hog's Wallow, West Virginia, eventually reaches the Atlantic. If you took all the man-made stuff that's in all the world's oceans and dumped it into the Med, it'd displace all the water and you could walk from France to Egypt."

I'd seen my share of crap in the water. While diving, I almost always came back with a length of monofilament, or a beer can, or something. And I'd seen my share of floating debris, too.

"Jimmy, the Mediterranean's probably a mile deep, on average," I said. "Some places nearly three miles deep."

Jimmy looked up solemnly. "Yeah, dude, I know."

My phone buzzed in my pocket. It was a message from Deuce.

C found something. Bring the boat. We may go to Bimini tomorrow.

CHAPTER NINE

E arly the following morning, Charity and I once more made the turn into Harbor Channel from my house. But instead of heading due north past Harbor Key, I turned the wheel a little to the right and held it there in a sweeping, three-mile-wide turn. When I straightened the wheel, we were heading south-south-east. I followed East Bahia Honda Channel to the high arch of the Seven Mile Bridge and Moser Channel. Passing under the bridge, we entered the open ocean and I turned east into the low, wind-driven swells.

Deuce had arranged a slip at a nearby marina and we reached Tavernier by mid-morning. Driving would have taken about the same amount of time.

Tony was waiting at the dock to help us tie off. Even though the *Revenge* was equipped with a security system, I left Finn aboard. I was not crazy about leaving my boat unattended at a strange marina. He couldn't get out of the salon, but I knew he'd raise so much commotion, any intruder would leave in a hurry.

"Hey, Jesse," Chyrel called when we stepped through the door into Deuce's outer office. "Hey, Charity."

The sign on the front read *Livingston and McDermitt*, but in my eyes, it was Deuce's security firm.

"I got that list together you asked for."

"Thanks." I took the sheets of paper from her, scanning through them. Each page was a vessel registry, each with a broadside view. There were dozens. Boats of all shapes and sizes, from luxury sailing catamarans, to charter boats like the *Revenge*.

"He owns all these?"

"Not exactly," Deuce said, coming out of the back office. "Armstrong Research owns the first dozen vessel registries you have there. The others are vessels that he has occasionally contracted."

"Contracted in what way?" Charity asked.

"The others will be here in a minute," he said. "Let's wait and go over everything together."

Deuce led us down a hall to a conference room. There were notebooks in front of eight chairs, arranged around an oval conference table. Each binder was filled with dozens of pages.

Chyrel had been busy.

Paul Bender came in carrying a large carafe. Andrew Bourke followed him with a tray of mugs. A moment later, Tom Broderick stepped through the door. Everyone shook hands while jockeying for position at the coffee dispenser.

Once everyone was seated, Chyrel began laying out what she'd learned in the last two days, moving through the notebook quickly. It was a lot to digest. Each of us would dig deeper into the binders later.

"And the facility on Bimini?" I asked. "What is it?"

"A shipyard," Deuce said. "Or it will be once the renovation and construction are completed. It used to be a marina and fuel depot. One of the few that could haul out large yachts. It's now owned by a shell company that's owned through several other nameplates, leading back to Jack Armstrong and Associates, the parent company of Armstrong Research. They're building a dry-dock facility there. Other dummy corporations are doing the same thing in a few other places around the globe, all of them large enough to maintain, repair, or even build ships up to 250 feet."

"This one on the top?" Tony said. "The *Ambrosia*? It's a 199-foot luxury mega-yacht originally built for a Saudi prince. Armstrong bought it three years ago and had it fully refitted for ocean-borne research, complete with a helipad and a submersible capable of depths of 10,000 feet. It's rumored to be incredibly fast."

"Not in the original specs I just read," I countered, tapping a finger on the top boat registry. "As built, I wouldn't think it capable of more than 25 knots."

Andrew nodded his head in agreement. "Probably not even that."

"But you think there's more to the new shipyard than what appears," I said.

"I think the new shipyards are for something more, yes," Deuce replied. "Bimini is a sport fisherman's paradise. You know that. You and Dad took me there when I was a kid. We stayed at the Compleat Angler, remember? What Armstrong's building there could be just a central place to keep *Ambrosia*, close to deep water. Or it could be something more. If we're going to have a working relationship with these people, I'd like to find out why Armstrong doesn't just own the shipyard outright. Why all the dummy companies?"

"All these other boats?" Charity asked. "Any idea what they were contracted for?"

"None," Chyrel said. "But Armstrong and Associates paid big. Well into five digits to each for the initial contract or charter. And the boats themselves? All different kinds, with no logical pattern."

I looked across the table at the former CIA analyst. She was grinning at me.

I grinned back. "You found an illogical pattern."

"Yes," she said. "Not the boats, though. The owners. Every one of those boats, the ones not owned by Armstrong, that is, they're all owned by people who have a few things in common. And they all share those commonalities with you. And with Deuce and Charity."

"What?" I asked.

"None of them will ever have to work a day in their lives," she replied. "They're all self-made millionaires and nearly all of them have some sort of military background, many in spec-ops."

"You said a few things in common," Charity said. "That's only two."

"Every single one of them has created some sort of charitable trust or foundation to help the less fortunate."

I glanced up sharply. "You mean like my Waterman Fund and the one I set up to help Keys Vets??"

"And Deuce's," Chyrel said. "And Charity's."

Charity was studying the file in front of her. When she looked up, everyone was staring at her. "What?"

"Your college fund for victims of abuse," Chyrel said.

Charity slowly closed the notebook in front of her, her blue eyes moving from one of us to the other. "That doesn't leave this room."

"Of course not," Deuce said. "All cards on the table, so we can find the connections. That's all."

"Charity received an inheritance when Victor was killed," I said, reminding each one about her loss. "Not just the sailboat she sold to me. She didn't need the money or want it, so she uses it to help other people. She told me all about it."

"Good on ya," Deuce offered. "And as I said, we're a team here, even if you're not on the payroll, which I'd like to remedy one day. We all have history together. Nothing leaves this room."

After glancing at my watch, I closed my notebook and rose. "Then let's go to Bimini. We can probably make it in time for dinner at Joe's Conch Shack."

"We'll all meet at the marina in one hour," Deuce said, also rising.

As everyone stood to leave, Chyrel looked up at Deuce. "Me too?"

"Yeah," he replied. "You could use some sun." He turned to the others. "From this point on, we're mission-focused. Our objective is a simple one; to find out if Armstrong is a good fit for us, as either a client or a possible employer. You all know my mission statement.

Integrity above all else. I won't do business with anyone who's not a straight-up white hat."

We left the office. Tony drove me and Charity back to the marina. Everyone had a go-bag on-site or in their car, but for a prolonged stay, up to four or five days, more gear and clothes would be needed. I had everything aboard that I'd need; enough to last a week. And Charity had had the forethought to bring all she'd arrived on my island with.

I unlocked the salon hatch and turned off the alarm system, letting Finn out. He was probably always going to prefer to pee on a tree, which, as most men will attest to, is a primal urge for all male animals.

"Thanks for that back there," Charity said, as we stepped into the conditioned air of the salon.

"What?"

"Telling Deuce and the others that you knew all about what I did with Victor's money."

"Victor's money?"

"Have you found the hiding spot in the salon bulkhead?"

"Yeah, I use it to stash a couple handguns, ammo, and a little cash."

"He only used it to hide cash," she said. "Bundles of hundred-dollar bills. His half of what we found after the money launderer's yacht sank."

"Gives a whole new meaning to the phrase."

Laughing, Charity flopped down on the couch. "So, this Jack Armstrong guy? He charters boats for some purpose we don't know, most of which are owned by former spec-ops guys turned wealthy philanthropists. That about sum it up?"

"Except for that little part about how he knew that me, you, and Deuce are in that same circle. I don't like my giving to be known by anyone."

Charity sat up. "Yeah, that *is* troubling. I went to great lengths to make sure that Vic's money was untraceable. I was surprised Chyrel found it. But she was trying to find a common connection tying me, you, and Deuce to these other boat owners. She was looking specifically at me, whereas he was just looking for anyone with my background. Digging blind." She sat forward, elbows on her knees. "That means Armstrong has some serious people doing his digging."

I felt the boat rock slightly—the only indication Finn gave when he returned. I opened the salon hatch and he came in, followed by Andrew and Paul.

"Stow your gear down in the guest stateroom, guys," I instructed. "Anywhere you can find a spot."

"How long will it take to get there?" Paul asked.

Paul Bender had come to Deuce's counterterrorist team from the Secret Service, unlike most of the others, who had some sort of military background. Paul wasn't at his most comfortable on the water.

"Three hours, tops," Andrew replied in his deep baritone.

Andrew, no stranger to operating any vessel from a kayak to a Coast Guard cutter, had come to Deuce's team from the Coast Guard's Maritime Enforcement, an elite team of anti-piracy operatives, who specialized in doing just what modern pirates did—boarding another vessel while underway from a small, high-speed craft.

"Should be a smooth crossing, Paul," I assured him.

Deuce and Tom were the last to arrive, right behind Tony and Chyrel. With everyone aboard, I started the engines, while Tony and Andrew tossed off the lines.

Charity took the second seat and the others took seats on the port and forward benches, except Tony and Andrew. They preferred to stand, each with one hand on a rail.

"I think when we get there, we shouldn't all be visible," Deuce said. "Just call it an abundance of caution."

I nodded, turning the *Revenge* out to sea. "No sense tipping our hand. This time of year is tournament season—Bimini Big Game Club has a wahoo tournament this weekend. So, the *Revenge* won't stand out. But most tournament charters are a crew of one or two and one or two clients. Or just a couple of guys looking for a trophy."

"And they're almost always testosterone-charged cowboys," Chyrel interjected. "Fish ain't the only trophies those good ole boys are interested in. I get it. Charity and I will stay below, right?"

"You four," Deuce said, pointing to the four men. "You'll take a cab from the customs building and we'll get a slip or anchor. Split up and recon the marinas on foot, but mostly listen—don't ask too many questions. We'll talk on the comm just after sunset."

I laughed. "Good luck finding a slip on Bimini this time of year."

"You got the rooms arranged?" Deuce asked Chyrel.

"All set," she replied, as I pushed the throttles forward.

The sun was still ten degrees above the horizon when we dropped anchor in the southern part of Bimini Bay, just off the Wild Quest docks, a place where tourists could swim with dolphins. Tucked in next to Wild Quest was Joe's place, and a small grocer just around the corner and down the road a bit. I'd found Joe's Conch Shack years ago. He could do things with conch meat that made my mouth water.

After going through customs, Tom, Tony, Andrew, and Paul took a cab to the hotel where Chyrel had booked the rooms. From there, they would fan out through Bailey Town and Alice Town with their ears to the ground.

Once we had the hook down and secure, Deuce and I joined the women in the salon.

"We're only 50 yards from shore," I said, emptying my pockets on the counter. "And ten yards from knee-deep water. I'm going to swim to Joe's and get something to eat."

"Are you ever gonna get a dinghy?" Chyrel asked.

"You can use one of the paddle boards on top of the fly bridge," I offered. "Just don't expect me to wait. Or there's some hamburger patties in the freezer. I'll arrange for supplies while I'm ashore."

"I'll go with you," Charity said. "It's okay to wear a bathing suit at this place?"

"Joe's never turned away a hungry swimmer that I know of."

A few minutes later, Charity joined me on the swim platform and we dove in. Finn remained on the boat with Deuce and Chyrel. They'd decided on burgers, and I guess Finn figured the burgers were a better bet than my bringing any conch back.

"That's it?" Charity asked, as we splashed ashore and I angled toward the little open-air shack.

Not really a shack, but more like a rusting tin roof with a counter in front and a small porch at the side under which were placed a couple of tables. Just off to the other side of the shack was a mountain of conch shells, probably numbering in the tens of thousands. Local kids gathered them in the shallow waters of the bay and on the leeward side, probably getting a quarter a piece for them.

"What he lacks in décor, he makes up for in flavor."

There were only a handful of people outside the place when we approached the counter, with its graffiti-covered support posts on either side. It was still early; the tournament boats were still out, scouting locations. I ordered a dozen scorch conch strips and waited while Charity ordered a conch and lobster salad.

The girl at the register had long braids in her hair. I extended a wet twenty-dollar bill and apologized.

"Iss okay," she said with a smile. "Half di dolluhs we get here are soggy like dat."

We ate quickly, washing it down with a pair of cold Kaliks.

"Did you see anything in the boats' registries that was out of the ordinary?" Charity asked as we walked toward the grocer.

"Nothing solid," I replied, as we reached the only road on the island and turned north. "The grocer's just a couple hundred yards down. I want to see about getting supplies out to the *Revenge*. All the power boat registries I looked at seem to be semi-displacement hulls, but many are underpowered for that to mean anything. The sailboats are mostly catamarans, or competition type sloops. So, fast, wannabe fast or off-the-grid, long range boats, would be the only connection."

An old man was just turning a key in the lock when we approached the grocery, called Bonefish Ebbie's.

When he turned toward us, I lifted a hand in greeting. "Hi there. We were hoping to pick up a few things."

"Sorry, suh," he said. "I have to get to me boy's school for a meetin'. Be 'round in di mornin'?"

"Yeah," I said. "I don't think we need anything that can't wait till then. You wouldn't happen to have a skiff to get what we buy out to our boat, would you?"

In some places, such a request would have been looked on with disdain, but tournament boats usually didn't have dinghies. Most tied up in expensive slips, leaving the stragglers to anchor out and swim to shore to get anything.

"No problem," he replied, noting our still-wet hair. "I can have me oldest boy take you back in di mornin'. I keep a small boat at di dock down at Wild Quest, just for dat sorta ting."

Charity and I walked back toward the little beach. She kept looking around nervously. I had to admit, my own internal alert was pinging about something, but I couldn't put my finger on what it was.

"What's bothering you?" I asked in a low voice.

She glanced behind us again. "I'm not sure. I just get a feeling that I'm being watched."

My head was always on a swivel, but I hadn't seen or heard anything to trigger it. I just knew that something didn't feel quite right.

"Yeah," I said. "I have a case of the heebie-jeebies, too. Maybe it's because neither of us has been around so many people in a while. Let's just get back to the boat."

We reached the beach where we'd swum ashore and waded back out into the water. When it was deep enough, we swam back out to where the *Revenge* lay at anchor. I relayed the plans for a morning supply run to Deuce and Chyrel as the four of us sat on the bridge to watch the sun go down. I also mentioned the odd feeling we'd both had.

"Trust your gut," Deuce said, nodding. "Dad always told me that."

"Me, too," I agreed, nodding.

As my platoon sergeant when I'd been stationed in Okinawa during my first enlistment, Deuce's father had drilled that lesson in to me. He was the one who'd been the first to pin my corporal chevrons.

Deuce grinned. "We all know that our instincts have kept us safe more than once."

"Armstrong would have to know we'd be curious about his operation," I said. "Should we be troubled that he knows that we know about his plans here?"

"I kinda don't think so," Chyrel offered. "I've been thinking about that and looking back at the data. The tracks are covered, but not so much that it looks like he's trying really hard. Does that make sense?"

"Sort of a test?" Charity asked.

"Could be," I said. "You said there were several people invited to this meet. Maybe he's just trying to see if anyone does their own investigation. When we talk to him, I'll be sure to ask."

Deuce's sat-phone rang and he dug it out of his pocket. "Julie." He stabbed the screen and held the phone to his ear. "What's up, babe?" He listened for a moment, then said, "Hold on, I'll put Chyrel on. he has a problem with one of your babies," Deuce said, handing Chyrel his phone, Chyrel put the phone to her ear. "What's up, Julie?"

She listened for several minutes. "Did you try a reboot?" she asked, then waved her hand as if to scare away a fly. "Never mind, of course you did. Dang, this will make things hard. Hang on."

Chyrel took the phone from her ear. "I might have to go back, boss."

"We just got here."

"Unavoidable," she said. "She's locked out of the comm system."

"We're probably good just using direct comm," he said. "At least until day after tomorrow."

"Yeah," Chyrel agreed. "But y'all are gonna need the linkup then."

Deuce looked at me and I shrugged. "You and I can make the run to the mainland tomorrow night. Be back well before sunrise."

Deuce took the phone from Chyrel and spoke into it. "Did you hear? Okay, that's what we'll do. We'll leave after dark. Arrange for someone to pick her up at the Rickenbacker Marina." He looked at me. "About midnight?" I nodded. "Yeah, midnight," he said into the phone." He listened a moment longer. "I love you, too."

Another tournament boat anchored nearby. The guy on the foredeck secured the anchor rode and then climbed up to the bridge. He sat with the captain, probably to watch the sun set and have a beer, same as us.

"Cheeky name," Charity said as the sun unceremoniously disappeared over the horizon. "He wishes."

I chuckled when I saw what she was looking at. *Droppin' Skirts* was stenciled across the other boat's stern.

"Could be referring to the skirt on a teaser or lure," I said. "You know, dropping the lures and teasers into the water."

Chyrel stood and stepped over to the ladder. "Like I said, cowboys with an overabundance of testosterone."

Charity followed her down to the salon and I offered Deuce a beer from the small cooler. We watched the stars wink on as darkness quickly enveloped us. The dark brought with it a profound silence that only a calm harbor could provide. Sounds from other boats around the anchorage reached my ears, as well as Chyrel and Charity's muffled conversation.

"Okay, so we pull an all-nighter," Deuce said, shrugging. "Leave after nightfall. It's not like we haven't done it before."

"No problem," I said. "It's barely five hours there and back. The guys can snoop around the restaurants and bars while we're gone."

"I'd really like to see this meet turn into something profitable," Deuce commented in the gathering darkness. "What's in it for you?"

"Charity mentioned it last night," I replied, my voice low. "When I asked *her* the same question. Something's missing from my life—hers too, I gathered—some sort of goal or direction, I guess. A challenge. I've been stubborn as a Missouri mule the last few months. Hanging on to something that's long gone."

"We're all mules in one way or another," he said, then took a long pull from his bottle. "You're not going through some kind of mid-life crisis, are you?"

I laughed. "No, that ship has sailed over the horizon."

"Rumor has it you've got a girl in every port."

My face flushed. "Rumor, huh?"

"Just something I picked up."

I played along, grinning. "And a backup port if need be."

He grinned at the obvious bravado. "Speaking of the mules," he said, pulling a small black box from his pocket. He opened it and put a small communication device in his ear. We called them earwigs, because the bone mic wrapping around the ear looked like a worm crawling into it. "We haven't called the mules to the barn. They should be within range of the comm."

"Let's go below," I said. "This close to shore, the bugs are starting to gather. You probably drew them in with the smell of that burned cow flesh you and Chyrel ate."

Deuce laughed and moved toward the ladder. "They weren't bad."

"Any left?" I asked, following him down.

CHAPTER TEN

The next morning, I woke late to the smell of coffee. Deuce was pouring a mug when I came up into the galley. He'd slept on the couch in the salon and the women had taken the guest stateroom, with its two single bunks. We'd all turned in early, and each of us had taken a three-hour watch through the night. Though my sleep and Charity's had been interrupted by our watches, we'd taken steps to ensure that we had all gotten a good eight hours of rest. It was nearly time for lunch.

"Just talked to Andrew," Deuce said, moving to the settee. "They're out walking the docks again, talking to people."

I poured a mug for myself and joined him. "Let's stay on the down low, like we're waiting for clients or something."

"If your and Charity's feelings were right, whoever was watching already knows she's with us."

"But they might not know Chyrel and the guys are."

"Me and the guys are what?" Chyrel asked coming up from below, with Charity right behind her.

"Here on the boat," I replied. "I think it's best if you're not seen."

"Overly cautious?" Charity asked.

"Something like that." I replied. "It's not paranoia if someone really is watching."

"Best not to show all your cards," Chyrel said.

I finished my coffee and rinsed the mug. "I'm going ashore and hit Joe's for an early lunch, then walk down to Bonefish Ebbie's for supplies."

"I was upwind of you," Charity said, "and that stuff you ate *still* burned my nose. And you're going back for more?"

"It's an acquired taste. I'll be back in an hour or two."

"Need help?" she offered.

"Nah, the fellow said he's got a boat that will bring me back out."

Finn followed me out into the cockpit. "You stay here," I told him. I knew he wanted to go ashore, but the beach was crowded with tourists. I wasn't worried that he'd intentionally hurt anyone, but he was a really big dog. Besides, if we were being watched, I didn't want Finn in harm's way.

Diving off the swim platform, I went deep and remained submerged as I swam toward the beach. I exhaled a little with each slow, measured stroke, off-gassing the carbon dioxide buildup in my lungs, as well as making me less buoyant. When I reached the shallows,

I stood and waded ashore, pushing the water out of my hair with both hands.

Scanning the beach, I saw no obvious threats. My eyes moved quickly across the faces of every person I could see, and none registered as familiar.

My eyes fell on a woman with wild red hair under a big white hat. She was sitting in the shaded part of Joe's shack. Though she wore dark sunglasses, her head was turned as if she were looking right at me—or maybe at the *Revenge* behind me. At first, I thought she resembled a doctor I'd once dated. But as I got closer, I could see that this woman was younger and shorter than Jackie.

I strode toward the counter, digging soggy dollars out of my baggies again. The redhead stood as I approached, removed her hat, and pushed her glasses up onto her head. She was small, a good foot shorter than my six-three. Her pants were that style that stopped below the knees—capri pants—I think, and she wore a light cotton top printed in green palm leaves, with white sandals on her feet. I doubted if she was even half my weight—barely a hundred pounds. Attractive, but young. Not a distraction I needed. She started toward the counter behind me.

With water dripping from my blue baggies, I waited at the counter. The redhead made me uncomfortable. Not that I thought her a threat. In a brief glance, I'd taken in her physical appearance and the breeze had outlined her loose-fitting top against her curves. She definitely wasn't carrying a weapon. But Deuce's *girl in every port* crack had made me uneasy. Had the last year been a mid-life crisis, as he'd suggested? I could feel the woman looking at me, studying me. A few months ago, a drunk me would have turned and made an advance. I'd been smacked more than once during that time. A lot more. Instead, I stood there dripping, waiting for Joe to look over.

"Got your famous scorch conch today?" I asked him, when he finally turned his head.

He just nodded, smiled, and filled a small bowl.

"And a Kalik," I added as the cashier, a young girl in braids, stepped up to the other side of the counter. I paid her and left a nice tip.

The redhead leaned on the wooden bar beside me. "What's the scorch conch? It looks good."

Turning, I started to respond but was suddenly lost in her eyes. My initial assessment had been based only on whether or not she was a threat. But now I could see that her eyes were bright and clear, abyssal blue, fading like sea ice to a tropical green. I felt I could dive in and never reach the bottom. She was naturally pretty, with a dusting of freckles, which she didn't try to hide with makeup. A wholesome, girl-next-door type.

Focus, McDermitt, I told myself. *So, a pretty girl is talking to me. No big deal. She just wants to know what I'm eating.*

Damn, I thought. *What am I eating?*

I looked down at my food, trying to remember what it was I'd ordered. When I looked up again, she smiled coyly.

Crap, I thought. *Did she just see that as me looking her over?*

"It's hot," I stammered, a bit embarrassed. "Really hot."

"How hot?" she asked.

Was she flirting?

I could feel my face beginning to flush. "Joe here makes the hot sauce himself, with locally grown goat peppers. Believe me, it will knock your socks off. But try it at your own risk. It packs some serious heat."

Dammit, I sound like a commercial.

She grinned. "I think I can handle it."

I studied her face a second. *No, she's not flirting,* I decided.

Somehow, for whatever reason, she'd been waiting here for me. Or maybe just waiting for whoever came ashore from the boat. I decided to play it out and see if I could find out anything.

She placed her order, and then added a Kalik, too.

I pulled the wet money from my pocket again. "Let me get that," I offered.

"No need."

"It would be my pleasure," I insisted, then tried to bait her, gesturing toward a picnic table. "If you'd care to join me?"

She hesitated for a fraction of a second, then nodded. "I'm Jesse."

"Poppy," she replied. The name suited her. She seemed puzzled, as if she almost expected a comment about her name. She had just a hint of an upper-Midwest accent, which she'd probably intentionally tried to suppress.

Joe placed a second bowl in front of us. I tucked my beer under my arm and picked up both bowls. "After you."

We moved through the crowd until we found a table with one end vacant and sat down across from each other.

"So, Poppy," I said, trying not to say her name in a way that might come across as derogatory or mocking, "what brings you to this tiny island paradise?"

She took a sip of her beer, a delaying tactic. She seemed somewhat nervous, so I just waited.

"I'm an intern," she replied. "I'm an ornithology major, but I got rotated into an internship here."

Giving her my most disarming grin, I said, "An ornithologist, huh? I can honestly say I've never met one." This was a lie; you couldn't swing a mackerel in the Keys and not hit one or two bird-watchers.

"Yep, I'm working on my first million. I figure by the time I'm forty, I'll be set for life."

A fiery attitude to go with the hair. If she was working for Armstrong, or doing some other undercover work, that attitude was real enough. "Well, aren't you a breath of fresh air?"

She shrugged and leaned forward in fake conspiracy. "I'm really just here for the sun and beer."

I couldn't help laughing. "You can't be serious? Kalik?"

She smiled. "Ah, there's something about the magic that comes with the sun, and the waves, and palm trees swaying in the wind. An ice cold, watered-down excuse for a beer can really hit the spot."

I couldn't figure her out. There was a plethora of younger men around, some practically within reach. While it's true that I'd slept around with more than a few young women this past year, I don't remember one that had initiated any flirtation. I chuckled loudly at the possibility of it. Others at the table glanced over at us. We looked at each other and laughed again.

She asked me the same question. "So, what brings you to this tiny island paradise?"

"Nothing," I lied, without hesitation. "I'm a lost soul, wandering the ocean blue, looking for meaning in it all."

"And have you found any?" Her eyes took on a note of suspicion.

"Nah." I decided to see how far she'd go, and slipped into my smug druggler persona, Stretch Buchannan. I lifted my bottle, admiring the condensation. "I think it's the beer. A stronger brew would help with the clarity, though. Kinda like peyote and a vision quest. Yeah, maybe that's what I need. Some peyote."

Putting down the beer, I speared a couple of pieces of conch and raised my fork. "I'd be willing to bet that peyote burns all the way down, like this conch. Cleans your spirit, inside and out."

Putting the spicy chunks of meat in my mouth, I savored the flavors, hot as they were, before chewing and swallowing. I nodded toward her bowl. "Go ahead."

She pushed the meat around in the bowl. "It, ah, looks really hot, that's for sure."

Maybe it was just that foreboding that both Charity and I had had last night, but I sensed that scorch conch wasn't really high on this lady's list of favorite menu items.

So, why is she approaching me? Did she work for Armstrong, maybe? Or whatever shell company it was that was renovating the marina just up the road past the grocer? Were they checking out any new arrivals? If so, they were about to get really busy. The tournament started in less than three days. More likely, Armstrong already knew about the *Revenge*.

She half-heartedly stabbed a tiny piece of conch. "Bottoms up."

It didn't hit her at first. It never did. Then her lips pursed and rather than spit it out, she swallowed it whole. "Yep, that's—" she moved her lips together, catching her breath "—that's a little hot."

Shaking my head, I took another bite, and grinned.

"I'm glad you're amused."

When she chugged the beer to douse the fire, I knew there had to be more. Why order something you knew you couldn't eat?

Charity was a gifted sketch artist and using my description, she could give Chyrel something to look for in

Armstrong's employee files. If this woman was attached to Armstrong Research, we'd probably find out, even if Poppy was a fake name. But I didn't think it was. Poppy was the sort of nickname one picked up in pre-adolescence. If she was just a pretty young girl who liked older men, well, that was an amusing thought, but something that I just didn't have time for. Hell, maybe she was a tournament groupie.

I quickly ate the last of my food, drained my beer, and started to rise.

"Well, it was nice talking to you, Poppy." I said. "Maybe I'll see you around."

"Yes," she said, a puzzled look on her face. "Thanks for lunch."

I tossed my bowl in a nearby trash can and headed up toward the road. Passing a large window at the dolphin place with the sun shining fully on the glass, I turned my head slightly, looking for the reflection. Poppy was following me across the dune, a good fifty yards behind me.

Without a backward glance, I turned the corner of the building and paused at the next window. Through it, I could look out the side window and study her, knowing she'd see nothing but a reflection. Any physical attraction I thought she might have had, no matter how remote, was off the table now. She'd been sent to surveille, to investigate.

Poppy stopped under the shade of a big royal palm, looking toward the corner I'd just disappeared around.

After a moment, she took a cellphone out of her back pocket and made a call. It didn't look like she was planning to follow me any farther, so I turned and hurried up the road to Bonefish Ebbie's Grocery.

When I walked in, the man I assumed was Ebbie looked up from his stool behind the counter. A look of recognition came to his face. "Not got yuh wife wit yuh dis afternoon?"

"Just me," I replied, not feeling the need to correct him. "I need to stock up for four people for a week."

He produced a military-grade duffle bag, or what we called a seabag in the Corps. "Just bring what yuh need up to di register, and I'll put everyting in dis. We use dese to take supplies out to boats."

"Got four or five more?"

He smiled, anticipating closing early. "More dan a dozen, Cap'n."

It took a couple of hours; Ebbie's grocery looked small on the outside, but it was packed with everything cruisers or fishermen might need. He didn't have any carts—they wouldn't fit between the aisles—but he had heavy-duty plastic baskets. Finally, after ferrying dozens of baskets to the counter, I paid for five full seabags of groceries and supplies, and a sixth one half full. Jerome, Ebbie's oldest son, helped me load everything onto the back of a topless electric golf cart and we headed to the Wild Quest dock.

I glanced around as we unloaded the seabags into a smart-looking center-console. Poppy wasn't anywhere around. It was mid-afternoon and hot. Most of the tourists had left the beach and Joe's was nearly vacant. Two guys sat at one of the picnic tables, drinking beer. They appeared to be watching the boats come and go and it didn't look as if they were together. Neither seemed to be especially interested in us.

In some places, seeing two men load a small boat with six large seabags would invite scrutiny. But it was daylight, and Jerome was probably well-known to a lot of people.

Once we reached the *Revenge*, Deuce helped carry the seabags into the salon, where Charity and Chyrel started putting everything away. Still, it took twenty minutes before I handed Jerome the last of the empty seabags, along with a twenty.

"Thank yuh, Cap'n," the young man said, tipping two fingers to his cap. "Hope yuh do well in di tournament dis weekend."

In the salon, Chyrel was talking to someone on the comm while working at her laptop. Charity stood in the galley, moving things from a stack on the counter into cabinets and storage boxes. She had a mischievous look on her face.

"What's going on?" I asked Deuce.

"Nothing," he replied, but the grin on his face said otherwise. "Chyrel's checking in with everyone. What little the guys have gathered from the locals is that the new shipyard is a blessing to the local economy. It's employing over a dozen locals during construction, and will likely hire more when they open, which is rumored to be soon."

"I've been thinking," I said, motioning toward the couch.

Charity joined us, and I kept my voice low, so as not to disturb Chyrel. "You gave me this idea," I said to Charity.

"I gave you the idea to go chasing a pretty, young redhead?"

I found myself stumped for a second. Then I remembered Poppy. My expression of bewilderment only fueled Charity.

"She's cute, but definitely not your type."

"I think she was watching us," I said, a bit too defensively.

"Oh, she was watching all right," Chyrel said, not looking up from her computer. "But she only had eyes for you, as Bond would say."

That was when I remembered the high-powered digital camera on the roof, and how Chyrel could connect to it with her laptop. We were close enough to shore that they could have counted the condensation drops on my beer. There was also a parabolic mic on board, but the boat's movement would have made it useless. However, the camera had image stabilization, so once locked onto something, it or the boat could move quite a bit, and the image would remain clear.

"Oh, for crying out loud," I said. "I'm serious."

Charity laughed. "Hey, what happens in Bimini stays in Bimini. We watched you look her over from head to toe when she smiled at you."

I turned toward Chyrel. "Did you record it? Can you run a facial recognition from here?"

Chyrel looked up from her screen. "You're serious?"

"Yeah, I'm serious. Look through Armstrong's personnel files if possible. I bet she works for one of his shell companies."

Deuce cleared his throat. "You mean you weren't hitting on her?"

"She's half my age," I said, again, too defensively.

Charity canted her head slightly, arching an eyebrow questioningly.

"Yeah," I said. "I've slept with a bunch of younger women this past year. Is that what you want to hear? But for every woman I slept with, I was shot down in flames by a dozen others. *This* girl approached *me.* Her name's Poppy."

All three grinned.

"Just get started looking her up," I told Chyrel. "And when you're done, I have another job for you."

"What?" Chyrel asked. "I can multi-task."

"Let's look at the first payment Armstrong and Associates paid these boat owners."

"Follow the money," Chyrel said, smiling, and getting to work on the keyboard.

"What are you looking for?" Deuce asked.

"A fellow speed junky," I replied, with a conspiratorial look at Charity.

It was getting close to dark when Chyrel finally called us to her spot at the settee. "Still working on Armstrong's personnel files. With all the different companies he owns and contracts with, it could take a while."

"What ya got on the boats?" I asked.

"I've put the initial payment alongside a picture and brief description of each boat, like you asked."

"Can you sort them by amount paid, lowest first?"

Chyrel clicked a few keys and the list rearranged.

"Just what I thought," I said, scanning down the list.

"What?" Chyrel asked, looking at the screen in bewilderment. "It's a random order now. And home ported all over the place."

"Not random," I said. "Not if you look at them from a specific viewpoint. See how most of the sailboats are near the top now. They received less of an initial payment."

"What's that tell you?"

"Sailboats are limited in speed. A displacement hull can only go so fast, no matter what you do to it. That's called hull speed and it's based on the length of the boat's waterline. Cats can go a little faster than hull speed but are still limited by wind speed."

"A payment to refit the boats!" Charity exclaimed. "Yeah, it makes perfect sense. You said all the boats were fast or had the right hull to be able to go fast."

Deuce stood and began pacing. "Armstrong Research paid these boat owners to upgrade their boats to be faster?"

"Or more efficient," I replied. "In the case of the sailboats, probably electronics upgrades, better sails, and a super-smooth hull repainting."

"Scroll to the bottom," Charity said.

Chyrel did so, and the last entry was an old Seaton raised-pilothouse trawler. The registry showed that it was equipped with a single GM diesel that produced 130 horsepower. It was a steel-hulled, long-range trawler, built with a semi-displacement hull more than 40 years ago. At 50 feet in length, I estimated a cruising speed around ten knots and a top speed of perhaps twelve. The owner of the vessel was a former Air Force Special Operations Command chief master sergeant. He'd been paid almost $100,000.

"That's a hell of a refit," Deuce said. "If what you suspect is true."

"Imagine a trawler," I said, "one that was designed to either go far *or* go fast. Forty years ago, they didn't have the technology to do both. With that single engine, that boat could cross the Atlantic, chugging along at 200 miles a day. Look how beamy it is. I bet a couple of modern, high-powered diesels could easily be added to that engine room. Engines that could get that old barge up to 30 knots or more."

Deuce leaned in and looked at the registry. "Weighs over twenty tons. It'd take some serious horsepower for that kind of speed."

"What would a couple of big engines cost?" Chyrel asked.

"It's not really about the size," I said. "This old Seaton is only a little bigger than the *Revenge*. I could replace both engines on the *Revenge* with a hundred grand."

Deuce looked out the port side windows. "His own rapid response fleet scattered all over the world, all capable of fast movement and long range. And they all look, and are used regularly, as private yachts. That sounds a little familiar."

"It's near sunset," I said, looking out toward the west. Then I turned to Deuce. "Let's get ready to depart. When we get underway, you hit the rack. I'll wake you when we get close to Miami and you can drive back."

CHAPTER
ELEVEN

An hour after sunset, Deuce stood ready on the bow. I activated the windlass and it began pulling the anchor rode aboard, the 50-foot chain clanking across the rollers and into the locker almost immediately. Charity sat next to me, her blond hair orange in the dim red glow of the single overhead LED light. The light from the radar and sonar panels, also red, did the same for her face.

With the anchor secured, Deuce came back and climbed up to join us on the bridge. We idled slowly through the channel into the ocean, with Deuce standing next to me, using the camera's night vision to help guide us to deep water.

"Wouldn't hurt to run dark for a bit," Deuce said, moving the camera to look straight ahead at normal magnification. He took a seat on the port bench. "Just until we're out of sight of the shipyard."

I reached up and switched off the navigation lights, as well as the red overhead light. The only glow now came from the console displays. It was illegal to run at night without lights, but the sky was clear, and the moon and stars illuminated everything around us for several hundred yards. I'd turn them back on when we were a couple of miles out.

"Twenty feet under the keel," Charity said. "And getting deeper."

As I pushed the throttles forward, the *Revenge* quickly gathered speed, climbing up on top of the water with ease. I backed off at 25 knots.

"Watch how fast it drops away," Deuce said, rising from the bench, and coming around to stand behind the helm seats.

"Whoa," Charity breathed after a few seconds. "It drops straight down. Beyond the sonar's range."

"That's what makes Bimini the gamefish capital of the world."

The speaker in the dash clicked and Chyrel's voice came over the intercom. "Can I come up now?"

"Yeah," Deuce said, pushing the button on the comm. "We're a mile offshore."

"Finn's asleep in the salon," Chyrel said, when she reached the bridge. Deuce moved over and she dropped onto the bench beside him. "I don't think he likes being cooped up all the time."

"No, he doesn't," I agreed. "But as big as he is, I don't want to risk some tourist mistaking his playfulness for something else and having him get a snoot full of pepper spray."

"He's a big ole baby," Chyrel said.

"You might as well get some sleep," I told Deuce, while setting the autopilot and checking the chart plotter. "We'll be in Biscayne Bay inside of three hours."

"Been a long day for me too," Charity said. "Think I'll catch a nap."

When Deuce and Charity moved toward the ladder, Chyrel came over to the helm. "Mind if I keep you company?"

"Sure," I replied. "Have a seat."

The two of us talked for an hour as the engines droned on monotonously. Though my eyes had adjusted to the darkness, my range of vision on the water's surface was limited to about a quarter mile, or 30 seconds. I glanced up at the night vision camera in the overhead console from time to time, just to see a little farther ahead.

Chyrel leaned forward, looking at the radar screen. "It looks like there's a stationary boat ahead and to the north."

Looking over, I studied the radar screen for a moment. She was right. The boat was eight miles away and more than a mile off our course, so there was no danger of collision. I double-checked the VHF to be sure it was on channel sixteen and the volume was turned up. It was. Sixteen was the emergency and hailing frequency, and if the drifting boat needed help, they'd use that. There just weren't many reasons for a boat to stop out here. Bottom fishing was out of the question; the bottom was a quarter mile or more below us.

Every now and then, I glanced over at the radar. The echo was small, probably a sailboat under 50 feet. The wind was so light that if they were under sail, they'd look stationary on the screen.

An hour out of Bimini, Chyrel turned toward me. "Are you ever gonna tell me what you ordered those DNA tests for?"

As I'd told Charity, Chyrel was the one I'd entrusted with two DNA samples last summer. One was from the bottle of water Savannah's daughter, Florence, had left behind.

"One of them was mine."

"And the other one? The water bottle?"

Looking over, I studied her eyes in the dim red glow of the console. I'd known Chyrel for several years and trusted her. There was no need for me to swear her to secrecy.

"Savannah's daughter had been drinking from that bottle."

"Savannah? Your old girlfriend, whose sister was killed?" A light seemed to come on behind her eyes. "Oh my God, you wanted to know if you were that girl's daddy?"

"I am."

Chyrel sat back in her seat. I glanced down at the radar. The stationary boat was moving. It was angling in behind us. Quite a few miles behind us but moving at our speed. Not a sailboat.

"You're that little girl's daddy?" She said it in disbelief, so I didn't respond. "What are you gonna do about it?"

Chyrel came from rural Alabama, the heart of the Bible belt. But she'd seen enough of the big bad world to know that her upbringing and small-town values were a far cry from the norm.

"Nothing," I said. "Or everything. It's not up to me."

The other boat was now running a nearly parallel course about six miles behind and a little to the north of our wake. It was still matching our speed. I glanced at the GPS; we were making 27 knots. I bumped the speed up to 35, knowing full well what the change in speed would do. And hoping that it wouldn't cause another reaction.

Chyrel looked at the radar, then over at me. "What's wrong?"

"Watch the distance to that boat back there," I said. "Is it falling back?"

"Yeah," she replied. "It's going slower than we are."

"Good. Keep an eye on it."

The intercom clicked, as I knew it would. "What's going on?" Deuce asked, as if on cue.

I pushed the button next to the speaker to open the intercom to the salon. "Probably nothing. A boat behind us."

"It's speeding up, Jesse," Chyrel said.

That was what I was hoping wouldn't happen.

"Go below," I told her, then pushed the button again. "Get up here, Deuce."

Chyrel started down the ladder as Deuce came out of the salon into the cockpit. Seas were calm, and the boat rode steady. Deuce said something to Chyrel that sent her inside, and then he climbed up, Charity right behind him.

"Charity," I said, firmly but calmly. "A boat is following us. Chyrel is a non-com."

She looked up at me for just a moment, then nodded. "Roger that."

Then she disappeared back down the ladder and I heard the salon hatch close. Though Chyrel had worked with the CIA and with Deuce's team, she was administrative, not a field agent; a non-combatant. Charity would make sure no harm came to her.

A moment later the intercom clicked. "We're in the forward stateroom, door locked."

Deuce took the second seat, studying the radar and chart plotter. He adjusted the radar and continued watching it.

"We're approaching territorial waters," Deuce said. "The boat behind us is matching our speed. Where'd it come out of?"

"It was stationary for a long time," I replied. "Maybe drifting in the Stream. After we passed, it fell in behind us, matching our speed. When I accelerated, it did too."

"There's something else out there," Deuce said. "Very small, off to the south."

"Heading?"

"Hang on—the echo comes and goes."

"False echo?"

"No," he replied. "It's definitely there. A small boat, the size of a skiff. At first, I thought it was a channel marker or something. But as we passed, it started moving on an intercept course, overtaking us. Less than a mile away now, at eight o'clock, angling to intercept."

Though I knew it was futile, I looked back over my shoulder. I could see nothing in the inky darkness except for the white wake we left behind.

"A thousand meters," Deuce said. "It's closing the distance, coming up on the port side. The other boat has also increased speed."

"Armstrong?"

"I don't know, but I don't like it." He reached into the cargo pocket of his pants and pulled out a night-vision scope. Turning to look out over the port side behind us, he scanned the water.

"What the—? It's a Zodiac! No lights, no markings, two people on board."

"Pirates," I said, pushing the intercom button. "Hang on to something!"

Jamming the throttles until I heard the superchargers engage, I turned hard to starboard, away from the Zodiac. The chines dug deep as the *Revenge* leaned into the turn, accelerating. I turned the wheel back slowly to the left, turning ever sharper, in a big one-eighty.

There wasn't time for Deuce to get down and set up the 50-caliber tail stinger stored under the false bottom in the couch. With only two people aboard the Zodiac and both Deuce and I armed aboard the *Revenge*, I liked our odds without it. The other boat was still too far away to be of any help to the Zodiac, if indeed these people were bent on stealing the *Revenge*.

"Guide me!" I shouted to Deuce. "I'm going to swamp them. It'll take the other boat three or four minutes to get here."

Holding the scope to his eye, he tried to reacquire the Zodiac. "Dead ahead. It's slowing."

Piracy is common in the Caribbean, the Bahamas, and all along the coast of Florida. Been that way for centuries. Modern pirates use fast boats and they practice how to board quickly and kill everyone in sight. They don't take captives; there'd be no ransom demand. They need boats to smuggle drugs, slaves, or any other kind of contraband. They use them up and scuttle them.

"Five hundred meters," Deuce said. "He's coming straight at us."

I eased the wheel to the left, giving the guy an out if he chose. Then I mashed the throttles to the stops. The twin superchargers roared.

"Hard to port!" Deuce shouted, just as the Zodiac came into my range of vision. He was swerving away to our starboard.

I turned sharply to the left, pulling back on the throttles. The *Revenge* displaced eighteen tons of water when she was empty. Loaded as we were, twenty. About half of that water would cascade away to either side. Nine tons of it hit the much smaller pirate boat at nearly 70 knots, our combined closing speed. I had no doubt as to the outcome.

I turned around and started back toward the now-overturned inflatable boat. The moon and stars provided plenty of light. Seas were nearly flat. I could only see one person in the water, not far from their boat. He was moving.

"Take the helm," I whispered to Deuce, as I stepped around the console to the forward part of the flybridge.

"Who are you?" I shouted down to the lone figure in the water just ahead of us. "What do you want?"

"What the hell, man," a voice called back. A woman's voice. "I was just trying to get to shore."

"Right." I shouted. If I pretended to be another pirate or smuggler, maybe I could throw these people off guard. The law of the sea required I assist. But if they were pirates, I could easily ignore that and sleep quite well. "You feds?" I shouted. "DEA?"

"What? No," came the woman's reply. I still couldn't see the other person, as Deuce put the engines in neutral.

"Didn't you see me?" the woman shouted, her voice somehow familiar. "You've flipped my boat. I'm going to need your help getting it flipped back upright."

"Where's your partner?"

"I don't know what you mean. Please, throw me a line. You can't leave me out here like this."

I climbed quickly down the ladder, as Deuce brought the *Revenge* alongside, just ten yards away. "Why were you following us?"

"I told you. I wasn't."

I'd had about enough nonsense. "Let me make some things clear, little lady. I have the high ground and you're in the water. Know how to tell if there's sharks in the water? Taste it. If it tastes salty, there's sharks in the water. So, you really need to start being a bit more forthcoming."

"Okay," she conceded. "Whatever you say. Just help me out of the water."

Leaning over the gunwale, I looked down at the woman's red hair bobbing in the moonlight around her face. "What the hell? What are you doing way out here?"

Opening the transom door, I stepped onto the swim platform. Knowing that Deuce would have his sidearm unholstered and covering me, I shouted up to the bridge, "It's all right, Deuce. I know her."

Now there was zero doubt in my mind that this woman had been sent to watch us. But to try and stop us way the hell out here in the ocean? A glance up at Deuce told me that he was ready for anything.

When I reached down to take Poppy's hand and pull her onto the platform, her other hand came up and grabbed my wrist. I was surprised and off balance. She braced her feet on the edge of the platform, and I knew I was getting wet.

I went with her pull. The water was my element and I'd be more in control. Just as I hit the water, I heard the salon hatch crash open and Finn came charging out into the cockpit, snarling.

When I surfaced at the swim platform, ready to grab at her feet, the woman I now knew was Poppy was gone, and someone was laughing behind me.

"Poppy!" a strange voice called out from the over-turned Zodiac. "Stop! Stand down!"

With my left arm up on the swim platform, I spun toward the new threat. My hand went quickly to the Sig still tucked securely in its holster at my back.

"Deuce!" the man in the water shouted. "What the hell, man? What are you doing in the middle of the At-lantic?"

"Dalton?" Deuce shouted, climbing down from the bridge. "You gotta be kidding me."

Levering myself onto the platform, I stood and looked back at the man now swimming toward us. Deuce joined me and helped him aboard, shaking his hand before they slapped one another on the back. I holstered my weapon.

Finn wasn't happy. He stood on the deck, just outside the salon hatch, the hair on his back standing up like a porcupine's.

"Sit, Finn," I told him. He obeyed, somewhat grudg-ingly.

"What's going on?" Poppy asked, standing beside the fighting chair.

Finn had calmed now that I was out of the water. I looked inside, but Chyrel and Charity were out of sight.

"Poppy," the stranger said, turning toward her. "This is Deuce. Formerly Lieutenant Commander Russell Livingston, Junior. He was the outgoing team leader when I first reported to Dam Neck."

"Commander," Deuce corrected him. "I was promoted after I left DEVGRU." He slapped the man on the back again, then gestured toward me. "You might have heard of my partner, Jesse McDermitt, former Marine Recon sniper. This is his boat."

"I've heard of you," the man called Dalton said, extending his hand. "You're the Jarhead who took down a warlord in the Mog with a thousand-meter shot. An honor to meet you, sir."

"Just Jesse," I said, shaking his hand.

His grip was firm and self-assured. It was obvious that he and Deuce had served together as SEALs. That was good enough for me. For now.

I turned to the redhead. "And who is this little spark plug? Poppy your real name?"

Dalton stepped forward. "My partner, Special Agent Poppy McVie."

I grinned. Not what I'd expected at all. "Special Agent, indeed."

"She's the brains of the operation," Dalton said. "I'm the brawn."

I faced Dalton. "What operation would that be that you're following us?"

"Well," he started, almost like a school boy, kicking at rocks, "we thought you might be running drugs."

Story of my life aboard the *Revenge*.

"This is Finn," I said. Finn rose and came to stand beside me.

Poppy knelt and cooed, "Hiya, Finn."

My dog has no fear of people. He'd never met anyone he didn't like and who didn't like him. He closed the distance between him and Poppy, allowing her to scratch the loose fur around his neck and ears.

Dalton studied Deuce for a moment. "Been a while."

"Yes, it has," Deuce replied.

"What brought you guys to Bimini?"

Deuce took a card from his pocket and handed it to Dalton, who turned it in the moonlight to get a better view.

"Livingston and McDermitt Security Consultants? You're a private eye or something?"

"Something like that," Deuce replied. "We're meeting a potential client. What's got you out here?"

Dalton said that they were working for U.S. Fish and Wildlife and gave a brief overview of what they were doing, collecting intel for other agencies and countries to use to make arrests. While he talked, Poppy made a short phone call, telling someone named Tom to head this way to pick them up.

After letting Finn back inside and closing the hatch, I leaned on the fighting chair, my arms crossed. "So, you're flying blind."

"Yep, that pretty much sums it up." Dalton replied.

I sensed a dynamic between these two, something outside of just being coworkers. It was in the way they looked at each other.

"Where were you headed, anyway?" Poppy asked, a hint of suspicion in her voice. "In the middle of the night, without your running lights on?"

I'd forgotten to turn the lights back on after leaving Bimini.

I grinned at Dalton. "You were right. The brains." I turned slowly back to Poppy. "Picking up a friend."

"And the lights?" She wasn't about to leave it alone.

"We were watching for dinoflagellates stirred up in this area," I lied. "They're bioluminescent. It's really quite something to see."

"Right, I've heard of that." She wasn't convinced

I nodded toward their inflatable. "Hey, let's get that boat flipped back over and get you on your way."

I didn't wait for a reply but climbed up to the helm. We'd drifted a good 50 feet away from the Zodiac.

"You might want to hold up a minute," Dalton called up to me. "I, ah, I wrapped a line around your prop."

I looked back down at him with grudging admiration. It's a trick I've used a few times, myself.

It only took a few minutes for Dalton to dive down and remove the line from the propeller. Then I maneuvered the *Revenge* closer to their Zodiac and together the three of us managed to right it and get the motor running.

Dalton and Poppy stepped over into their boat and waved goodbye.

Waving back, I said, "We'll be back in Bimini for a few days. If we see anything, we'll let you know."

Dalton put the boat in gear and shouted back, "Appreciate it."

A larger vessel had slowed, then stopped, holding position about a quarter mile away. The Zodiac took off, heading toward their stern. I waited until Dalton and Poppy were aboard and the boat had turned back toward Bimini. When it did, I took the night-vision scope from Deuce and looked at the retreating boat.

"*Droppin' Skirts*," I said, handing the scope back.

Deuce took it and looked toward the sport fisher. "The same boat that anchored near us last night."

When I opened the hatch to call Chyrel and Charity out, Finn went straight over to the transom door and whined. The inside latch was bent, and the hatch wouldn't stay closed.

"All that excitement get to you?" Deuce asked him, as he opened the transom door.

I called through the salon that the visitors were gone, while I wrestled with the latch. It would need to be replaced, but I managed to bend it back enough to keep the hatch closed. Finn relieved himself on the platform. When he re-boarded, I took the washdown hose and rinsed it off before letting him back into the salon. He looked ashamed when I struggled to get it open.

Deuce and I went up to the bridge to get underway and Charity soon joined us. "Chyrel's working on something," she said. "We were listening on the intercom. You buy their story? Fish and Wildlife can't make arrests in the Bahamas, whether it's drugs or poaching."

"Until a few minutes ago," I said, "I would never have thought they had undercover agents. He said they only gather evidence, anyway."

"Dalton was with DEVGRU for a short time after I took command," Deuce replied. "He's a good man. Grew up in Montana, I think. A real outdoorsman. You know, hunting and fishing to survive. He could track an ant across solid rock."

"So, Fish and Wildlife would be a calling for a guy like that," I said.

"That and other things," Deuce said. "We lost some good people in Afghanistan, and Dalton lost his dad while we were there. Had a heart attack trying to get a bagged moose out of the woods. Yeah, I could see Dalton moving toward a park ranger sort of life. His natural ability and talent would be quickly evident, and he'd move up."

Bringing the *Revenge* back up on plane, I reengaged the autopilot. We were less than ten miles from Biscayne Bay, so Deuce and Charity both decided to just stay awake. We'd be at the dock in less than half an hour.

Still five miles out, Chyrel came up to join us. "They are exactly who they said," she reported. "Fish and Wildlife has a special operations branch. Their undercover assets gather intelligence on illegal animal smuggling and poaching. Some of them come from military spec-ops. They operate worldwide."

"It's that big a problem?" I asked. "Animal smuggling?"

"Apparently so," Chyrel replied. "I took a little stroll through Fish and Wildlife's files. Their encryption is so nineties, by the way. Dalton and McVie have been responsible for the takedown of some major animal smugglers and poachers. She's the daughter of a Navy admiral, a doctor. Her dad was an animal rights activist until he disappeared in Africa several years ago. In the area where he disappeared, there had been an uprising of Al-Shabaab activity."

I glanced over at Chyrel in the subdued light. "Al-Shabaab?"

The mention of the radical Islamic terrorist group got Deuce's attention, too. "Any connection to the father?"

"Not directly," Chyrel said. "At least nothing official. He was looking into recent elephant poaching activity. An adult elephant's tusks can weigh more than a hundred pounds each and both male and female African elephants have them."

"Two hundred pounds of ivory," I said, making the connection immediately. "What would that bring on the black market?"

"Over $1000 a pound."

"Whoa," Charity said softly. "A quarter million for one elephant. Was Al-Shabaab responsible for the poaching?"

"No way to tell," Chyrel replied. "Everyone and their brother are on the take in that area."

"What about Dalton?" Deuce asked. "I know his SEAL history, but since then?"

"Not a lot on Dalton, but being a former SEAL, that's expected. Married and divorced. No real home." She grinned. "I found a juicy little tidbit, though."

I rolled my eyes. Chyrel was like a worm when she was digging for information. There was little she wouldn't find. "Juicy, huh?"

"Dalton's ex-wife just remarried."

"And how's that juicy?"

Chyrel turned to Deuce. "She married a guy named Rod Whitaker."

Deuce looked at her and nodded. "No surprise. She always struck me as a barracks bunny."

The term wasn't new to me. Deployment separation took a toll on families, something I knew all too well. The months alone sometimes sent wives into a tailspin; infidelity wasn't uncommon. Sleeping around with men in the husband's unit didn't happen often. But it did happen. Apparently, this Rod Whittaker guy was Dalton's former teammate.

Chyrel turned to me. "Whitaker is—"

"Married to Dalton's ex," I finished for her.

Chyrel went on to tell us about a few of the projects Dalton and Poppy had been involved in, sometimes risking their lives, to protect animals. To me, that seemed a very thankless job, yet a tremendously noble one.

An hour later, we were coming back out of Biscayne Bay, after leaving Chyrel with Julie. Once clear of the busy port, Charity elected to stay on the bridge with Deuce for a while, after I turned the helm over to him and went down to my cabin for a nap.

CHAPTER  TWELVE

By the time I woke up for the second time, it was late morning again. It was rare for me to sleep in, but not knowing what we were getting into, we opted to ensure that each of us got at least eight hours of rest.

The sound of the engines had awakened me when Deuce had slowed, approaching Bimini. I'd helped get the hook down and then the three of us had turned in for another nap.

Surveillance was always a boring job. Andrew and the others were ashore, working in teams. Tony and Tom circulated among the local shops and stores, while Andrew and Paul mingled with the tournament fishing crowd and tourists. Their job was to listen; to get a feel for the new shipyard, and maybe who was coming and going there. They didn't ask any direct questions, but steered conversations to the shipyard whenever they could. It was the only lead we had.

By mid-afternoon, we decided the most likely purpose of the private facility would be as a place where boats could be refitted for speed without drawing attention.

A few locals had said that was what they'd been told by people working there. It was being built as a facility to bring boats in for engine upgrades.

I was itching to get ashore, as was Finn. I'd spent the day going over the systems on the boat, making sure everything was in order.

"We oughta top off the fuel tanks," I told Deuce, after coming out of the engine room.

"Where do you think the meet will be?"

I thought about that a moment. "If I were setting this up, I'd advise each person who was attending so that they had just enough time to get there."

"If it's in the Gulf, we're screwed," Deuce said. "We're 200 miles east of where Armstrong would think we are."

"Not really," I said, getting a bottle of water from the fridge and guzzling half. "The advertised top speed of a Rampage with the smaller engine setup is 35 knots. Jimmy and I were making over 50 the other day. The meet's in less than 48 hours. So, somewhere in a 1600-mile radius from your office."

"And shrinking by 100 miles every three hours," he said. "Still, that's a lot of ocean. If we got the notification, can we move 1800 miles in two days?"

"It won't be," I said. "At least not if I were setting it up. I'd know the range of the boats involved. A Rampage 45 only has a 300-mile range at cruising speed. It'll be somewhere within 150 miles of fuel. He'd have no way of knowing the *Revenge* is a lot faster, carries more fuel, and has greater range."

"Yeah," he agreed. "So, we should take on fuel."

Twenty minutes later, we were nearing the fuel dock at Bimini Big Game Club. As we approached, I saw Poppy first. How she could work undercover with her conspicuous hair color, I had no idea. She was talking to Dalton. Or they were arguing. She seemed upset.

As I maneuvered toward the dock, Dalton offered to help tie off, then talked to Deuce about fishing while the dock hand dragged the fuel hose over and started the pump.

"How much do yuh think it gwon take, cap'n?" the young man called up to me on the bridge.

I turned on the dash instruments and checked the fuel gauge. "At least 300 gallons," I called out. I knew Dalton and Poppy were there for a reason, so I asked the dockhand if I could move to the end of the dock after fueling while we waited for someone.

"Long as someone stay aboard, ya mon. Gotta move if a big one come in. I be back in a few minutes. Di pump isn't very fast. Sorry 'bout dat."

Climbing down, I stepped up to the dock next to Dalton, while the pump ate up my wallet. He was shorter than I recalled, but it had been dark. His easy movements spoke of a fit body under his baggy clothes.

"How's the investigation going?" I asked him.

"We've got another lead," he replied, then turned to Deuce. "I was just heading over to recruit Whit. He's here on the island."

"Rod Whitaker?" Deuce asked, glancing at me. "He's here?"

"Yeah, on his honeymoon."

Deuce's glance was a question. If Dalton didn't know that his old SEAL buddy was now married to his ex-wife, he'd certainly find out if he went to ask for his help. Deuce and I simultaneously nodded to one another.

"Whatcha need?" I asked.

"Need to board a vessel. No footprint."

Deuce again glanced over at me. He and I could communicate a lot with just a look. He wanted to offer our assistance. I nodded again.

I looked out over the boats anchored in the bay. "We're just killing time for a day or two," I said. "Need any help?"

"Could be like the old days," Deuce added.

Dalton nodded. "Yeah. That'd be great. But I still need Whit."

"Didn't you say he's on his honeymoon?" Deuce asked. His concern was evident in his voice, even if Dalton didn't catch it. He wondered if the younger man knew who his old pal's new wife was.

"Yeah, but the boat," Dalton said. "We think they're Russian."

Deuce nodded, seeming to understand. "Roger that. C'mon aboard. Let me show you some gear we've got that might be what we need."

Stepping down into the cockpit, I opened the salon hatch, and waved our guests inside. Dalton and Poppy both took in the interior with the usual expression.

Gaspar's Revenge is a true fishing machine aft, and her hull loved the blue water. But inside, she was a luxury apartment.

Looking forward, I saw that my stateroom hatch was closed. Charity was keeping her presence concealed. Not that these two weren't to be trusted. It's just the way we operated.

"Have a seat," I said, sweeping a hand toward the couch on the port side. "Care for a beer?"

Deuce glanced over. I shot my eyes to the couch where Dalton sat, then down the gangway to my stateroom, and nodded. He picked up on what I was conveying and nodded back. I was giving him the okay to divulge our assets. To a degree. I trusted Dalton, but Poppy was a wild card.

"Hey, uh," Poppy said to me. "Dalton said you were in the Mog. That's Mogadishu, right? Africa."

I nodded, wondering where she was going. "Yeah."

"How long were you there?"

"Too long," I replied. "As soon as you're wheels down you've been in that hell-hole too long."

"You ever spend any time around South Sudan?"

Where was *this leading?* I looked over to Dalton, who looked a bit bewildered also. Did she know something that he didn't? Something she couldn't possibly know? I had to be careful here. I didn't know what, if anything, she might know. But I was a civilian now and she and Dalton were agents of the federal government. It didn't matter that it was Fish and Wildlife or the FBI, lying to a federal agent could get a person in deep shit really fast.

"Not officially," I replied, noncommittally.

Dalton cleared his throat. "Not now, Poppy."

She folded her arms and glared at him. *No*, I thought, *this doesn't have anything to do with my time in the Mog.* This was personal.

Passing around a few Red Stripes, I leaned against the counter separating the salon and galley, appraising the unlikely duo. "Deuce says you're good to go, Dalton. That's good enough for me." I nodded to where Poppy sat fuming. "Under the bench Poppy's sitting on, I have three Draeger PSS 7000's, all fully charged, inspected, and ready to go."

Dalton let out a whistle. "Wish we had your funding."

"Personal gear," I said, with a half-grin. "I can also add noise-makers, if you're not carrying."

"We're good there," Dalton said. "And I have access to some gear at the dive shop, too. But, um, just out of curiosity, what kind of noise-makers?"

I grinned. "Ma Deuce is below your seat."

"No way! How?"

"Custom-built titanium tripod with a center post that fits into the fighting chair's deck receiver. Got some full-auto long guns, and plenty of pistols and ammo. In case of an apocalypse there's an electric mini-gun, as well."

Dalton's eyes showed his admiration. In minutes, the three of us worked out a simple plan to get aboard the suspected boat. He explained that they were investigative only and would leave no trace that anyone had gone aboard. Our plan was just the basics. One of the first rules of combat is that the battle plan rarely survives first contact with the enemy. Better to plan simple and be ready to adapt to conditions as they change.

Dalton produced a paper chart and spread it out on the settee. The boat he wanted to infiltrate was anchored half a mile northeast of the northern tip of the island. I would have preferred to take the *Revenge*, anchor close, and swim from there. But that would be too conspicuous.

We chose an entry point four miles up the coast from where we were. It was a desolate beach way past Bailey Town, just before the island's northern point. Carrying tactical-type dive gear, on foot, after midnight, was out of the question. It would be way too obvious. Dalton said he could get a golf cart and a couple of seabags to carry our gear.

"I appreciate the equipment and backup," Dalton said. "But this—"

"Your op," Deuce said, cutting him off. "You call the shots. Jesse and I can provide the equipment and help you get there. But we're just backup. We'll stay in the water."

Dalton grinned. "Thanks, Deuce."

"Hey, what about me?" Poppy asked.

Deuce shook his head.

I looked over at her and crossed my arms. "Nope."

"What do you mean, *nope*? This is my op. Dalton and I are partners."

"Yeah, no," I said, looking over at Dalton.

She didn't like it. If she were a Saturday morning cartoon character, steam would have been blowing out of her ears.

Dalton held up his hand. "Poppy, listen. It's nothing personal."

"It's just a *guy* thing." Sarcasm dripped from her voice.

Dalton shook his head. "No, no." He looked at me for help, but I just shrugged. "No," he told her. "It's a military thing. They're not comfortable with you because they don't know you like I do, that's all. These men have trained together, fought together."

This seemed to just add fuel to the fire. No doubt she was a true redhead. Dalton took her arm and whispered something to her; a challenge. He told her he'd take her instead, if she could tell him what Ma Deuce was. Not a good tack in my experience. Especially with a redhead whose temper was already flaring. She stared back at him defiantly.

He said aloud, "*Ma Deuce* is an affectionate term for the M-2 50-caliber machine gun, developed by Browning in the 1930's to destroy tanks. It's still employed today."

"Men and their gadgets," she said, unimpressed.

Definitely not a good idea to belittle your partner, I thought. There was a lot more going on between these two than just working together.

"Yeah, well, what am I supposed to do? Hang out here and babysit Finn?"

"Finn can take care of himself," I said. Then I decided to push her to see what kind of reaction I'd get. And to take some of the heat off Dalton. "You're welcome to hang out on the boat, looking pretty." I winked and added, "That's something you seem to excel at."

She started to move toward me but hesitated. "Would you like to spend the rest of your life speaking in a falsetto voice?"

Somehow, I knew she wasn't just mouthing off.

"Wow, she is quite the little spark plug," I said to Dalton. "You got your hands full, don't you, buddy?"

"You don't know the half of it," Dalton muttered.

"What? You don't like your normal speaking voice either?"

Dalton clamped his mouth shut.

Poppy threw her hands up and left without a word. Dalton turned and shrugged. "I'll go find Whit and be back here before midnight."

After Dalton left, and I was sure he was going after Poppy, not Whit, Deuce folded his arms on his chest. "What the hell was that? Pushing her buttons, the way you did?"

Looking over at him, I shrugged and answered his question with one of my own. "I just wanted to see their reaction. Tell me something, would you chase after a co-worker who left in a huff over being left out of a tactical decision?"

"Depends on the co-worker and what they contributed."

"What if the co-worker was Julie?" Charity said, as she passed between us and went to the couch, where Finn lay.

"That's different. Julie's my wife," Deuce replied, rinsing his mug in the sink. He stopped and looked up. "Hey, you think maybe there's something going on between Dalton and Poppy?"

I grinned at him. "That's what I like about you, man. You don't miss a thing."

Having agreed on the vibe we'd picked up between Poppy and Dalton, Deuce and I studied the area where the boat was anchored.

"Neither of us works for Uncle Sam anymore," Deuce said. "It's against the law to board a boat at anchor without permission. Carry a gun while doing it—and we will be carrying—and it's called piracy. It doesn't matter if Dalton's an agent of the government. He doesn't have a warrant. So, why are we considering this?"

I glanced up from the chart. "For the jazz."

He headed over to the coffee maker and refilled his mug, offering the pot toward me. I nodded.

"You sure you're not taken by that girl?" he asked, filling my mug.

I rolled my eyes and was about to say something when Charity interrupted me.

"He's not." She'd been sitting quietly in the corner of the L-shaped sofa in the salon. She grinned at me and winked. "Maybe at first, over at the conch shack. But Poppy and Dalton are an item, whether either of them knows it or not. Jesse sees that."

I looked over to where she was gently stroking Finn's neck as he slept at her feet. "Yeah, I kinda got that impression."

"For the *jazz*, huh?" Deuce said, shaking his head. "Dad used that expression a lot."

Taking a sip from the mug, I looked over the rim at him. "Yeah, I know."

"Just for kicks then?" he asked. "That's it? This could be dangerous."

"No," I said, thinking back on what the two had told us of their investigation. "Not for kicks. For the dolphins."

"For the... dolphins," Deuce repeated.

Charity smiled and joined us in the dinette. "Very noble, Jesse."

"Meh. Defending the weak is just the right thing to do. It's what the three of us have done most of our lives."

"Most of *yours*, maybe," she said. "You're old. Only about a third of mine."

"Seriously," I said, "Wild animals should be left alone."

Charity cocked her head. "You own a charter fishing business."

"Yeah, so? We catch and release, for the most part; and we tag certain migratory species to help the eggheads. What we don't release is food. I don't fish for trophies. Besides, if what they suspect is true, this is like something right out of the Cold War.

"Cold War?" Charity asked.

"The Soviets captured and trained dolphins for the military," Deuce said. "We did, too. But ours were primarily used to help locate lost swimmers or underwater mines. The Soviets trained dolphins to locate subs and brush up against their hulls. Then they attached explosives to the dolphins to test the delivery method, how much they could carry and if the amount of explosives was enough to destroy a sub."

"Magnetic mines?"

"Contact detonation," I replied.

Her eyes grew wide. "Contact—?"

"They had plenty of old subs to test with," I told her. "The Russians claim that they shut down the program, but ten years ago, I heard a news story about the Russian Navy selling these unwilling kamikaze dolphins to Iran. Those people make a sport out of torturing people."

She looked over the chart I had turned toward her. To a sailor, very little on land is of any significance. That's why nautical charts don't show roads, or much of anything not right on the coast. But with a glance, a seasoned sailor could detect reefs, shoals, obstructions, and sounding lines. The way the lines curved and separated, then came together, packed densely, indicated a steep drop-off. After a moment, she returned to the couch and sat down again.

"No real places to hide anywhere around here," Charity said. "So, they're hiding in the vastness of the open ocean. A boat like that wouldn't fit in with the other boats around here to be able to hide in plain sight."

Getting our gear from the dry storage under the aft part of the couch, we assembled everything and checked it over, each of us inspecting all three rigs.

Finally, Deuce looked at his watch. "Close to midnight. I wonder how Dalton is making out with Whit."

"I meant to ask," I said. "Why is a fourth person needed?"

"Rod Whitaker is fluent in Russian and can recognize different regional dialects. And he reads Cyrillic."

I glanced up at him with a grin. "So do you."

Deuce shrugged. "Be nice to see him again. Not sure how his and Dalton's reunion will go, though."

"What's Dalton's first name?" Charity asked. "Or *is* that his first name?"

"G," Deuce replied.

"G?" I asked. "That's a letter, not a name."

"It's all he ever went by," Deuce said. "And it's all that was on most of his files at Dam Neck."

"*Most* of them?" Charity asked.

"It struck me as weird, way back then," Deuce said. "So, I dug out his original enlistment contract. His first name's Garrett."

"Garrett Dalton?" I said with a chuckle. "You're kidding."

"I don't get it," Charity said.

"A movie with Sam Elliot and Patrick Swayze," Deuce said. "They played a couple of bar bouncers named Garrett and Dalton."

"Dalton kinda looks like him," I said.

"Anyway, the kid qualified for any kind of high-tech job he might have asked for," Deuce continued. "ASVAB's off the chart in every category of testing. He chose combat swimmer."

The Armed Services Vocational Aptitude Battery was a test that helped the military determine what job skills a potential recruit brought to the table.

"And then SEAL training," I said. "Was he good?"

"Yeah," Deuce replied. "Very good. Smart, disciplined, and one of the most vocal people I've ever met when it came to freedom and the American way."

"Ahoy, the boat," came a call from outside.

Charity looked aft, then at Deuce. "Should I make myself scarce?"

"No need," I said. "Think you can pilot the *Revenge* out of the harbor by yourself?"

"Huh?"

"It'd be a good idea to have a boat to pick us up if things go south," Deuce said.

"Why does south get a bad name?" I asked, tossing Charity the keys as I moved to the salon hatch. "The souther I go, the better I feel."

Finn was right beside me when I opened the salon hatch.

"Make it quick," I told him. "We have to move the boat."

"Permission to board?" Dalton asked, as I stepped down into the cockpit. Dalton and another man, whom I assumed was Rod Whitaker, were standing on the dock.

"Granted," I said, looking past them to the roofless golf cart at the foot of the fuel dock. Finn leaped past the two men and loped off down the dock. "Come on in. I see we get groceries from the same place."

Dalton grinned as they stepped down to the deck in unison. The other man was of similar height and build as Dalton, fit and muscular. He carried a black, zippered bag.

"Nice-looking dog," the man said. "Yellow lab?"

"Mostly," I replied. "With a little pointer mixed in."

Dalton introduced me to Whitaker, and we shook hands. "Whit was our team shooter," Dalton added.

"Not as good as you," the young man said. "One of your confirmed kills is still talked about in sniper schools all over the world."

For all the good it did, I thought, waving the two men inside.

"Whoa!" Whitaker said, stepping up into the salon.

Dalton stepped up beside him. "I told you."

Upon seeing Charity, both men stopped just inside the hatch.

"Whit," Deuce said, stepping toward them with his hand out. "Good to see you again."

Whitaker shook Deuce's hand and the two men embraced, slapping one another on the back. "Good to be seen, Commander."

"Just Deuce, okay." He turned to Dalton. "Where's your partner?"

"She's following up on another lead."

Charity rose from the couch and Deuce extended a hand. "This is another of my co-workers," he said, stepping back. "Whit, Dalton, meet Charity Styles, former Army captain and chopper pilot."

"Ma'am," Dalton said, shaking her hand.

"An honor," Whit said, smiling broadly. "Sydney Olympics, right?"

"Uh, yeah," Charity replied, shaking Rod's hand in turn.

Dalton looked puzzled. Rod explained. "Know how today's competitive swimmers stay fully submerged after diving in?"

"Yeah," Dalton said. "Somebody finally told them about hydronic physics."

"She was one of the first to do that." Whit turned back to Charity. "And none has ever done it with more grace. You always had the lead when you surfaced. You're the reason I became a SEAL."

I'd never seen it happen before, but Charity's face flushed.

"Our gear's over here," I said.

My three Draegers were laid out on the couch, along with fins and full-face masks. Rod opened a zippered bag and took his own rebreather out, laying it on the sofa with the other three. His was a civilian model made by ScubaPro. Good equipment, not a lot different from the Draegers used by the military.

Though Deuce and I had already gone over my three, each of us checked and rechecked all four units. Satisfied that the gear was ready, and each of us was familiar with each other's, we put everything in the seabags Dalton had borrowed from Ebbie, along with his golf cart.

Taking Charity to the chart on the dinette table, I pointed to the spot where Dalton had said the suspected Russian boat was anchored. "Right here's where we're swimming to," I said. Then I moved my finger to another location just before the tip of the island. "We'll enter the water from the beach, right here."

"Where do you want me?"

Moving my finger again, I pointed to a spot nearly a mile offshore. "I already programmed two positions on the chart plotter. Here and where the Russian boat is anchored. Don't drop the hook, just use the station-holding feature on the GPS and the autopilot will keep you in place. You should be able to see a lot with the camera. It's deep water all around, at least 40 feet, with no shoals or reefs. If we need you, we'll call."

"Call?" Whit asked, looking over our shoulders.

Deuce opened a box on the counter and passed out five earwigs. "These are waterproof to 50 meters," he said, then looked at Whit. "Do you have a full-face mask?" The man nodded. "Good. Just turn this on and put it in your ear. It allows water movement around it, so there's no danger of pressure pushing it in too far. You have to twist it around your ear a little, to get the bone mic under the seal of your mask, but we'll be able to talk."

Reaching into the box again, he removed and distributed five antenna tethers. "Float these behind you. The tether is only 15 feet and the little float ball houses the antenna."

"Who the hell do you guys work for?" Dalton asked.

"Ourselves," Deuce and I both said at the same time.

"The earwigs work on a very low frequency," I said. "That allows underwater comm of about twenty feet between divers. The antenna patches the comm to a satellite link."

"There will be others listening," Deuce cautioned them. "We have four of our co-workers here on Bimini. One of them, a man named Andrew, will be on duty. You'll recognize him by his deep voice. He's a former senior chief with the Coast Guard's Maritime Enforcement. Anything you want to know about boats or boarding tactics, he can tell you. He'll be in a hotel room with a digital telescopic camera connected to a laptop and should be able to see the target as well as Charity can, out on the boat."

Both men nodded, and Deuce continued. "Our comms will also be monitored from my office in the Keys, by a woman named Chyrel. She's our intel tech and will be on a secure computer. She's got a bit of a southern accent. The answer to anything is at her fingertips."

"The answer to anything?" Whit asked.

"Just about anything, Whit," Deuce said, turning to face the man. "You remember how I work. All cards on the table. Face up, so there's no surprises for anyone. There was one thing my intel tech couldn't tell me— your wife's due date."

"You know—?"

"Everything," Deuce said.

"I do, too, Commander," Dalton said. "He and my ex being married won't affect us working together."

Deuce grinned at Whit. "So long as we're all on the same page."

He then turned to Dalton. "Being an agent for Fish and Wildlife notwithstanding, what we're about to do is illegal, right?"

"You ask that now?" Dalton said.

"Cards," I said, as the three former SEALs grinned at one another, sharing some secret. "Never play poker with friends. We just like everything on the table, face up. That's just how we roll."

CHAPTER THIRTEEN

We left the golf cart on the dune, 100 yards from where the beach turned around the northern tip of the island. There wasn't anyone around as we suited up.

"Poppy's not your typical animal lover," I said to Dalton.

He looked over at me in the moonlight, cinching his rebreather in place. "Yeah," he agreed, shrugging. "She comes by it naturally, I guess. She told me that her dad was a wildlife photographer."

I wondered if Poppy even knew about her father's more activist-type role in central Africa. "Yeah," I said, scoffing a little. "A wildlife photographer."

Dalton's puzzled look told me he didn't know. "What's that supposed to mean?"

"We learned he was on the South Sudan border with Congo when he disappeared," I told him, watching for a reaction. "More as an *activist* than a photographer."

Dalton stepped closer, checking my gear as I checked his. "What do you mean, *activist*?"

"Elephant poaching," I replied. "Possibly connected to Al-Shabaab."

Even in the dark, I could see in his eyes that this was something he didn't know. "How good is your intel?"

"The best," I replied, grabbing my fins from the back of the cart.

"Same way you found out about Alison and Whit?"

"Yep," I said, turning to join Deuce and Whit to walk into the water.

Deuce touched the button on his earwig, activating the device. "All comms on," he said. We each did likewise. "Comm check."

"Base up," came Chyrel's voice over my earwig.

"Jesse," I said.

The other two men gave their names and then Andrew chimed in. The hotel room he was in was half a mile from the shipyard and a mile from our location. He had north-and west-facing windows in the tenth-floor hotel room. The powerful telescope was on a tripod.

"All comms are good," Chyrel said. "And Andrew's telemetry is excellent. Hey, Dalton and Whit."

"If I'm looking at the right boat," Andrew said, "it's a derelict-looking work or research vessel, dark hull, and light-colored topsides, about 80 feet in length, with only a few lights on. But there are people moving around."

"Two guys," Dalton said. "We were hoping for that. Listen in and get a little scuttlebutt. Can you see clearly enough to warn us if there's someone on the aft deck?"

"Yes," Andrew replied. "I think only one person is awake though. I wouldn't count on picking up on anything said, unless he talks to himself."

"You guys cover all the bases," Whit said.

I shrugged. "We try to leave little to chance."

"We'll swim at a depth of ten feet," Dalton said. "Due north from here for 200 yards. Once clear of land, I'll surface and get a visual from there and take a bearing."

"Roger that," Deuce replied.

We quickly donned our fins and masks, making one last check of our equipment before submerging. I'd never worked with either man before, but knowing they were as well-trained as Deuce gave me comfort. We'd all trained in the same way, using some of the same equipment, and sometimes in the same place for the same op.

I brought my right arm out in front of me, gripping the elbow with my left hand. With my compass right in front of me, I turned north and started finning slowly into deeper water. The four of us moved into a loose diamond formation with Deuce at the rear and me on the left side. Each of us had a small float trailing behind us on fifteen-foot tethers. As long as we remained within ten feet of the surface, we'd remain in contact with Chyrel.

We stayed close, within eyesight of each other in the near blackness. The moon, which had been ever-present since we arrived, was now hidden behind high clouds. This made no difference to us as we swam through the dark water, just a couple of feet between each of us.

When I'd counted the right number of kicks for the distance, all four of us stopped at nearly the same time. Knowing the number of kicks required to swim a certain distance was something all combat swimmers learned, in both the Navy and Marine Corps.

I hung motionless in the water with Deuce and Whit, while Dalton slowly surfaced. The sea is never a quiet place but wearing the rebreathers, it was a lot quieter. Still, there were clicks and chirps, as well as faraway sounds from the much deeper water just offshore.

"Zero-four-two degrees magnetic," came Dalton's voice over my comm. "Approximately 1000 yards."

"I see you," Andrew's voice said. "Give us a second."

"For what?" Dalton asked.

"Got it," came Chyrel's voice next. "Three thousand and sixty-four feet to the back of the boat."

"Huh?" Whit said.

Chyrel explained. "Andrew's telescope is connected to his computer and he's recording. His computer is connected to mine via satellite. I see what he sees and use ranging software to get the distance. Your range is three-zero-six-four feet to target."

"Dayum," Whit said.

"I told you; everything." Deuce said. "Dalton has the lead. Jesse on the left flank. Whit, you take the right."

"And the CO in the rear with the gear," Dalton said. Even over the tiny speaker in my ear, distorted by the water, I could hear the mirth in his voice.

Again, we swam in a straight line, each of us following our own compasses and maintaining peripheral eye contact with the others. We kicked and counted. Our kicks were in rhythm with our internal clocks. One full kick, down and then back to the top, every four seconds. The slow pace, roughly two miles per hour, was to conserve energy. Our destination was only twenty minutes away. We'd be back on shore in an hour.

There was no talk over the comm. Within the first couple of minutes, our kicks synchronized. After just fifteen minutes, we began to sense we were close. The water began to get a little brighter ahead, lights from the yacht shining down on the surface. Finally, I could see the looming hull dead ahead. The boat drew six feet at least, black in the dark water around it. We moved toward the stern.

Our plan was simple. Deuce and I would be backup, while Dalton and Whit boarded the boat. They'd spend no more than ten minutes finding out anything they could. Then we'd return the way we came.

If anything went wrong, if they were discovered, they'd both go overboard instantly on whatever side was closest. With Deuce and I holding their gear, we'd meet up under the hull, just forward of the props, where the two younger men could suit up, then we'd dive to the bottom and head back to the beach. If it got really squirrely and we had to call Charity in, we'd swim due north, away from land. It'd be the last direction the people on the boat would suspect.

At the stern of the big boat was an impressive work platform, a foot above the water. It was large enough to be a dance floor. We split up into two-man teams, moving to either side of the platform. Whit was with me. He methodically got out of his gear, handing me his equipment, beginning with his fins. I hung everything over my left arm, as we hovered just below the platform. There was enough light to see by, but that also meant there was enough light to be seen.

"Be careful," I said, as Whit began to remove his mask.

Andrew's voice came over my earwig. "I don't see anyone on the aft deck."

Whit rose and grabbed the edge of the platform, levering himself slowly and quietly out of the water. I looked over to see Dalton doing the same on the port side. Deuce and I rose at the end of the platform until the tops of our heads were out of the water, while we hung on the edge of the platform, adding another pair of ears and eyes.

Deuce and I both had weapons drawn. Dalton and Whit carried suppressed MP-5s. It was a tense ten minutes, but finally the two men reappeared and slipped quietly into the water.

I handed Whit his mask first. We submerged a few feet as he got it on and then cleared it of water. The purging sound came over my comm, followed a second later by the same sound from Dalton.

"It's them," Whit said, strapping his rebreather back in place. "We got 'em."

Slowly descending toward the bottom, Whit and Dalton got their fins on and we started back the way we came, again silently following our compasses and counting kicks.

After a few minutes, Andrew said, "No activity on the stern. I think you got away unnoticed."

"Until someone sees a puddle of water at the comm center," Whit quipped.

After another twenty-minute swim, we turned due south, knowing we'd come ashore very close to the same place we entered. When we finally reached shallow water, Dalton surfaced to scan the beach.

His head quickly came back down, as if he were ducking a fast ball thrown high and inside. "There's another golf cart on the beach."

"Hang on a second," warned Andrew's voice over the comm. The seconds ticked by. "Two women," Andrew finally said. "One pregnant, the other with red hair."

"Dammit, Poppy," Dalton muttered.

"Take a little advice from an old salt?" I said. "Don't make a big deal about it. They were worried."

We submerged and spread out, swimming along the sandy bottom toward the beach. I came across a tangle of rope, covered with barnacles. Not a dock line, probably part of a float line used by some local fisherman. I dragged it along, unwilling to leave it in the water.

In three feet of water, we all stopped and removed our fins, then rose slowly and walked ashore, like a bunch of night divers out having fun. Hopefully, if we were seen by anyone, they wouldn't notice the lack of bulky scuba tanks.

The wind had picked up since we'd left. I checked my watch. It'd only been an hour. Way off to the south, cloud to cloud lightning, what some call heat-lightning, lit the sky for a moment. A storm was brewing.

The pregnant woman, whom I figured could only be Dalton's ex, and now Whit's bride, ran toward us carrying towels. She went straight to her husband and kissed him.

"How'd it go?" Poppy asked Dalton. I could sense a need for physical contact, but she wasn't overt about it. "What was the delay? Are you all right?"

Deuce and I started shedding our gear. I put the barnacle-covered rope in the sea bag, followed by our gear, including our wetsuits. The air was chillier. We toweled off and pulled our dry T-shirts back on.

"You were worried about me?" Dalton asked, grinning.

"Well, yeah," Poppy stammered. "I mean, no. Of course, there was no need to worry. I just—you're late."

Dalton's grin grew wider. He shed his gear and I took it, putting it in the same bag with mine and Deuce's.

"We got the right boat," he told Poppy. "They're definitely our guys. Buckets of fish and shrimp on board. Two men. Russians. And interestingly, military."

"Military?" Poppy asked, surprised.

Whit nodded his head, dropping his rebreather onto the back of our cart. "I'm sure of it. They had military communication equipment and the documents I saw, their directive, most definitely in military format."

Poppy turned toward Whit, worry on her face. "What was the directive?"

"Well, they sent an update," he began. "'Four responding to calls. Number five stubbornly refusing to engage. Do we abort? Leave number five?' The response was to leave no evidence. They have three days to get the fifth dolphin to respond, or they are to destroy it and leave the area."

"And when was that?"

Dalton and Rod answered simultaneously. "Yesterday."

"What in the world is the Russian military doing in the Bahamas training dolphins?" Poppy asked aloud. It was obvious she didn't expect an answer; more as if she were voicing her thoughts.

Rod and Dalton looked at one another, both shaking their heads. I put Whit's gear in the other seabag, figuring we'd split up and they'd be going back with Poppy and Whit's wife. Deuce collected the earwigs from the two men before saying goodbye.

"Everyone, stand down," Deuce ordered, after the others left. "Thanks for the assist."

"Want me to return to the fuel dock?" Charity asked.

"No," I replied. "Head to the spot where we anchored, just off Wild Quest. We'll swim out to you."

By the time Charity got the *Revenge* in, the wind was picking up and there were whitecaps on the deep ocean just beyond the entrance to the bay. I stayed on the comm with her and talked her through the procedure, directing her to a different anchorage. The wind blowing out of the south would move the *Revenge* more than the tidal current.

As she dropped the hook and backed down on it, Deuce and I started to swim the seabag out to the boat. I'd return it to Abbie in the morning, once the storm passed.

We were just pulling ourselves up onto the swim platform when Andrew called on the earwig. "You guys need to get somewhere you can look at the weather."

"We are looking at it," Deuce said. "It's all around us. What's up?"

"The local Bimini weather service there doesn't have much," he said, as I removed our dive gear from the sea bag and dropped it into a fish box. "The National Weather Service in Miami is calling it a big, late winter storm. Could get rough. Small craft warnings are up throughout the northern Bahamas. Seas are forecast to be six to eight feet through the day."

"Winter storm?" I said.

"Technically, it's still winter," he said. "For a little more than a day, anyway."

Grabbing a couple of towels from the cabinet, we hurried inside, drying off. Finn greeted us at the door. Unsure how long he'd been inside, I stepped back out and opened the transom door.

"Don't fall in," I told him, as he stepped out to do his business.

The bay was choppy, and the boat was rocking, causing water to come up through the slats in the swim platform. Finn looked up at me with a sort of forlorn expression. He had his own head on *Salty Dog* and we'd never spent this much time on the *Revenge* without a shore excursion. He probably missed his creature comforts. I didn't bother with the washdown when he stepped back through the transom door. The sea would take care of it. We ducked back inside just as another gust of wind rocked the boat.

"Will we be okay here?" Charity asked, drying her hair. Her clothes were dripping onto the deck.

"Yeah," I replied. "Might be a bumpy night. That's why I had you anchor here. I can let out more scope if we need to; even a second anchor. Was it raining out there?"

"I came through a squall just as I turned between the outer markers," she said. "I got the Isinglass down and the bridge zipped up, but it was over by then."

"Go get out of those wet clothes," I told her. "And get some rest. The sun'll be up soon."

Deuce looked at his watch. "Yeah, about three hours."

"If you don't need me," Andrew said, "I'm gonna turn in."

"Yeah," Deuce said. "Thanks, Andrew. Get some sleep. You too, Chyrel, if you're still on here."

"I am," she replied. "Just waiting till y'all were all safe. G'night."

A gust of wind howled, rocking us again. Then a sudden downpour beat on the roof for a few seconds and was gone.

"If there's any chance we'll need to put down a second anchor," Deuce said, "maybe the sooner the better."

I went over to the laptop, still sitting on the settee cushion where I'd left it. I pulled up the nearest weather buoy. It was west of Bimini about ten miles.

"Seas west of here are three feet with seven-second intervals," I told Deuce. "Wind's a steady twenty knots with gusts to 25." I closed the laptop. "Yeah, let's do it. There's a 40-pound plow anchor in the engine room and a second rode in the anchor locker; 250 feet. We can drop it a little to the south of the main anchor."

The rain was coming down in sheets by the time we had the second anchor down. With 250 feet of rode out to each anchor, the last 50 of each being heavy chain, I felt more comfortable about riding the storm out.

After a quick shower to warm up, I dressed more appropriately for the coming weather; jeans and a heavy cotton work shirt, which I fully planned to sleep in. I left the laptop on in the salon and set the anchor watch alarm on the GPS. It would go off if the boat moved more than 100 feet. I went to bed exhausted.

CHAPTER FOURTEEN

Sleeping on a boat in a storm isn't easy. It feels like you're underway as the vessel rises and falls over the waves—at least it did on the *Revenge*. Bigger, ocean-going boats usually located the master stateroom below a raised pilothouse, the center of both pitch and roll, but my stateroom was in the bow. Counting on the GPS alarm to alert us, I'd managed to get only a few hours of fitful sleep, and I woke at mid-morning.

I had to brace myself as I went up to the galley. The rain was no longer pelting the roof, but the wind was still blowing. From the port side, I could see whitecaps on the bay. Offshore, it was sure to be a mosh pit.

Charity sat on the settee, her hair disheveled. She was dressed as I was, in jeans and a long-sleeved shirt, and only nodded as I stepped sideways into the galley.

"In the sixties," was all she said.

Deuce was asleep on the pullout. In his fifteen years of service, he'd probably slept aboard naval vessels quite a bit, fair weather, and foul. And Julie had grown up on boats. Together, they'd sailed their Whitby ketch thousands of miles on auto-pilot straight through the night numerous times, and I'm sure they'd encountered bad weather. But they had grown up in the electronic age and completely trusted their equipment and alarms. I hadn't, and every unusual bump had jarred me awake.

Filling a mug from the coffeemaker was tricky. It was spill proof, but I wasn't. I dropped a towel on the floor and moved it around with my foot, then just left it there for the next spill. Bending over would probably have caused a head injury. I joined Charity at the settee.

"Squids can sleep through anything," I said, nodding toward Deuce.

"You Jarheads, too," she whispered. "I passed out from exhaustion an hour ago, but the boat jerked hard and woke me up."

"I'm not asleep," Deuce said, his back to us.

Turning over, he rose and pulled on the same T-shirt he'd worn after showering last night. Odds were we'd be getting wet soon.

"Any word from Andrew?" I asked, noting the earwig in Charity's right ear.

"I was talking to Chyrel," she replied. "I don't think Andrew's up yet. But the others are. Tony said that they were going to go out and help with whatever they could."

"Help what?" I asked.

"The storm was bad," she replied. "There's damage all over the island."

"Good idea," Deuce said, while folding his blanket. "I don't think we'll find out anything more here. I've been giving it a lot of thought and I've decided that Armstrong is probably solid."

I looked at my watch. "The meet is in just a little over 24 hours. The circle is down to about 700 miles."

After closing the sofa bed, Deuce stretched, then went to the galley for coffee. "And we're a good 150 miles from my office, which is where Armstrong thinks we are."

"That's a worry for tomorrow," I said. "But I'm betting the meet will be somewhere in the northern Bahamas." I glanced outside again. "This storm should have passed by now."

Charity clicked a few keys on the laptop and said, "Tell them what you told me, Chyrel."

"Hey, boss." Chyrel's voice came over the laptop's tiny speaker. "Hey, Jesse. The National Weather Service is saying it's one of the worst winter storms in 50 years."

"It's not winter," I said for the second time.

"Technically it is," Chyrel replied. "Winter ends at the time of your meeting with Armstrong tomorrow, wherever that's gonna be."

"I know, but there's rarely a winter storm this far south. Is there a tropical low involved, maybe?"

"Negative," Chyrel replied. "It's just a big-assed nor'easter that wandered south."

Deuce sat next to Charity. "Any idea when it will pass?"

"You've seen the worst of it," she replied, as a weather map appeared on the screen. "It'll be windy, and seas are still gonna be rough."

"How rough?" I asked.

The *Revenge* was built for heavy seas, but not at high speed. She could handle four-foot swells at 30 knots, but any bigger than that, we'd have to go slower.

"Forecast for the opening of the tournament is three to five."

Nodding to Deuce, I finished my coffee. "She can handle that. I'm going to check the anchors."

Finn followed me to the hatch. "Has he been out yet?" I asked Charity.

"No, I just came up."

Opening the wet locker by the hatch, I got Finn's vest and leash. He sat next to me and allowed me to suit him up for foul weather. I didn't worry about his swimming ability. But I know from experience that when you're in the water in stormy seas, a boat can disappear from sight very quickly.

We headed out into the dwindling storm. Wind whipped around the sides of the house and water dripped off the bridge overhang onto the cockpit deck as I moved across it to open the transom door.

"Make it quick," I told Finn.

Labs naturally love the water. Rain is just liquid sunshine to them. But Finn was a little uneasy on the swim platform. The *Revenge* was bobbing up and down at the bow as foot-high rollers passed beneath her, causing the stern to rise and fall, and water to splash up through the wooden slats of the platform. Rain falling on his back was no problem, but he didn't like the water splashing up from below. He managed to take care of his needs despite the conditions and came back aboard. I waited with him under the overhang until he shook off the water, then let him back inside, his leash trailing behind him.

Climbing up to the bridge, I checked the tracks on the chart plotter. We'd moved slightly. The track showed us moving back and forth in an arc, but then the arc shifted a little, no more than five or ten feet. But it appeared as if the anchors had both dragged some. At least the storm was letting up. Here and there, patches of blue sky could be seen between the scudding clouds.

I climbed down and went forward, holding onto the hand rail, the wind whipping at my hair and clothes. On the foredeck, I had to keep one hand on the side rail for balance. The wind was blowing at a speed of at least 30 knots, with gusts up to tropical storm strength.

Winter storms in the North Atlantic were treacherous and came up quickly, but by March, they've usually calmed down. Soon after March would come hurricane season.

I checked both rodes. They pulled tight with every wave but were holding fast. Surveying the bay, I noticed two boats driven up onto the shore behind us—both small, open, and made of wood.

There were no lights on in any of the nearby buildings. A mile to the north, I could just make out the Hilton. There appeared to be lights there, at least. That's where Andrew and the guys were staying.

There were quite a few more boats like the *Revenge* anchored in the bay—big sport-fishing machines. Some boaters preferred to ride out a storm at anchor, rather than tied up in a slip. Not every captain took precautions against an approaching storm; in fact, some of the owners of the boats still at the dock probably weren't even on the island. If a boat broke free from a dock, it could do a lot of damage to the docks and any boats around it.

Before going back inside, I grabbed a fresh towel and dried my hair. Occasional raindrops and seawater were blowing in the wind, so I wrapped the towel over my shoulders to absorb some of the cold dampness. The temperature had dropped fifteen degrees since yesterday. It was going to be a rough day; cool and windy, with nothing to do. I found myself wondering what Dalton and Poppy were up to as I stepped into the salon.

Deuce looked up from the laptop. "Andrew just checked in. Trees and powerlines are down all over the island. Their hotel has their own generator, so they're good."

"Yeah," I said, heading to my stateroom to change. "I bet they even have room service."

The wind continued to howl. I hung up my damp shirt and put on another one. It was too rough to cook, so we ate fruit for our breakfast.

Deuce's cell phone buzzed, and he picked it up, checking the display before stabbing the screen with a finger.

"Hey, Andrew," he said, then paused. "Hang on, let me pull it up."

"What's up?" I asked, as Deuce opened my laptop.

"Your redheaded friend is renting a Wave Runner," he said, as he moved the mouse around and clicked on the keyboard.

"In this slop? She's nuts."

A full-screen image from the camera in Andrew's room filled the display. He was looking back toward the shore near where we were anchored. I could see the *Revenge* in the foreground, and I recognized the marina.

"Bimini Big Game," I breathed, seeing a flash of red in the midst of the gray rain and sea.

The camera slowly zoomed in on the rental dock. A man and woman were trying to balance something as they got onto a Wave Runner. The woman was small, with wild red hair; Agent Poppy McVie. The man with her wasn't her partner, Dalton. They both turned and looked in the direction of the camera, but I'd never seen the man before. They had a cooler and a Y-shaped contraption of some kind. The man got on first, in front. Whatever the thing was that Poppy was juggling with the cooler proved to be too much, and she tossed it on the dock. Then they dismounted and changed seats, the man now behind Poppy and the cooler between them. With a toss of a line, they moved away from the dock and accelerated.

"Where are they going?" Charity asked, leaning over my shoulder.

I had my suspicions. I had no idea what was in the cooler, but I didn't like it. "Stay on her, Andrew. I think she's about crazy enough for a frontal assault on the Russian boat."

The Wave Runner crashed through the first wave as they exited the bay and became airborne. For a second, I thought she'd lost it, but after launching over a second wave, Poppy slowed down and turned north.

Outside, the wind was slowly dying down, but it was still a good twenty knots. "Keep an eye on her, Deuce. I'm gonna go pull one of the anchors. Just in case."

When I got to the bridge, I activated the windlass and took in some of the plow anchor's rode. When I started back down the ladder, Charity stepped outside.

"Stay there," she called up, stepping up onto the side deck. "I'll get the safety."

In seconds, she had the safety off, and I toggled the windlass again. Hauling up 200 feet of rode took a few minutes. Finally, the anchor broke free of the sand and the Revenge drifted back on the main anchor rode.

"Hang on!" I shouted down to Charity as the rode tightened, bringing the Revenge to a sudden stop.

I continued retrieving the plow and when I saw the red chain links on the last ten feet of the 50-foot chain, I toggled the windlass on and off until the anchor was on the pulpit. Then I climbed down the ladder, went forward, and while I lifted the 30-pound anchor, Charity unshackled the chain, letting the end drop into the chain locker.

After stowing the anchor, I headed back inside. "What's going on?"

"Hard to make out," Deuce said. "They keep whipping past the boat, throwing some kind of objects at it."

I watched the monitor for a moment. Whatever the guy was throwing, they were about the size of grapefruits and in various bright colors.

"Water balloons?" I asked.

"Something like that," Deuce replied, mesmerized by the action unfolding nearly five miles away. "But dirty brown water."

Poppy started to turn the Wave Runner when a muzzle flash from the Russian boat caught my eye. "Gunfire!"

We watched in horror as someone on the boat continued firing. Poppy turned the machine suddenly and roared off, leaping over the wave tops with abandon. She turned south, back toward the marina. In seconds the pair on the Wave Runner were out of range of the shooter, but still fighting against wind and waves.

"What the hell were they doing?" I wondered aloud.

Andrew's voice came over the speaker. "That lady's certifiable." His deep baritone seemed to lend absolute credibility to his words.

I watched the Wave Runner racing away from the Russian boat as Andrew zoomed in with the telescope. Poppy was standing, leaning out over the handlebars. Her knees were bent, absorbing the jarring shock of the waves as her machine bucked beneath her. With a determined look on her face and a death grip on the machine, she clenched her teeth against the wind, her wet clothes clinging to her body and snapping in the wind at her back. She looked over her shoulder once, red hair flying behind her as if her head were ablaze. Her whole attitude screamed of defiance and passion.

In a state of panic, the man on the back must have given up on the cooler and released it. Now in the lee of the island, he simply held onto Poppy as they raced across the calmer water, hopefully headed back to the marina.

I breathed a sigh of relief when Poppy pulled the Wave Runner up to the dock and the man got off the back. He and Poppy talked for a moment while she still sat on the machine. Her companion kept shaking his head, arguing with her.

"She's going back out there," Charity said.

"Hoist anchor," I ordered, turning away, and heading toward the aft hatch. "Make ready to depart. We're going out."

"Are you nuts?" Deuce said. "You don't even know if she's—"

"She's leaving the dock," Charity said, as I stepped out into the cockpit and quickly climbed the ladder.

I fired up the engines as Deuce came out and made his way to the foredeck. Within minutes, we had the primary anchor up and I pointed the *Revenge* toward open water.

"Here," Deuce said, when he reached the bridge.

He handed me an earwig. I turned it on and put it in, adjusting the bone mic around my ear.

Andrew's voice came over the comm. "She's trying to grab something off the boat."

"What's happening?" I asked, mashing the throttles down.

"That crazy lady," Andrew said, his voice awestruck, "she charged right at that boat with someone on deck shooting back at her. Charged straight into the gunfire, man! She's fighting with the rifleman! Holy shit! She just yanked the guy right off the boat! The boat's underway and she just yanked something off the stern. She's bearing away now."

I turned the wheel and headed north at 30 knots, the fastest I dared go in these conditions. It was rougher ahead, beyond the island's northern tip

"Where are they?" I asked.

"Close to where the Russian boat was anchored. It pulled the hook after she and the guy left. It's now heading north and she's coming back toward you, a good mile from the north end of the island."

"That girl's irrational," Deuce said.

"Wait one," came Andrew's voice again. "She's slowing. There's smoke coming from the Wave Runner."

"Guide me to her," I told him.

"Dead in the water. It's going down, man."

"Jesse," said Chyrel's voice in my ear. "I got her location: half a mile north of the tip of the island."

Deuce navigated through the chart plotter screens to input latitude and longitude, then said, "Give me the numbers."

As he entered the location, I turned slightly northeast around the island's north beach, where we'd dived. Ahead, I could see the Russian scow moving away.

"Take the helm," I told Deuce and started for the ladder. We'd be there in a matter of minutes.

I opened the salon hatch and looked inside. Charity was at the settee, eyes glued to the monitor. "You or Andrew keep an eye on that boat," I said. "Let me know if it turns back."

"Roger that," both voices said over my comm.

"I got the boat, Andrew. Too hard to keep the girl on this pitching camera."

Finn stood at the hatch, ears up and eager. He still had his vest on. It would inflate instantly if it hit the water. Even without one, he used to pull the Trent kids around the lagoon, the two of them clinging to his neck or fur. And Poppy didn't weigh much more than Carl Junior.

When I opened the hatch wider, Finn came out and joined me in the cockpit. "Stay right there," I told him. "Be alert."

Finn had learned a lot of keywords and hand signals. *Alert* was one of them. His butt hit the deck and his head came up, ears raised, as he looked and listened for anything. When it came to retrieving something from the water, Labs didn't have to be taught anything. It's what they did. As a kid, I had a big black Lab named Shadow.

My friends and I would throw tennis balls for hours, until our arms hurt, and Shadow would bring them back every time. If I ordered Finn to fetch, or simply tapped his forehead and pointed, he'd launch himself into the waves, not even waiting to see what I wanted him to bring back. If it was in the water, a Labrador Retriever would bring it back.

Deuce shouted down from the bridge. "Coming up on the starboard side. Twenty yards."

I leaned out over the gunwale, looking forward as Deuce reversed the engines. Three-foot wind waves rocked the boat—remnants of the storm. On the flats of the Bahama Bank, these would dissipate by the end of the day. But right now, beyond Poppy's bobbing head, waves were lined up in regimented rows.

Poppy looked even smaller in the vastness of the rolling ocean. I waited until a wave rolled under the boat, lifting, and rocking the *Revenge*, and then I leaned over the gunwale before the next one arrived.

"Hey, you need a lift?" I called out, as Deuce shifted to neutral. I started to reach down, then hesitated, remembering the last time we'd been in this situation. "This is my last dry shirt," I said with a grin.

She rolled her eyes. "Really?"

The next wave lifted her, breaking slightly around her head. I waited for it to roll beneath the boat, knowing that the next one would be seven seconds behind it. Reaching over, I took her extended arm, wrist to wrist, and lifted her bodily out of the water and onto the gunwale. Even soaked, she couldn't be half my weight. She swung her legs over and slid to a cross-legged position on the deck, totally spent.

"She's okay," I shouted up to Deuce unnecessarily. He was still wearing his earwig. I lowered my voice. "Back to the bay, fifteen knots."

"Aye, aye," he replied.

"Do you want some alone time?" Charity teased over the comm. "I can hide out in the guest bunk."

"Har-dee-har," I said, turning back to Poppy. Finn greeted her happily, licking her face and wagging his tail.

"Where's Dalton?" I asked.

"So much for small talk," she replied, taking the fur on Finn's neck in her hands and rubbing her nose to his. "Is he always like this?" she asked him. Another delaying tactic.

"He's your partner, right?"

"Yeah, but—I dunno," she said, then yelled up to the bridge, "Is he gone?"

Deuce shouted back. "Hightailing it out of here."

"I was just working a lead," she said, answering my question, but not really offering anything. "On my own," she added.

The girl would make a lousy poker player.

"Uh-huh," I said, eyeing her suspiciously. "You've gone rogue."

"Well, that depends on your definition of—"

"We watched you out there," I said, pointing aft. "Throwing whatever it was at their boat. What the hell are you up to?"

She stared at Finn for a moment, as if he might give her something plausible to work with. He didn't. He just stared back at her.

"Stink bombs," she said. "We hit them with stink bombs, okay?"

"Stink bombs," I repeated.

"Dalton and I don't agree on the course of action, exactly. So, I was doing my own thing."

"Uh-huh," I said, waiting. "And?"

"And, I admit, I'm a little unorthodox. But hey, I've got a pretty good track record." She looked up and pursed her lips. "Mostly."

"Uh-huh," I said again, leaning against the gunwale, and crossing my arms. This girl had fire, no doubt about it. Using a jet ski and stink bombs to chase off armed Russians took guts. She seemed about as predictable as a firecracker with a short, smoking fuse. But it was the passion I'd seen in her face as she'd raced away from the Russian boat that stuck in my mind.

If Dalton doesn't get off his ass...

I shook the thought away. Opening the mini-fridge, I took out two water bottles. "And what exactly was the purpose of this unorthodox stink bomb attack?" I asked, handing her one. "If you don't mind me asking, of course."

"It was cover," she said, putting the bottle to her lips, and chugging down a couple of swallows. She wiped her mouth with the back of her hand. "Thanks."

Poppy turned her head, looking up at me sideways. "I needed to get close to the boat to disable their... diver recall transducer."

Her lower lip twitched slightly, as if thinking about smiling.

"Why?" I asked.

"Because I learned that's how they communicate with the dolphins. They can summon them anytime they want, from great distances."

"Wish you'd've mentioned it," I said, grinning. "We have one on board. We could've blasted a signal to cancel theirs."

She stared up at me for a moment. "But for how long?"

I just shrugged.

"I had to destroy it."

"Uh-huh." I seemed to be saying that a lot. Not really agreeing, but leaving the door open for her to add more information. I took a pull from my own water. She didn't elaborate. "I'm going to take a stab in the dark," I started, "and guess that Dalton didn't think this was a good idea."

"You know," she said after a deep breath, "a ride back to the dock would be greatly appreciated. Thank you."

"Sure thing, little lady."

I watched her sitting there as I drained about half my water. Then, without saying anything else, I climbed up to the bridge. Deuce moved over to the second seat and

I took the helm, throttling up to twenty knots in the lee of the island.

"She's gonna get herself killed," Deuce said.

"Definitely not rational," Charity said over the comm. "But love isn't rational all that often."

"Pull in over there," Deuce said, pointing toward the mangrove shoreline. "It's five feet deep just a few feet from shore."

I glanced over at him. "Why?"

"We're just killing time out here until tomorrow, anyway," he said. "She seems to like you and could use someone to talk to. I know from experience that Dalton wouldn't be that person. I don't mind helping other agencies, but if those two don't get their heads in whatever game it needs to be in, they're of no help to each other. She'll listen to you."

As we passed the northern tip of the island, only 100 feet from the lee shore, the wind and waves dropped to almost nothing. I turned toward shore and slowed, moving close to some deep-water mangroves.

"What's up?" Poppy shouted from below. "Where're we going?"

I brought the boat to a halt in a shallow, sandy spot. Glancing down, I could see Poppy was on her feet. Finn was curled up in his usual spot by the transom door.

"Finn's gotta take a whiz," I replied.

She gazed down at him lying on the deck, then looked back up at me, hands on her hips.

I released the windlass brake and dropped the anchor, along with a good 30 feet of chain. Meanwhile, Finn had jumped to his feet in anticipation.

"See?" I said, grinning.

Deuce said he'd wait on the bridge as I headed down the ladder. When I reached the cockpit, I turned off my earwig. Finn jumped back and forth, tail wagging.

I opened the transom door and bent to remove his vest, scratching his ears. "Find us something to snack on while you're out there."

He shook his fur into place and barked before jumping into the water. Then he submerged for a second before popping up again. Looking around, he spotted a small, sandy shoreline, and struck out toward it at a fast swim, using his thick tail as a rudder.

I leaned against the transom, one foot crossed in front of the other, hands in my pockets, in as non-threatening a pose as I could muster. "So, how long have you and Dalton been working together?"

"About a year and a half," she replied, looking past me at Finn.

"Yeah? How's it going?"

"Right now? Well..."

"Uh-huh," I said once more, looking over my shoulder. Finn had reached the beach and trotted out onto the sand, his nose to the ground.

"What was that about the snack?" Poppy asked.

"You like clams?"

"No."

"That's right," I said, looking back at her. "Deuce mentioned you pitched the conch I bought you."

"He had eyes on me, huh?"

I nodded.

"Yeah, well, sorry about that. I'm a vegetarian. I was so caught up in—" Her eyes trailed off toward shore. "Doesn't matter."

I followed her gaze. Finn had disappeared into the mangroves.

"Right now, I think he's just looking to relieve himself," I told her.

A moment later, Finn returned to the water's edge, sniffing around in the sand above the high tide line. Then he waded out into the water and began pawing at the bottom. His head went under for a second and when he came up, he had a clam in his mouth and started swimming back toward the boat.

"I've never seen anything like that," Poppy said.

"Yeah," I said. "He's something to behold." Turning to face her, I crossed my arms. "You were saying, about you and Dalton?"

"You know how it is. Sometimes you don't see eye-to-eye."

There was a lot more to it than that. I knew it, but did she? "Looks more like a lover's quarrel to me."

"Oh, we aren't—"

Holding my hands up, palms out, I said, "Not my circus, not my monkeys." I leaned toward her slightly.

"It's obvious the man cares about you. A lot. In case you didn't know."

Her eyes were remarkable; they seemed to pull a person in. I waited.

She matched my stance, crossing her arms and staring back defiantly.

Sometimes, it's better to back off, I thought. *Who the hell am I to give relationship advice?*

"And I can see you are one stubborn woman," I conceded, having known my fair share. "I've known a few like you over the years. Fierce. Lord almighty."

Some of the fiercest were also the gentlest, as I recalled, thinking of Charity, and one or two others I've known.

"Anyway," I said, "I can't stand by and watch you get yourself killed. Those men out there are Russian military. This ain't a game."

I could see that I'd struck a nerve.

"Thanks for the advice," she said, her tone now like ice.

"What I'm saying is—"

"Yeah, I got the picture."

I frowned down at her as Finn reached the swim platform and deposited his clam, distracting both of us.

He turned and swam in circles for a moment, then dove under. He swam to the bottom and pawed with his front legs, coming up a moment later with another clam.

"Good boy," I told him, as he dropped it on the platform with the first one.

He turned and went down again.

"Your dog's cute," Poppy said. "But I'd really like that ride back to the dock now, please."

I sighed. "Sure thing. C'mon, Finn."

As Finn climbed onto the swim platform, I headed back up to the helm. I waited till Finn moved his clams, one by one, from the platform to his bucket.

"Mind closing the door?" I asked.

She reached for it, as if she were going to slam it shut. Then she looked up at me and smiled, gently closing, and latching the transom door.

"You turned off your comm," Deuce said, as I toggled the windlass switch and started the engines. "Chyrel got the courier dispatch. You were right. The meeting location is just 25 miles from here."

CHAPTER
FIFTEEN

Word had spread rapidly around the bay, and the marina was abuzz. When we dropped Poppy off at the fuel dock, we learned quickly that although some of the entrants had bugged out ahead of the storm, the tournament was still on. More importantly, several boats weren't returning, so we moved the *Revenge* over to a vacant slip at Bimini Big Game Club.

Leaving Finn on the boat, the three of us met Andrew and the others for dinner at the club.

"I just don't agree," Tony said, once we'd ordered. "He'd have no way of knowing where anyone was. The very nature of a boat is that it moves."

He had a point. The courier had delivered the coordinates almost 24 hours before the meet was to take place. From Tavernier to the meet location was only about 80 miles—barely three hours, at cruising speed.

"Maybe he's allowing for daylight operation only," I said. "Eighty miles, starting in the morning, makes sense."

"I'm with Tony on this," Paul Bender said. During his time with the Secret Service, Paul had received a PhD in forensic psychology. He usually only listened whenever we met over something, and didn't often offer an opinion, so his ideas were always well thought-out. "The more I see, read, and hear about Armstrong and his business dealings," Paul continued, "the more I'm certain that he's on the level. My bet is he sent the same message to all parties concerned at a time that would allow everyone to get there on time without rushing. He's finished investigating us."

"Some of the registrations for those boats I looked at showed a top speed of only ten or fifteen knots," I said.

"But we don't have any idea where the other boats are coming from," Tony added. "Nor how many."

Everyone looked toward Charity. She shrugged. "All Bremmer said was that there would be others at the meeting."

Our dinner arrived and after the waiter left the table, Deuce asked me when we should leave.

"Twenty-five miles?" I said. "I'd like to skirt around the location, about ten miles from it, check things out with the radar, then come back to it from the west. Let's pull out of here after the tournament boats, about 0900."

"And after?" Deuce asked.

"No telling how long this will be," I replied. "And I'd kinda like to see how Dalton's investigation goes. Let's figure on returning here for the night. Unless anyone has to be somewhere."

"I like that idea," Bender said. "I can hang back here and keep an eye on things with the telescope."

Deuce nodded toward Tom to get his attention. "Why don't you stay with him?" he suggested. "You might be able to see what people are saying."

Tom Broderick had been my company commander when I retired from the Corps. Years later, he'd been injured on the battlefield, losing his hearing, and severely burning the side of his face. During his recovery, he'd quickly adapted, learning American sign language and lip reading. The Corps had medically retired him just over a year ago.

"Roger that," Tom said.

"Andrew and Tony," Deuce said, "you're with us. Chyrel can use the camera on the boat and patch it through to Tom to watch any other boats; maybe pick up some cross-talk before we actually meet these people. The location's in deep water, too deep to anchor. If we're to leave the boat and go to Armstrong's for the meeting, he has to know we have an extra person aboard, so there's no need for covertness. We'll come back here after the meet and head home Sunday morning."

We ate dinner, but my mind kept going back to the question Poppy had asked me about using my recall system: *how long?*

Yeah, she'd destroyed the sound system the Russians used to call the dolphins, but you could pick up sound transducers at any of the bigger marinas here in the Bahamas, or back in Florida.

She knew that, I thought, while chewing a bite of very delicious cobia. Whatever those Russians were training the dolphins to do, they weren't going to give up that easily. They could come back with another transducer and just call the dolphins to them. Poppy was asking me how long I'd be willing to devote to blocking their calls. I had no illusions about Poppy's passion for protecting animals. Her work was something she would devote everything to.

I wondered how close the dolphins would have to be to hear the Russian's call. The navy used the Tongue of the Ocean for acoustic research, partially because it was really deep and almost completely shut off from the surrounding ocean by shallow banks. The banks isolated the mile-deep water of the TOTO from acoustical interference from the outside, and kept anyone from listening in. So-called Russian *fishing boats* sometimes carried very sensitive acoustic equipment.

Bimini was right on the outside western edge of the bank, about 100 miles west-northwest of a deep canyon called Northwest Channel. There the bottom dropped quickly, from about twenty feet on the bank south of Chub Cay, to over a mile deep in the TOTO. Not a sheer drop, like the Grand Canyon. The slope varied, but a mile out, the bottom dropped a mile deep. That was a steep drop in any book.

To the west of Bimini, the raised limestone karst making up the Bahamas dropped down to the continental shelf, where the bottom was roughly half a mile deep. Acoustically, Bimini was open to the whole eastern continental shelf, from Canada to Cuba. Our dive the previous night had been right on the edge of the bank. Where Charity monitored us from the *Revenge*, a mile away, the water was 2000 feet deep. The sounds we'd heard during the dive could have come from hundreds of miles away, maybe thousands. It was far noisier out there than in the TOTO. The Russians would have to be moderately close to the dolphins for the transducer to override the surrounding cacophony of the deep ocean.

Thinking like a fisherman, I knew the banks to be mostly devoid of anything except vast, shallow sand flats. There were patch reefs here and there, but they were like an oasis on a desert, few and far between. There was plenty of life out there, but not what fishermen were after, nor dolphins. Little cover meant fewer fish. The sandy banks were home to things that lived below the sand, and the things that hunted them. Not gamefish.

Nor was it the ideal hunting habitat for wild dolphins. They hunted along the deep ledge, only occasionally coming onto the shallower banks. That was what drew the dolphin-watchers and dive encounters, like Wild Quest. The Russians would only have to cruise the edge of the Bahamas karst until they got within range. It was unlikely they'd search the TOTO, since it was so far away from here, and monitored by the United States Navy. And I doubted the dolphins could find the TOTO across miles of shallow banks. They'd have no reason to go out there, so the Russians would be less likely to look for them there. It might be a good place for Dalton and Poppy's team to relocate the dolphins.

It was cover, Poppy'd also said, talking about why she'd thrown stink bombs at the Russian boat. *Cover for what?* I wondered.

Fish and Wildlife wasn't like Homeland Security or the Department of Defense, with their unlimited funds, but stink bombs? Surely, they carried guns and could call in the Coast Guard. Why balloons filled with something brown and stinky when she was an undercover agent for a government agency?

But she'd said *cover*, not *under*cover. She'd said she'd thrown stink bombs at the Russians as cover. To conceal the fact that she worked for the U.S. government? Acting as some sort of eco-warrior? To protect someone else? Maybe draw the heat away?

"Earth to Jesse," Charity said, nudging me.

"Huh?"

"He does that sometimes," Deuce said, standing. "I said we should get some sleep."

"Sorry," I said, rising also. "I was just thinking about a dolphin I swam with a few days ago."

When we returned to the *Revenge*, I still had questions in my head. The slip we were in had the stern to the southwest. The bridge was still buttoned up against the rain, but open to the rear. I went straight for the ladder and Tony followed me up. It was nearly sunset.

"Did you know Dalton?" I asked, handing him a Kalik from the cooler.

"Nah," Tony replied. "I reported to Dam Neck about a year behind Deuce. Remember he said that Dalton left there about the time he arrived."

"And Rod Whitaker?"

"Met him once," he replied. "He was rotating out when I arrived. Deuce seems to vouch for them. That's good enough for me. You're awfully interested in Dalton and agent McVie."

"I admit their relationship has got me thinking. Tasha's your first wife," I began. "Julie is Deuce's first. Both of y'all waited a long time. That's good."

"Ah, I get it now," Tony said, leaning back, and looking toward where the sun might still appear from the clouds before it dropped below the horizon. "I can't speak for Deuce—er, yeah, I guess I can; he told me once. The military life isn't conducive to a marriage. His words, and I agree."

"That's very true," I said.

"Your first marriage didn't work out and you think that's proof," Tony said. "You want those two to be together just to show, if only to yourself, that future warriors can have a normal family life. Even eco-warriors."

"Eco-warriors," I repeated, recalling again the image of Poppy on the Wave Runner. Though she was physically small, she had a warrior's heart, no doubt about it. And because of that, she also wore the mask and had to suffer taking it off around people who always had the same face. Cops had that problem on a daily basis. I could never figure how they did it.

"I couldn't imagine having a wife back when I was a SEAL," Tony said. "More than a few times, we had to deploy really fast."

"It wasn't easy," I said, as the sun burst from behind a cloud for a second, then disappeared again. "And it'd never be a normal life. Sandy and I were married for six-and-a-half years." I took a pull from the cold beer.

"You were gone a lot?"

"And then some," I replied. "It was surprising that we lasted as long as we did. Three weeks after our wedding, I went to Lebanon for six months. That was when our barracks was bombed; couldn't even call her for a week."

"Had to be hell for her," he said. "The not knowing."

"She was pregnant, too," I said, remembering. "Then she was thrust into the notifications group once she did learn that I was safe. The chaplain was overwhelmed; we'd lost 220 Marines that day. He went to all the survivors' spouses first, to ask for their help."

Tony sat forward. "That's not normal."

"No, it's not," I agreed. "Nor is it usual for a single battalion to lose 220 men in one day. We weren't prepared. There or at home. Sandy hated having to do it. A new life growing inside her, a husband she knew was safe, and she had to be one of the women to tell another wife, a friend, that her husband wasn't coming home."

Tony exhaled slowly. "I never considered anything like that."

"Yeah," I said, softly. "It wasn't anything she'd bargained for either." I took another pull from my beer. "I was home from Beirut just three months when I got orders to Parris Island for a two-year tour on the drill field. During that time, Sandy and I saw each other in passing, and that was about it. I was focused on the job, working more than 100 hours a week. After that, we were transferred back to Lejeune for three years. It was almost normal, except—you know—when it wasn't. We rarely talked. We were back at Lejeune only three months when I was sent off for a six-month WestPac cruise. When we got back, I was home for just six weeks and suddenly deployed to Panama with orders to not call or write anyone. She was informed the next day and left before I got home."

"Man, look, you were deployed or otherwise engaged for half the time you were married. That's not on you, man."

"Well, I was kind of a non-functioning spouse the other half," I said. "That was all on me. Before we got married, whenever I came back from the field or a deployment, we hit the town; me and my buddies, you know. We had nothing to hide from each other, we'd been through it together. Married, your mind has to shift from a high-revving top gear into a low idle in first. And you have to do it in the time it takes to deplane and meet your wife, who's rushing toward you on the tarmac. Things become detached. The real is no longer real. They don't and *can't* know." I tipped the bottle to my lips again and swallowed. "America's not at war; her military is. America's at the mall."

Somewhere in the marina, a conch horn blew, followed by several airhorns. The sun had set on another day, invisible to us. But sunset times, like the moon phases and tides, are ingrained in all sailors.

I yawned.

"You better get some rest," Tony said. "You're starting to get a little melancholy."

"You're right. I'm getting too old for this."

We were up early the following morning. The sounds in the marina—people talking and laughing, captains starting their engines for a final check—were too loud to ignore. I took a mug of Hacienda la Minita coffee up to the bridge and did my own systems check, if for nothing else but to maintain appearances.

Tony and Andrew had returned to the hotel to get their gear packed up but promised to be back by first light.

The docks were full of people, all moving in different directions. There were carts loaded with provisions and ice being wheeled out to the tournament boats. Empty carts went back for more. The tournament boats were easy to spot. Their decks were ablaze with lights, and some of the boats even sported underwater lights. The *Revenge* had all that, but I sat in the darkness.

The official start time was 0900, but the marina was a beehive of activity before the sun even rose; anglers and captains wanted to be out on the water when the time came. Tony and Andrew made their way down the dock, dodging the activity. I waved them aboard as they neared the stern.

"Drop your gear inside," I said. "Coffee's on."

"I got a dozen sausage biscuits," Tony said, lifting a paper bag.

I grinned. "What's everyone else gonna eat?"

With the sun rising over the far side of the bay, boats started throwing off lines and heading out. The five of us watched from the fly bridge while we ate. I was in no hurry to jockey for position in the bay entrance with tournament fishermen.

We waited at the docks until the time came for the tournament to be underway. Most of the boats were out of the bay before I started the engines. Andrew and Tony went down to untie the lines.

It was time to go see what our future might hold for us.

Charity looked back at the nearly empty bay, it's dozens of million-dollar fishing machines out on the ocean now. "I don't get it. A fish is a fish. Why all the excitement?"

"Bimini attracts a lot of wahoo fishermen. The fish's name alone should tell you all you'd need to know about catching them. Deep-running lures are trolled at much higher speeds than you'd troll for other fish. My best results were at around fifteen knots, but I'd had bites as fast as twenty. That's not all that fast to a fish that can triple that speed for short bursts while attacking prey. When a wahoo hits, the line screams off the reel, as the fish hits top speed, usually in the opposite direction. The line stripping off the reel at 80 miles per hour has to be seen and heard to really understand. The excitement of a wahoo bite is like no other, and exclamations come naturally. Hence the name."

"And this place is some kind of wahoo Mecca or something?"

"What makes Bimini such a good spot for game fishing, especially wahoo, is the underwater terrain. Wahoo are pelagic hunters and like to hang out on the deeper side of ledges where the bottom drops steeply to about 300 feet. The closer to vertical, the more they like it. And that type of terrain was exactly what you have for miles and miles along the Great Bahama Bank. Weaving back and forth across the ledge, trailing lures about ten or fifteen feet below the surface, always draws the big wahoo up to investigate."

Idling the *Revenge* out of the protected harbor, I punched the speed up to twenty knots. Seas built quickly to three or four feet once we were outside the protected waters of Bimini Bay. At that speed, the *Revenge* was just barely on top of the water, bow still a little high and stern low.

Once clear of the bay's entrance, I turned southwest, toward deeper water. Clearing the southern part of the island, big four-and five-foot rollers appeared, coming out of the south. The *Revenge* took each one on the port bow, the wide Carolina flares deflecting the water up and away from the boat.

At the edge of the almost vertical wall, I turned south-southeast to follow the underwater ridge. The tournament boats had done the same thing, going north and south of the island. The waves were nearly right on the bow and the *Revenge* took each one in stride, climbing up the face of the oncoming wave while simultaneously plowing through it with her bulk. Then she'd emerge, the spray flying away for twenty yards, as she'd tip her bow slightly, and ride softly down the shoulder.

All the while, I was fixated on where I was headed, not just physically, but metaphorically. To say I was apprehensive about this meeting would be an understatement. What Charity had said was the stone-cold truth. If I didn't find some direction, a mission to give my life meaning, I'd slide back into oblivion.

The first couple of months of my year-long bender had been full of new experiences. I'd vowed not to turn away from anything new just because I'd never done it before.

It'd started simply enough. My first need, I'd convinced myself then, had been speed and distance. Soon, it became just a search for speed. I sailed *Salty Dog* hard, putting up every sail she could carry, stressing the rigging and sails beyond what was prudent. I rarely reefed. I'd sought out wind and found it in abundance off the island of Mayaguana in the Southern Bahamas. Limping into Abraham's Bay, I'd discovered four other boats seeking refuge.

I'd stayed with them for a week, two single women among the group of four couples, and paired guests. I'd slowly and intentionally peeled off what little of the mask remained. The two women, both more than a decade younger, did their best to melt the hard, crusty remnants of the facade with liberal doses of rum and warm flesh.

It soon became a need, a way to prove my own virility. I went through phases where I wanted to be with large groups of life-loving people, then craved days of solitude. After about eight months, my mind had started to become dull to the excitement of any new treat that happened across my bow.

But my mind wasn't dull now. I concentrated on the water, and we continued south for an hour, putting us due east of the meeting location by about twenty miles. We occasionally passed tournament boats as they turned north, running back over a bite, or just transiting to another spot. We gave each one we encountered a wide berth.

To a casual observer, we looked, with our outriggers extended, just like every other boat crashing through the rough seas. But if anyone looked closer, they might see that we hadn't dropped any lures. Nobody looked close. Captains were focused on their instruments, swerving their boats back and forth over the probable spots for wahoo. Mates were tending the lines, and fishermen were in the fighting chairs, also watching the lines.

With no other boats in sight, I made a slow, lazy turn toward the southwest. Andrew, being the most experienced radar operator on the boat, was in the second seat. His eyes moved back and forth, studying the radar image and chart plotter.

After ten minutes, I straightened up, heading due west on a course that would take us within five miles of the location we were supposed to be at in less than two-and-a-half hours.

The minutes ticked by. Finally, Andrew looked over at me. "We're within range of the coordinates for the meeting. There's nothing there."

Sitting on the port bench with Charity, Deuce looked down at his watch. "The meeting, the precise time of the equinox, is in two hours."

"Thirteen-thirty-two," Tony confirmed, standing just behind me and Andrew.

Charity had been watching the distant horizon ahead of the *Revenge*. She turned and looked at me. "The instructions were to *arrive* at those coordinates at that precise time." She shrugged. "Maybe points are taken off for being early."

"Then that's exactly what we'll do," I said, slowing the *Revenge*, and bringing her down off plane. We continued west, at a speed mahi or tuna fishermen would run. "Keep me within radar range of the target location, Andrew. In case someone arrives there early."

We circled clockwise, keeping the GPS waypoint for the meet on our starboard side, within five or six miles. I changed course several times, moving in and out of a precise circle around it, as if we were simply another fishing boat, positioning to find the bite. After an hour, we were roughly west of the coordinates and just 21 miles from Biscayne Bay.

"Multiple echoes," Andrew said. "I count two vessels nearing the territorial limit, outbound. One coming out of Biscayne Bay and another out of the Palm Beach area. I've been watching the first one for a few minutes."

Charity looked over at him. "How come?"

"It's on a course directly toward the meeting location."

"Bearing of the second boat?" I asked, glancing at the radar screen.

Andrew watched it closely for a moment, then looked up. "Both are on headings that will intersect at the coordinates for the meeting. They're both moving at speeds that will put each there at about 1330 hours."

"They're going to the meet," I said.

"Let's have a look at them," Deuce said, peering over the bow toward the boat we'd soon intercept. "Chyrel, bring the camera up."

"Roger that," came Chyrel's voice over my earwig. "You'll need to get within three miles and give me a heading."

"Pan to dead ahead," I said. "We'll use the radar to point us. When you see it, lock on with the image stabilizer, and I'll turn away."

As we drew to within three miles of the vessel, Chyrel was able to locate it with the powerful zoom lens of the roof-mounted camera. Still two miles away, I turned back east, circling behind the first boat to come up astern of the second.

"It's a trawler yacht," Chyrel said over the comm, as we moved away from the northernmost boat. "About 40 feet. Might be an Albin; same lines. Blue hull, white topsides with a blue Bimini top on the bridge and a trunk cabin. The name on the transom is *Shallow Minded*.

"Is it on the list?" Tony asked. "The boats that Armstrong has contracts with?"

"No," she replied. "I'm checking Coast Guard registry now."

I began a wide turn that would bring us to within two or three miles of the boat. When we were parallel with its course, and slightly behind it, Andrew instructed Chyrel to turn the camera, estimating the direction from the radar image.

Looking in the direction the radar indicated, I saw an empty sea. But right on the horizon I noticed an occasional flash of reflected light. After a few minutes, Chyrel found it with the camera. "Looks kinda like yours, Jesse. Maybe a little bigger. Light blue hull, really long, white foredeck and a tuna tower above the bridge. Name on the stern is *Reel Fun*.

Turning sharper to port, I made a looping turn and crossed the wake of the second boat nearly four miles behind it. We circled back around the meeting spot counter-clockwise, keeping it roughly four to five miles away, while Andrew stayed glued to the radar screen.

Chyrel's voice came over the comm. "You're not gonna believe this boss. I just found the registry for *Shallow Minded*."

"And?" Deuce and I said together.

"It's a Monk 48 trawler, US flagged, built in 1970 and home-ported in Riviera Beach."

"Why wouldn't I believe that?" Deuce asked.

"Ownership of the vessel was recently transferred to Rodney Whitaker."

In my mind, I could picture Chyrel grinning at her desk.

"Whit?" Deuce wondered. "He just bought it?"

"Previous owner was Cyrus Whitaker," Chyrel replied. "A relative?"

"Check into it," Deuce said, looking at his watch.

Glancing at the clock on the GPS, I grinned at him. "We're six miles away," I said. "We can be there in twelve minutes, just at cruising speed."

"No sign of any other boats?"

"Nothing on the radar," Andrew replied.

I looked back at Tony. "Go down and bring in the outriggers."

When he was coming back up the ladder, I turned the *Revenge* toward the waypoint on the chart plotter and punched the speed up to 30 knots. The GPS's estimated time of arrival at the waypoint showed we'd be a minute early.

"Whoa," Andrew said, still looking at the radar.

We were less than five miles from the coordinates.

"What is it?"

"Something big," he replied. "Overtaking us from the south."

Overtaking us?

I looked over at the barrel-chested man next to me. "How big?"

Andrew looked up at me. "Big enough and fast enough," he said, "that you don't want to deal with his wake. And it's headed to the same place we are."

With a glance at the radar screen, the echo was unmistakable. A very large ship, as big as an island freighter or small cruise ship, was going to pass us less than a mile away.

"ETA?" Deuce asked, standing, and looking aft.

"About four minutes ahead of the scheduled time."

"Armstrong himself?" Deuce asked, rhetorically.

"The *Ambrosia*?" I said.

Chyrel found the ship with the camera only seconds before Tony did with the binoculars. Within minutes, neither was needed, as the ship behind us and off to starboard plowed effortlessly through four-foot swells, steadily eating up the distance between us.

I looked over my shoulder at the speeding ship. It was the *Ambrosia*, no doubt about it. All 199 feet of her.

"How fast is she going?" I asked, in complete awe.

"Huh?" Andrew said. He was turned around in his seat, watching the quickly approaching vessel.

"Her speed?" I said, a bit more urgently.

He spun around and checked the radar. "Sorry, um—holy shit."

"Yeah, that's about how fast I was guessing," Tony said, beaming from ear to ear as he watched the *Ambrosia*.

Andrew looked over at me. "Forty-seven knots."

"*Seriously?*"

"But she's got a tail wind," Andrew offered.

All of us looked back at the massive, black ship as it encountered the wake from the *Revenge*. The big waves hit the side of the ship's bow, each successive wave coming faster than the previous. Giant mists of spray shot up and away like a water cannon on full auto. Our eight-foot wake had no effect on the ship.

Instinctively, I turned the wheel to bear away. Andrew was right. I wanted to be a mile away before I encountered a following wake like that thing produced. When I reached for the throttles to accelerate away, Deuce stopped me, holding up a finger.

"Maybe everyone doesn't need to know," he said, looking forward.

We were quickly approaching the two boats out of Florida, both just two miles ahead. I turned back to our original heading, trusting that the behemoth would slow before swamping my boat.

As it came abreast, a good half a mile away, I heard it—the high-pitched whine of large turbine engines. I stood at the helm and joined the others, staring in amazement at *Ambrosia*. To see such a large ship moving at twenty knots would be an astonishing sight. To see it passing us twenty knots faster than our 30 was nothing less than awe-inspiring to a boat guy. I wanted to see those engines. The turbines slowed as the boat moved ahead of us.

"Another boat coming in fast," Andrew said. "Well, not as fast as that, but a good 30 knots. If it came in a straight line, they're out of north Florida or maybe Georgia."

"Us, Whit, and two others invited," Deuce said. "And Whit's on his honeymoon."

"Wonder if he's alone," Charity said, as the five vessels began to slow as we all converged.

That was a concern. Had Dalton also been invited? Poppy? Probably not her. But Dalton would probably be a shoo-in.

Chyrel said she was moving the camera to see. "Just him on the fly bridge," she reported.

"Dalton could be down below."

"I'll move closer," I said. "Maybe he'll recognize us."

Ambrosia slowed and finally came to a stop. The other three boats converged as I pulled back on the throttles. The clock said it was 1330; two minutes before spring. And the waypoint on the chart plotter was 800 feet ahead.

A crackling static from the overhead console caught my attention. The noise nearly covered a weak signal. "This is the research vessel *Ambrosia*. Do not reply."

Slowing to idle speed, I started to reach for the mic anyway. We were just a few hundred yards from the farthest vessel, which I could now see was a big Viking convertible, probably 60 feet. That made five boats occupying the same small part of the ocean. Communication was paramount.

Before I could get to the mic, the voice repeated, more clearly, "This is the research vessel Ambrosia. Do not reply. I repeat, do not reply. We are broadcasting on a low-power transmitter with a one-mile range."

There was a pause, then the radio squawked again. But it was a different voice. "Happy spring, captains. A tap of the horn to acknowledge you hear me."

I touched the horn button on the dash and heard two others in quick succession. Then came a low sound, obviously a conch horn. It was from Whit on *Shallow Minded*. We were coming up alongside him, just fifty yards away.

The radio crackled. "Beginning at my bow," the voice said. "Captain of *Oceanis Three*, please bring your vessel to our stern to discharge two guests."

The Viking's horn blasted for a second and it began to move. I glanced over at Whit. He was reaching for something on the dash.

"Whit!" I called out.

He turned and looked at us for a moment before recognizing who we were. He'd only seen the *Revenge* once, at night.

"You alone?" I called over, just loud enough for him to hear.

"Yeah," Whit called back.

I turned around. "Tony?"

"Roger that," he said, stripping off his shirt and emptying his pockets.

If Whit were alone, there'd be nobody to stay aboard as we drifted in the ocean. With the bottom half a mile below us, anchoring was out of the question. Tony knew this and didn't have to be asked.

A moment later, he dove from the swim platform and swam half the distance to Whit's boat underwater. He surfaced for a breath and went under again. Whit met him at the stern of *Shallow Minded*. They said a few words and then Whit helped him aboard. Both men were SEALs, so not really strangers.

The fishing vessel out of Biscayne Bay was called up next—the *Ambrosia* asked for one guest. Then Whit and finally us. Seven guests going aboard the big ship.

When we were called, Andrew skillfully piloted us toward *Ambrosia*. She was more impressive the closer we got; everything clean and polished. On *Ambrosia's* lee side, we were out of the wind and the waves were diminished greatly. Andrew brought the *Revenge* alongside, port-to-port with the much larger vessel. Deuce, Charity, and I stood in the cockpit, gazing up at it.

I'd studied the specs of the ship. Round portholes sat just below our eye level, running nearly the length of the ship, about five feet above the waterline. Originally, the lower deck had held sleeping quarters for the crew, the galley and scullery, and tons of storage area. The main deck was just above our heads, the front fourth of it being open foredeck. Aft, the house was a partially covered cockpit. Originally, the owner and VIP staterooms, and a big lounge and dining area that opened to the cockpit for outdoor dining had been situated on the main deck. Above that was the bridge deck. The bridge itself was full beam, the ends extending past the house like wings, to provide a clear view aft from both sides, and the front glass was reverse-angled to better shed water. The bridge deck lounge area, situated behind the bridge, had originally included a large, well-appointed bar, a stage, and even a hardwood dance floor. No telling what the current layout was now, though, since all the windows were completely black.

Andrew reversed the engines as we neared a massive work platform hanging off the stern. It was steel, with a diamond-plate, non-skid surface. Very industrial-looking, the complete opposite of the luxurious appearance of the former mega-yacht the Saudi prince had tired of after only a year. A set of steps went up either side to the cockpit. Between them, I could see a large hatch, and an area behind it that had originally housed two 24-foot tenders, four personal watercrafts, storage for dive gear, a compressor, and a ton of storage for water toys. The working-class platform didn't mesh with the aristocratic stern it was attached to.

Colonel Travis Stockwell stood on the platform, next to a smaller man with balding hair. Stockwell was in jeans and a denim shirt. The other man wore khaki tactical pants with a windbreaker over a white but-ton-down shirt. I noticed that they both wore black tac-tical boots.

Andrew kept the *Revenge* just a foot or so away from the platform as the three of us stepped over.

"Welcome aboard," Stockwell said, as Andrew moved the *Revenge* away. He turned to the smaller man. "Mister Bremmer, you remember Charity. This is Deuce Living-ston and Jesse McDermitt."

"Charlie Bremmer," the man said, extending a hand to Deuce. We shook hands all around and Bremmer mo-tioned toward the ladderwell. "Please join the others," he said. "There are drinks and snacks. I'll be with the four of you throughout your visit."

Up in the semi-enclosed cockpit, *Ambrosia* looked more like the elegant yacht she'd been designed to be. The decks were polished teak and another hardwood I didn't even recognize. It took a sharp eye and knowl-edge of a change to spot where the original expansive lounges and settees had been removed. They'd been re-placed with a long table, probably hinged at the bulk-head, which was now covered with white linen and trays of light food, snacks, and drinks.

Whit stood by a table with four other men. One was dressed the same as Bremmer. The other three "guests" appeared to be typical boating people, dressed for comfort on the water.

"Please help yourself," the Bremmer clone said. "I'm Walter Knox, Charlie's partner. Our host will be here shortly."

Bremmer and Knox disappeared through a hatch into the ship's interior. The three of us moved toward the others, Deuce edging close to Whit.

Two men stood together, obviously the two from the big Viking, as they wore matching fishing hats with the name *Oceanis III* stenciled on them. One was about my age, a good twenty or thirty years the other's senior. The older one had graying hair, cut short, a stern demeanor, and broad shoulders. His partner was of similar height and build with dark hair and eyes. The third man, who'd boarded from the boat with the tuna tower, was maybe 30. His hair brushed past his collar and he sported a neatly trimmed but very long goatee beard. All three had a certain look about them. They were former military.

I approached the older man, my hand out. Not really because I wanted to know him, or assert dominance by being first to talk, but mostly to give Deuce a chance to talk to Whit.

"Jesse McDermitt," I said. "Captain and owner of *Gaspar's Revenge*."

He took my hand, his grip firm and sure. "Barkley," he said, his accent southern. "Ed Barkley, of the *Oceanis*. This is my son, Zach."

Coastal Georgia, I was guessing from his accent. Maybe a working-class background. He'd earned the big Viking he'd arrived on. I shook hands with both men and turned to the third.

"DJ Martin," the bearded man said, shaking my hand. "I've heard of you. You're out of Marathon, right?" I nodded. "I'm on *Reel Fun* out of Key Largo."

The Barkleys quickly removed their fishing hats, as Charity and Stockwell joined me. I made the introductions.

The younger Barkley looked at Charity nervously. "You probably don't remember me," he said, shaking her hand.

I could see Charity tense, but I was probably the only one to notice.

"Have we met?" she asked.

"No, ma'am," Zach Barkley replied. He turned his eyes to the deck as they misted over. "Not really. I doubt you even saw me. I was on your bird when you went down."

"You were on my—?"

"Yes, ma'am. You were flying us out. I'd been shot up pretty bad."

"I thought everyone on board had—"

"All but me," he said. "When they came, they dragged you out first and carried you off. Then one by one, this big, ugly Taliban with a scar across his cheek shot your co-pilot and my wounded buddies in back. He was aiming at me when he was driven off by some other soldiers who saw us go down."

Charity's eyes seemed to glaze over at the mention of the scar-faced man. She'd told me about him. She'd also told me how she'd eventually killed the man after being held captive for two days, repeatedly raped and tortured.

The faraway look in her eyes dissolved and I saw tears forming. She pulled the younger man toward her and the two hugged tightly, both sobbing.

When they finally broke apart, the father stepped in and hugged Charity. "Zach told me everything," I heard him whisper. "I can never undo what you went through, but for saving my boy, I'm forever in your debt, ma'am."

The two separated awkwardly, Charity still sniffing, as the hatch opened, and Jack Armstrong stepped out into the cockpit. The latest photo of the man was years old, but it was him. So much for the rumors of his demise.

"Gentlemen," he said, then nodded to Charity, "and ma'am." He spread his arms wide in a welcoming gesture. "Welcome aboard *Ambrosia*."

He looked more fit than he had in the photographs I'd seen. His eyes were also different, somehow. It was the same man, of that I had no doubt, but I felt a stronger presence in the man now standing before me. Nothing like the mild-mannered businessman in the pictures I'd seen. His eyes revealed a driving purpose.

Armstrong's gaze moved around the group, making eye contact as if he knew who each of us were. I suspected he did. Finally, his eyes fell on Charity and Zach Barkley.

A sad smile touched the man's face. "I see that the two of you have finally met."

CHAPTER SIXTEEN

The tour of *Ambrosia* was short and didn't include the engine room or what used to be the sky lounge area, with the stage and dance floor.

The bridge was nothing short of phenomenal and definitely not original. Everything about it was state of the art, perhaps even ahead of that, with equal redundancy for everything—two of every instrument and electronic device. The captain, a stalwart looking man about sixty, told us that the only things original to the upper deck were the cherry and maple planks and the magnetic compass. I glanced forward and saw it centered in front of the helm on the expansive dash. He appeared a professional captain in every way, but inside that demeanor, I sensed an old salt. Hence the magnetic compass. It was old, much older than the boat, and was probably owned by the captain.

His name was Nils Hansen. He'd explained that the aft part of the deck was the nerve center, from which Mr. Armstrong ran all his businesses. Though his name hinted at a Nordic heritage, he had no discernable accent.

After touring the bridge, we were led to a conference room, large enough for twenty people. There, Armstrong laid out his proposal. He told us of his ideology in a very concise way. It meshed with my own. He explained what he and his associates had done, were doing, what they had planned for the future, and how each of us might fit in. There wasn't a question-and answer-session. Nor was there any mention of a salary.

In short, Armstrong and several other like-minded multi-billionaires had simply had enough of the way things were being handled around the world. The political games and ongoing debate and deliberation brought security only to the length of the continuous discussion, while never really fixing the problem. There were faster, more expeditious ways to set at least a few things back to right in the world, he'd said. His concerns were many, including environmental, political, and tyrannical abuses.

Though the meeting itself was short and to the point, there was something intangible about the man himself. His words definitely lit a fire in me, and the blaze was welcomed.

"Part of the reason you're here," he'd told us, "is because money is not important to you, except for how each of you can use it to do good things for other people. A notion I happen to share."

On the return trip to Bimini, none of us had said much of anything about the meet for the first half hour. I know I had a lot to chew on and figured Deuce and Charity did as well. Tony and Andrew picked up on it and didn't ask any questions. They were both salaried employees of Livingston and McDermitt Security. Before I knew it, the chart plotter told me we were only four miles from the entrance to Bimini Bay.

"We'll be at the dock in fifteen minutes," I said to Deuce. "Should we get everyone together?"

"Tomorrow," he replied absently. "I need to talk this all over with Julie, and that's gonna take a while. In fact, I think I'll get a room; I need to think about this before I even call her."

"Me too," Charity chimed in. "Need to think, that is." She looked over at me. "Mind some company?"

I nodded. "Yeah, it's a lot to swallow."

Tony and Andrew looked at one another, then at Deuce.

"We'll lay it all out to everyone once we think it through," he told them. "But the three of us each have our own personal decisions to make."

"No pressure," Tony said. "I've been with you for ten years, and you know where I'll be ten years from now."

Andrew nodded.

Once we got backed into the slip and had the *Revenge* tied up, Deuce left with the others.

Charity and I went down to the salon. I opened the hatch and Finn came out onto the deck, anxiously eyeing the docks and buildings.

"Wanna go to the club to eat?" I asked Charity, reaching for Finn's leash. "Or eat in?"

"I'm not really hungry," she said. "Maybe just hang out here?"

"I think after I walk Finn, I'm just gonna go up and watch the sun go down."

"Should I put a couple of beers in the cooler?" she asked. "Or coffee?"

"I could drink a beer or two," I replied. "We'll be back in five minutes."

The sun was low and most of the tournament boats were back, weighing their catches. Finn was distracted and took ten minutes.

Once I had him back in the salon, I climbed up to the bridge. Charity was sitting in the second seat, spun completely around, with her long, tanned legs up on the aft rail. There was a cooler filled with ice beside her and several small bowls on top.

"Lobster bites and fruit," she said.

The helm seat was also facing backward. I joined her, looking toward the bright orange orb slowly sinking toward the sea.

"How did Armstrong know?" Charity asked, once we were settled on the bridge.

"How did he know Zach was on your chopper?" I asked, popping a chunk of broiled lobster into my mouth. "Or that we'd been working with Dalton and McVie and knew Whit?"

"All of the above."

"It's nearly impossible to be invisible anymore," I said. "We leave electronic tracks everywhere. Chyrel has taught me that much. My guess is that Armstrong has his own *Chyrel*, maybe a whole team of them. As for working with Dalton and Poppy..." I pointed a finger straight up.

"You think he has his own satellite?"

"He said some things that made me think that," I replied. "Poppy attacking the Russian boat? Couldn't see that from shore."

"Andrew did."

"Well, technically, I guess he could have seen it," I said. "If he'd had someone looking through a telescope from 100 feet up, like Andrew was, *and* he knew exactly when and where to look. If he was watching us, he was watching Whit. Maybe he was seen with Dalton and Poppy. To keep tabs on that many people would take more people than are on the island. I'm betting Armstrong has a satellite at his disposal."

We watched as the sun sank slowly toward the horizon, becoming a rustier shade of orange, both of us lost in our own thoughts. There were clouds sitting low, lit in shades of pink and orange, as the sun slipped into the sea's embrace.

"Would someone like Jack Armstrong lease a satellite?" Charity asked. "Or do you think he'd have his own launched into space?"

"That's a very good question," I said, rising from my seat. "Let's go down and ask Chyrel. You saw the technology they had on that bridge. I'm thinking he owns one."

In the salon, I powered up the video comm, hoping that Chyrel would still be in the office. She was. Her face appeared on the screen—just her against a white background. Nothing to identify where she was, or what time of day it was there. She was in the conference room.

"Hey, Jesse. What's up?"

"A duck's butt, when he eats," I replied. She smiled. "I bet you probably know this. Satellites with the ability to look down from space? Are they registered somehow?"

"Satellites? Well, yeah, sorta. Everything that's launched into space is recorded and tracked by NASA's collision-avoidance computers. But surveillance satellites? Well, even though the launch and location are known, nobody wants the other guy to know just what all their satellites can do."

"Has Armstrong ever launched a satellite, or maybe funded one?"

Chyrel's eyebrows came up. "That'll take some time to find out."

"Let me know, okay?"

"I will," Chyrel said. Then the screen went blank.

Suddenly, the boat rocked, and the salon hatch flew open. My hand went instinctively to my back, where my Sig rested in its holster. Charity's hand moved too, but I stopped her when I saw who was standing there. Finn's head came up, but when he realized the visitor in the hatchway was no threat, his tail began to thump against the deck.

I rose and faced Poppy. "What the hell?"

Her eyes shot to Charity, then looked back at me. "I need your help," she blurted.

I cocked my head. "Well, okay."

When I glanced down at Charity, she looked highly amused. "I'll be right back," I told her.

I took Poppy by the elbow and guided her out of the salon and back up to the dock. I didn't want to scold her like an errant schoolgirl, but there were some things you just don't do.

"Boarding without permission could get you shot," I said bluntly.

"Sorry, but I really need your help."

I didn't see fear in her eyes, so whatever it was wasn't life-threatening. I waited for her to collect her thoughts.

"Tonight," she began, "would you and Deuce do your recon-incursion thing you do with those fancy rebreathers you have, and foul the prop on that Russian boat?"

So, they did return.

I had my doubts about whether Dalton knew anything about her plans, although it was a good tactic. I'd used it myself. Dalton had, as well. I remembered she'd also attacked the same boat with nothing but stink bombs. And they'd shot back with guns. I wanted to know more.

"Deuce is gone," I said. "But I might."

"You can do that alone?"

I arched an eyebrow in mock indignation. "Uh, yeah."

"Okay. Didn't mean to offend."

"No offense taken."

"All right, then," Poppy said nervously. "Um. Don't use a dock line. Has to be something they'd get entangled in by accident. Plastic, old fishing net, something."

"Uh-huh."

She handed me a flash drive. "Then, at dawn, would you play the sounds that my team recorded through your diver recall system? It's track seven."

I nodded slowly, waiting. "I could."

"If we can call in the last dolphin, we can get her satellite transmitter off."

"Her?" I asked, wondering how she'd learned it was a female dolphin.

"Yeah, well, she's the clever one," Poppy replied with a half grin. "I figure she must be female."

I smiled. "Ri-ight."

"I'll meet you out there," she said. "You play the pied piper and I'll do the rest."

I waited, wondering if there was more. It was a lot to ask, but I was intrigued.

"Will you do it?" Poppy finally asked.

"For you?"

"For the dolphins?"

I could feel the grin broadening across my face. I had no idea what the Russians had planned for the dolphins but didn't think it could be anything beneficial to the animals.

I agreed, and Poppy stepped up onto her toes and kissed my cheek. She explained how her team planned to dart the last dolphin so they could remove the tracker, and that she'd be in the Zodiac ready when I led the dolphins toward the north shore.

Inside, I explained to Charity what Poppy wanted me to do. I'd need help. The swim was nothing. I could anchor within a mile and cover that distance in less than twenty minutes. But I couldn't leave the boat unattended.

"I'll do it," Charity replied without hesitation.

"You will? I thought you didn't like her."

"I've just been teasing you about her," Charity said. "She works for Fish and Wildlife. I admire that. And I love dolphins."

"Would you be so willing if they were saving sea slugs?"

Charity laughed, then got serious. "When?"

"Before dawn," I said. "At least a couple of hours before, to give me time to foul their prop and hopefully lure the dolphins away."

"Then we should go to bed."

"I thought you'd never ask," I said, with a sly wink.

Charity's face flushed slightly. Something else I'd never seen her do. She started to stammer something, and I grinned. She punched my shoulder.

"Go get some rest," I told her. "I have a feeling tomorrow will be a long day."

"Remember, we have to meet with Deuce and the guys in the morning. And I still haven't decided."

"I haven't either," I said. "Gonna just sleep on it, I guess. We'll be back by sunrise and maybe it'll be done by then."

CHAPTER SEVENTEEN

We'd dropped the hook less than a mile from the Russian boat, with a good three hours of darkness left. We were very near the edge of the drop off. Once more, we acted out the illusion with the lights, as if anchoring for the night and going to sleep. Just in case anyone was watching.

"Stay with Charity," I told Finn, after suiting up in the darkened salon. "I'll be back in an hour."

"Put your mask on and check the comm," Charity said.

Pulling the mask up over my face, I adjusted the bone mic and said, "Comm check."

I heard her response over the earwig and in my other ear. "Loud and clear. Be careful," she added. "If anything goes wrong, bail. You don't have anything at stake in this."

I nodded and slipped out the hatch. I stayed low as I moved across the deck and then down onto the swim platform. There, I sat and put on my fins and rechecked my equipment. I tossed the little float out and it trailed behind the *Revenge*. The current was almost nonexistent.

Slipping into the water, I took a bearing on the Russian boat, then quietly dropped below the surface. The last time I'd done this alone, I'd been shot. I wasn't going to let that happen again.

Charity's voice came over my earwig. "Still working okay?"

"Loud and clear," I said into the full-face mask. "When I get close, I'm gonna go deep and come up under the boat. So, you won't hear me until I get close to the surface again."

Following my compass, I swam toward the Russian vessel, maintaining a depth of ten feet. If they saw me, I was under no illusion that they wouldn't shoot. But the water would stop a bullet before it reached half my depth. I counted my kicks for the next twenty minutes. Soon, the water glowed slightly ahead and to my right. The light was coming from the Russian boat.

"I have a visual," I said.

"Roger that," Charity replied, whispering needlessly. "Minimal lights inside, only the anchor light visible on the outside. I haven't seen any movement."

"Guess they're not suspecting a stink bomb attack at night."

"What do you have to foul their prop with?" she asked.

"A tangled hunk of nylon rope I found. It's covered with barnacles. Probably been in the water for years. Going deep and silent."

Bending at the waist, I finned closer to the bottom. The boat was again anchored in 40 feet. When I entered a dark space between two areas of light, I figured I was under the keel and slowly began to rise, feeling for the hull with both hands high above my head.

Finding it, I turned toward the stern. The big prop was silhouetted against the dimly lit water from the anchor light. This would be a piece of cake. There was no need to tie the rope to a strut. I didn't need to disable the boat. If anyone on board came down, I wanted them to think the barnacle-covered float line had just drifted close and got tangled in the prop. The captain would know he was fouled as soon as he engaged the transmission and would immediately shut the engine down. By then, the line would be hopelessly tangled and would take a diver quite a while to saw through with a knife.

I unclipped a carabiner from a D-ring on my rig, removed the stiff coil of half-inch crusty rope, then reattached the carabiner to my gear. It'd taken me ten minutes to untangle the heavily encrusted line, measuring a good twenty feet. I got to work, threading it through and around the blades, leaving enough of a tail to make a helluva racket when the prop started spinning.

Satisfied, I descended to the bottom and checked my compass, then swam slowly away from the Russian boat on a reverse heading toward the *Revenge*, nearly a mile away. Well clear of the lights, I angled up to ten feet to let the little float surface.

"Mission accomplished," I said, without losing count.

"Roger that," Charity said. "No movement and no new lights on."

I swam on quietly, enveloped by the sounds of the ocean. The clouds had cleared out before we'd awakened, leaving the moon and stars alone in the night sky. There was enough light that I could make out the bottom, detecting dark patches of coral or an occasional sea fan.

About halfway back to the boat, I heard a series of fast clicks and suddenly a dolphin glided past me. It disappeared just as quickly, but the clicks and high-pitched whines remained. It was watching me, not in the literal sense, but using its echolocation to *see* me by sound reflection.

Finally, I heard the unmistakable sound of an anchor chain rattling. I surfaced, just the top of my head rising above the water. The *Revenge* gently bobbed in the foot-high swells left over by the storm.

Reaching the swim platform, I climbed aboard and removed my mask and fins.

"No problem?" Charity asked, standing in the cockpit.

"None," I said. "But I did see a dolphin."

"I thought there was one around. I kept hearing its blow, but never saw it. Is this gonna work?"

"No idea," I replied, stripping out of my rebreather and wetsuit. The early morning air was cold on my skin. "Did you get the file uploaded to the recall system?"

"Yeah, it's all set."

"I defrosted some bait fish," I said, nudging a bucket by the transom door, and accepting a towel from her. "Let's give it a try."

Stepping over to the console above the cleaning station, I activated the diver recall for five seconds.

"How can you tell if it's working?" Charity asked.

I pointed to a small modulation meter on the controls. "You can't hear it on the surface, but this tells me the sound is going out to the transducer."

We both looked all around, not really expecting anything. I turned it on again for a few seconds longer.

There was a whooshing sound aft and we both looked back. A dolphin, maybe the one I'd encountered underwater, was fifteen feet off the stern, just its head above water.

Charity and I both moved to the transom. The dolphin dropped below the surface and reappeared a little closer, but still well out of reach. I pulled a whole bluefish out of the bait bucket and tossed it. The small fish floated on the surface as the dolphin looked at us, ignoring the offering.

It was wary. I liked wariness. I couldn't help grinning.

The dolphin took the bluefish and disappeared below the surface.

"And that's supposed to be a wild dolphin?" Charity asked.

"Trained a little," I replied. "But yeah, still wild. Let's get underway."

After Charity secured the anchor, I brought the engines up to a high idle, setting a course that would take us close to the north end of the island. We moved away at seven knots. I knew dolphins could swim at that speed for long distances, but I didn't want to go too fast and lose them. There were others around, too, and we needed them all. So, we played the sounds on the diver recall, then tossed baitfish to the one following us. It was working. The dolphin stayed about fifty feet back. After less than a mile, I noticed something. When Charity played the sound from the transducer, the dolphin moved in closer.

"There's another one," Charity said over the comm.

I looked back and sure enough, a second dolphin had joined the first. Charity played the recording, shut it off, and tossed a fish in the water. The first dolphin came charging up even before she threw the fish. When she did it again, she threw two fish, and both dolphins closed the distance before the fish hit the water.

"They're so smart," she said, as if to herself.

Leaving the recall system on, I set a course for the west side of the island. The dolphins followed us; we could see them every now and then. Halfway back to Bimini, they were joined by three others.

Rising, Charity looked aft. "I don't believe this. It's working."

The sun began to warm the air as we approached the northern tip of the island. Poppy said she'd find us, but so far, I hadn't seen another boat.

"There," Charity said, pointing.

The same Zodiac that Dalton and Poppy had intercepted us with was slowing as it came toward the *Revenge*. As it neared, I could see Poppy. She was with another woman and the man she'd been with when throwing stink bombs at the Russians.

I knew it, I thought.

Dalton wasn't a part of this dolphin-kidnapping conspiracy. But it had worked. Now all she had to do was get the tracker off the last one. I waved, and Poppy waved back. I gave her a thumbs-up and looked back at the five dolphins following in our wake.

As we got closer, Poppy motioned for me to slow down. The other woman on the boat held a rifle. I assumed it was a tranquilizer gun.

The man driving the Zodiac turned in a big circle and came up alongside the pod of dolphins. The other woman in the boat handed the gun to Poppy and my threat level came down a notch. She said something to her and Poppy nodded, settling onto the forward seat and watching the dolphins. She was studying them intently, apparently trying to discern which one was still tagged or maybe timing their surfacing pattern.

Finally, she fired. It was a hit. When the dolphin surfaced again, Poppy let out a yell. The others on the Zodiac joined her. I pumped my fist in the air, celebrating with them.

The dolphin with the dart in the base of its fin soon began to slow. The rest of the pod slowed also. I pulled back on the throttles to a dead idle.

The two women on the Zodiac were talking, both with worried looks on their faces. Though I couldn't hear them over my engines, I quickly realized their concern. The tranquilized dolphin could drown.

"Someone will have to get in the water with the dolphin," Charity said. "To keep it on the surface."

I nodded, watching the event play out. Jumping in too soon would spook the dolphin and it might dive deep before succumbing to the drug. Going in too late might mean it could sink before they got to it.

The dolphin slowed, exhaling lazily.

Poppy picked up a mask and fins and motioned me to come to a stop. I put the *Revenge* in neutral and drifted, watching. The man at the little boat's helm maneuvered closer, crowding the now semi-conscious dolphin toward my boat. There was some sort of sling on the deck, which the other woman tied a line to as Poppy got in the water.

When the woman handed the sling down to Poppy, I had a pretty good idea what she was going to do. With the other dolphins agitated and zipping in and out between the two boats, Poppy grabbed the sling and dove. In the clear water, I could see her moving toward the dolphin. She wasn't going to make it and be able to get the sling around it.

Without waiting, I stepped over the rail and dove from the bridge, knowing that Charity would be available if I needed her to move the boat. I swam slowly down toward Poppy, who was struggling beneath the dolphin.

My approach startled her. Using hand signals, I told her what we should do. Then I took half the sling from her. Looking up, I could see the dolphin above us, barely moving, and jerked my thumb toward it. Without a mask, everything was blurry. But the water was so clear, I could easily make out shapes.

When we surfaced, we were on either side of the large mammal. It moved lethargically in the sling. But it was still a good three times my weight and this was its habitat. A sudden movement could injure me or Poppy, or even both of us.

The sling had straps on both bars, and cutouts for the pectoral fins. We brought the bars up over the dolphin's back and lashed the two poles together. Being wrapped as it was seemed to calm the dolphin, or maybe it fell asleep.

The Zodiac came closer. Poppy threw the line from the sling to the dark-haired woman and then moved out from between the dolphin and the little boat. I helped nudge it closer to the Zodiac, where the woman tied the lines off to two small cleats.

"That will keep her snug while the sedative wears off," the woman said, obvious relief in her voice. "Good job, guys!"

I turned and swam back toward my boat with Poppy following me. When Finn met us on the swim platform, tail wagging, Poppy gave him a quick scratch behind his ears.

The fiery little redhead stood dripping wet on my deck. "Thanks for all your help."

I shrugged. "It was either that or watch you drown."

"What? I could've—"

I grinned at her. "I'm kidding. You're obviously a more-than-capable young lady."

"I don't know how you'd know that. I swear, I've been benched this whole operation. Not to mention my head has been—"

I just smiled down at her. "Forget it," she said, waving a hand as if shooing a fly.

"I don't know anything about that," I said. "But I do know a good agent knows how to best use the tools at her disposal. In this case, well, it's been me." I paused. "Did I just call myself a tool?"

She nodded. "Thanks. I figured you'd say something wise like, *know thyself*," she said with a wink.

I laughed. "Yeah, that's what I meant."

I stared into her deep, blue-green eyes for a moment. An uncomfortable moment. I wanted to be tactful, but I also wanted to know if she'd been given the details about her father we'd shared with Dalton.

"Hey, about Africa," she said, tickling the fight or flight neurons in my brain once more. "I was wondering if you knew anything about what was going on in the South Sudan round about the time—"

"What's all this about Africa?" I asked, maybe a bit too suspiciously. I strove for a more neutral tone. "Why do you and Dalton have so much interest?"

"What do you mean? Dalton asked about it?"

I had no way of learning if she'd always known, or if Dalton had told her. "Oh, nothing." I could see in her face that she wasn't going to let it slide. "Dalton asked me about it is all. My time there."

"Africa?"

"Just general stuff." I said, waving it off. This wasn't something she should hear from me.

"I got it!" the woman on the Zodiac yelled, diverting our attention. She held something up in the air. It was small, and I assumed it was the tracking device.

Poppy gave her a thumbs up, then turned back to me. "As soon as that dolphin is swimming on her own again, I've got to go."

"I had a feeling there might be a few more steps in your plan."

Her blue eyes were sparkling. "You'll keep them away from the Russian boat for the rest of the day?"

Deuce and the rest of the guys would be expecting me at the dock. But with one phone call, I could probably get him moving, and he was resourceful enough to find a way for them to get out to the *Revenge* as we passed by.

"An easy promise," I replied with a shrug. "I can't think of anything I'd rather do."

She stood on her toes and kissed my cheek once more. "I knew you weren't an evil drug runner."

I tapped her lightly on the shoulder with a forefinger. "And I knew you weren't an ornithology intern."

"What?" she said, eyebrows raised. "I know a lot about birds. I could pull that off."

"No doubt in my mind."

The sadness returned to her eyes. "So, when Dalton was asking—"

"She's already waking up," the other woman shouted.

Poppy looked toward the Zodiac. The dolphin was beginning to thrash around. "I gotta go," she said. I nodded, and she threw her arms around my neck. "Thanks. I mean it."

"You take care of yourself," I whispered in her ear. "And take it from me—true love doesn't come along very often. So don't blow it."

She pulled away, cheeks blushing. "Right."

I held her gaze, staring into the depths of her eyes. "I mean it. When you get to be my age, you know these things. Right now, you think your career is everything. You gotta make something of yourself, you've got something to prove. But in the end, it's the people we love, our relationships that matter."

Tony was right. I wanted to see those two work things out so they could have everything they wanted, even if they didn't know what that was yet. Shaw once said that youth was wasted on the young. But I hoped not on all of them.

She nodded.

"We need your help," the man at the helm of the little inflatable shouted.

Poppy turned and looked over at the Zodiac. The man and woman were untying the lines holding the poles together. The dolphin was becoming more agitated.

She turned back toward me. "Are you some kind of guardian angel? I ask, because last night, I was sure I'd lost my marbles."

I chuckled. "Actually, I've been called that before."

Turning, I started up the ladder. "Let's get you back on that Zodiac."

I started the engines and maneuvered over to the smaller boat. Poppy stepped over and helped her companions get the dolphin loose from the sling. From my vantage point, I could see the dolphin go deep for a moment, pausing to look up at the two boats, and possibly the people on them. I had no idea what went on in a dolphin's mind, but they were supposed to be very intelligent animals. I wondered if she understood we were helping her or thought us just another bunch of surface-dwellers who hurt her.

With two powerful kicks of her tail, the dolphin leapt from the water, twisting, and making a huge splash. The other dolphins joined her, all of them seeming anxious.

"They're free," I heard the other woman on Poppy's boat say. "They know it. I know they know it."

Not yet, I thought, though I did get the feeling that the one dolphin understood our intent.

There was another step in Poppy's plan. When I was maneuvering the *Revenge*, she'd shouted up to me to draw the dolphins away from the Russians, and to follow her lead when she called me on the radio later. And I was to ignore the request she would make and just continue heading south. So, I put the *Revenge* in gear and turned toward Gun Cay. Charity went down to the cockpit and turned on the diver recall.

As I was reaching for the phone to call Deuce, Charity looked back and asked, "Where do you plan to lead those dolphins?"

"South," I replied, punching Deuce's number on the contact list on my sat-phone. "See what I meant? Things are going south, and that's a good thing. We'll play it by ear after that."

Deuce answered on the first ring. "Where are you?"

"North end of the island," I replied. "We have a change in plans. Can you get someone to bring you out beyond the mouth of the bay?"

"Why can't you come in?" he asked. "We're at the dock, packed and ready."

"I'm leading the dolphins away from the Russians. I'll explain it all when you get aboard. We're thirty minutes from the mouth of the harbor."

"Roger that," Deuce said and ended the call.

We continued south at a snail's pace. The dolphins weren't used to my boat and I didn't want to spook them. Still a mile from the mouth of Bimini Bay, the VHF radio crackled to life. It was Poppy.

"*Gaspar's Revenge, Gaspar's Revenge.* Do you copy?"

Taking the mic from its holder, I keyed it, and said, "This is *Gaspar's Revenge.* Acknowledge and step up to channel seventeen, one-seven."

She acknowledged, repeating the channel. "Seventeen, switching to channel seventeen."

Her enunciation of the channel number was a little obvious. She wanted someone listening to follow us to the other frequency. I changed channels and she hailed me again.

"*Gaspar's Revenge* here," I replied.

"Jesse. Can you come help? Some dolphins have beached themselves."

I looked back and smiled. All five dolphins were following obediently behind us. Even the clever female. After the drugging, I would have thought she'd want nothing to do with any humans. Were they intelligent enough to discern the various motivations of individual humans? I imagined her back there, explaining to the other four that the human with the crazy red hair was their friend for taking off the trackers. And now her friend was leading them away from the bad people who had hurt them.

Misinformation was another tactic that worked well, if done right. Poppy wanted the Russians to think the dolphins had stranded and died. The final step in her plan to get the Russians to give up and leave.

"What?" I said, false alarm in my voice. "That's terrible. What can we do?"

"We need men to help carry buckets, to keep them cool. I don't know though, they're in bad shape, really distressed."

"Tell me where."

"The beach on the north side of the island," Poppy replied. "Inside the bay."

"Okay. Keep your chin up. I'll be there as soon as I can."

A mental image of Poppy's face came to my mind. She was beaming. Smug satisfaction lit her features.

◆ ◆ ◆ ◆

Shortly after, Ebbie's son's boat approached and came alongside. We slowed, matching speed, with fenders out on both boats. With Charity's help, Andrew stepped over the gunwales first, followed quickly by Deuce, who climbed immediately to the bridge.

He looked back at the dolphins following us. "How?"

"Would you believe me if I told you they thought I was one of them?" I asked. He gave me a mocking look, one eyebrow raised. I smiled. "Poppy recorded the sounds the Russians were using to train the dolphins. We're playing it over the diver recall system."

With both boats bobbing in the one-foot swells, Andrew helped Tony over, and Paul quickly passed the bags to the two men, who then passed them on to Charity. Once all the gear was moved, the two men helped Paul aboard. Ebbie's son looked impressed until

Paul clumsily went across. He saluted me again and moved slowly away as the others climbed up to the bridge. With another look back at the dolphins, the kid raised both hands, thumbs up. As Rusty would say, those who live by the sea have a special affinity for it and its creatures.

We idled steadily south, the dolphins following behind us, as I explained to my friends about our evening visitor and my early morning swim.

"It might work," Paul said. "But it won't make any difference. Even if the Russians think those five stranded and died, they'll just do it again somewhere else."

As I looked over my shoulder, the five dolphins rose and fell in our wake in a very rhythmic pattern. "It'll make a difference to those five."

We continued south.

Deuce looked over at me. I knew the dolphins were no longer paramount, they were safe. Dalton's and Poppy's mission was a success. I could see that Deuce's mind was turning toward other things. After all, we'd come all this way with the intention of discussing our future. I could see it in his eyes; he'd decided. I nodded my head slightly, and we both looked at Charity.

"I need to get back to California," she said, as if reading our minds.

I was a bit disappointed. I'd hoped that she'd come back to the Keys. She had friends there. And her excitement at doing something meaningful had a lot to do with whether or not I would commit.

She grinned at me. "I'll need someone to help with the lines in the canal locks."

"I think I could use a Pacific vacation after this," I said, smiling back at her. "When?"

"Right away."

Tony leaned forward from where he stood behind me and Andrew. "Will one of you tell us what the hell you're talking about?"

"Yeah," Andrew echoed, his voice punctuating his interest like thunder. "What's with all the cloak and dagger?"

CHAPTER EIGHTEEN

As we continued south, Deuce retrieved his laptop and plugged it into the USB port on the stereo, so the sound would go through the stereo speakers. He got Chyrel on the comm then placed the device on the far corner of the bench seat, so everyone could see everyone.

Tom was in the office with Chyrel and they expected Julie any minute. She added a speech-to-text extension to the link, so Tom could read what we discussed. Once Julie arrived in the office, we spent the next two hours outlining what Armstrong had told us.

For the most part, the others listened. Chyrel interrupted at the start. "What did Armstrong say that made you decide, Jesse?"

"It wasn't so much what he said," I began. "The talking heads in DC say the same stuff every day. I think it was more the man than his words. He has an indomitable conviction; a certainty that what he's doing is right and just. I sensed an unwavering moral compass."

"For a man who doesn't talk much," Charity said, "you sure do have a wonderful way with words. I picked up the same kind of vibe from Armstrong. And the dweeb, Bremmer, too."

I looked again at the dolphins following us. I still couldn't believe we'd pulled it off. "It's doubtful that any of us will be the catalyst that brings about real world-wide change." I nodded toward the dolphins rising and falling behind us in a sort of rhythmic dance. "But we can make a small adjustment here and there, you know, just take the pressure down a little to make life better for someone, one person at a time."

What Armstrong had proposed, and what the three of us had decided, was like some sort of mix between *The Undersea World of Jacques Cousteau* and *Ironman*. The three men with us on the boat listened intently, occasionally asking pertinent questions, as did Chyrel and Tom. Julie had already talked with Deuce at great length the night before, but she did ask a couple of specific questions.

"I agree," Deuce said. "Having met the man now, I have no doubt about him." He looked at me for a long moment. "You're not fully in, are you?"

"You know I'm not much of a joiner," I replied. "I'll tell him yes, as long as that caveat remains that I can also say no at any time."

He nodded and smiled wryly. "Some things never change."

Deuce looked one-by-one at each of the three men on the bridge, getting a nod from each. "Whatever you decide," Tony said.

"Same here," Tom said over the speaker.

"And me," Chyrel added.

Julie smiled on the screen. "What Uncle Jesse says. And all communications go through me."

"A hundred percent, babe," Deuce said. "All cards face up on the table, at all times."

We were a couple of miles off Gun Cay. I glanced over at Charity. "Time to say goodbye to the dolphins."

"We'll be home shortly," Deuce said, moving toward the laptop. "Chyrel, keep the audio open." He ended the video link and closed the computer.

Charity went down to switch off the diver recall and dumped the last of the bait fish in the water. I turned the *Revenge* west and brought her up on plane, accelerating to full speed.

Dolphins can swim faster than my boat's top speed, but only for short bursts. Soon, we reached the karst shelf and the bottom quickly fell away below us. The five dolphins were far behind. I kept it at full throttle for ten minutes, the superchargers screaming, then backed off to 30 knots.

"Okay," Deuce shouted, I can hear again."

"So, kinda like old times?" Chyrel asked over the stereo speakers.

"But privately funded," Deuce said.

"And not just terrorists," Tony added. "You dug up enough data on some of the projects they conducted."

"I still have some doubts," I said. "But I liked what I heard."

"What kind of doubts?" Charity asked.

"I'm in," I said. "I guess I just have some doubts about whether Armstrong can pull off anything really monumental in the grand scheme of things. But I'm definitely down with the intent."

"I'd say that what y'all just did with those dolphins was pretty big," Chyrel said. "And the bread crumbs Armstrong dropped? Getting us here at the same time as the Fish and Wildlife operation? He really played us well."

"Yeah, he did that," I said, looking back toward Gun Cay, now over the horizon with a new pod of dolphins in attendance. I grinned. "I *will* say this, if it's always this satisfying, I'm good."

The others chimed in, affirming what I'd said.

"Big echo, six miles ahead, and off to starboard," Andrew said.

I leaned over to look at the radar screen. "Probably a freighter. Nowhere near our rhumb line."

"Give me a direction," Chyrel said. "I wanna practice with that camera some more."

For the next several minutes, Andrew fed Chyrel information, while she searched the far horizon for the freighter. I turned slightly toward it, to get within four miles, the farthest I calculated the horizon could be.

"Got it!" Chyrel exclaimed. "I think."

I looked up at the monitor. Right on the horizon, I could just make out the bridge and upper part of a ship. The camera zoomed in, and although the image was grainy, it appeared as if the ship was running partially submerged, the deck and hull invisible over the horizon. As we got closer and Chyrel zoomed in more, we could see it was an island freighter of some kind.

"Hang on," Chyrel said over the speaker. "I've been wanting to try something."

"What?" Deuce asked.

"I'm going to patch the image from the camera into a program I wrote. See, it's a four-K dpi camera, but when it's zoomed in real tight like this, we're seeing a lot fewer pixels. This program will search through all the blank spots and fill them in based on the pixels around them."

"Yeah," I said. "That makes perfect sense."

"Just watch the screen, Jesse."

All of us gathered around, watching the closed-circuit monitor. It looked sort of like TV did when I was a kid, unless the station you were watching was pretty close. Growing up in Fort Myers, we could pick up three TV channels, but only WFLA in Tampa came in clearly. This looked like a rainy day watching the Orlando or Miami stations.

We were within four miles of the ship, so we could see all of it now, at least through the camera. I glanced in the direction the radar showed the ship to be, and it was a mere spot on the distant horizon.

All I knew about the camera on the roof was that with it you could count the hairs in a squirrel's mustache at 100 yards. It had image stabilization and could be locked onto an object. So, you could count the squirrel's mustache hairs as it scampered from branch to branch. And with infrared and night vision, you could do it in almost complete darkness. A hundred yards was nothing compared to four miles, but the ship was a bit larger than a squirrel's mustache hairs.

"She's slowed," Andrew said. "Now making only about three knots."

The image remained grainy and fuzzy. On the screen, I could tell we were looking at probably the aft two-thirds of what I would guess to be a 300-foot ship—the zoom was that powerful.

Suddenly, a horizontal line moved up and down the screen, sharpening the image with each pass. It was clear enough to see dozens of barrels along the edge of the aft deck. I could also see a crew of four men, each one tethered to the ship. They were moving from barrel to barrel with a large dolly on wheels. Two men tipped a barrel and the dolly went under it. Then the other two pushed down on the handles of the dolly, levering the barrel over the low gunwale.

"Are you seeing this?" Chyrel asked.

"Yeah," Deuce said. "Start recording."

"What are they doing?" Charity asked, leaning in, with her breasts pressed against my shoulder.

Deuce leaned in closer too. "They're dumping what looks like standard 55-gallon industrial steel drums. Doesn't matter what's in them, it's illegal dumping."

I glanced at the chart plotter. "Illegal where? We're twenty miles from the Florida coast and that's the nearest land."

"That'd be the London Convention," Chyrel said. "Or, more precisely, the *1972 Convention on the Prevention of Marine Pollution by Dumping of Wastes and Other Matter*, which all North American countries, as well as most of those in South America and the Caribbean, are signatories to."

"I have an idea," I said. "Andrew, isolate that ship's position and mark it as best you can, and plot his course from there. Chyrel, get the ship's name and home port as I turn aft of it."

Deuce chuckled. "I like your idea. Also, Chyrel, try to get a closeup of one of those barrels' labels. If you can clean up the image, maybe we can tell what they're dumping."

I turned across the ship's wake and passed two miles astern. By getting distance and range from several locations of the slow-moving ship, Andrew was able to triangulate and pinpoint within a few hundred yards both its position, and the line where they dumped the barrels.

I slowed and watched the ship moving away. "It's headed toward Miami."

"Got that info," Chyrel said. "Ship's name is *Argosy*, home port is Miami, and it's owned by Trinity Shipping."

"See if you can get its schedule, Chyrel," I said. "Deuce is gonna call Jack Armstrong."

"Why me?"

"You're the boss," Tony said.

"Maybe we should wait until Chyrel knows what the labels say."

"Give me just a minute," she replied. "I don't think the small print will be clear, but I can tell you its *toxic waste* for sure."

"How can you tell?" I asked.

"Several barrels have yellow and red hazmat labels," she replied, now in what I called her full-tech mode, in which her accent was almost indiscernible. "Those are health hazards and unstable compounds, respectively.

Deuce went down to the salon to make the call. A few minutes later, he returned and looked around at all of us. "Can we remain on station?"

Everyone nodded.

"What'd he say?" I asked.

"*Ambrosia* will be here in less than an hour."

Using the pinpoint that Andrew had estimated, I turned to a precise course away from Government Cut and the busy Miami port. Moving at idle speed of three knots, the same speed the freighter had made, we estimated how long it was from the time we'd first spotted the barrels going in and the time Andrew fixed their position. We'd watched the men pushing the barrels overboard for about eight minutes, leaving a debris field nearly half a mile long.

I dropped another pin on the GPS. We continued for several more minutes and I dropped a third. They'd been in the process of dumping the barrels when we first saw them, so the third location was just an estimate of where they might have started when the ship had slowed. We now had a line almost a mile long, hopefully right on top of where they'd dumped the toxic waste.

One thing I'd noticed on the *Ambrosia's* bridge was the sophisticated sonar system. Captain Hansen had said it could map the sea floor to within a couple of inches, so finding a bunch of barrels shouldn't pose much of a problem.

She arrived at a more sedate cruising speed this time. Although *Ambrosia* was capable of covering vast distances in little time, it was something Armstrong said he only employed on occasion. I know it'd made an impression on me; a 200-foot ship passing the *Revenge* like she was on the hard wasn't anything I'd likely see again.

Andrew handled the *Revenge* as Deuce and I stepped over onto the big work platform. Armstrong himself was there to greet us, Bremmer at his side.

"You're certain it was toxic waste?" he asked, without preamble.

Deuce handed him a flash drive. Armstrong handed it to Bremmer, who inserted it into a small tablet. He tapped the screen a few times and handed the tablet to his boss. Armstrong watched it carefully, a stern expression covering his features.

"Come on up to the bridge," he said to me and Deuce, as he handed the tablet to Bremmer. "Get the coordinates on that flash drive to Captain Hansen."

Bremmer went ahead of us as Armstrong led the way to the bridge. The captain was studying the chart plotter as we entered the upper deck area. The hatch to the room aft the bridge was open. Where there had once been a party lounge, stage, and dance floor, half a dozen people now sat bent over computer screens, with several others watching over their shoulders.

"Course laid in," Captain Hansen said. Armstrong nodded, and the captain turned to two men beside him, one at the helm and the other staring into a sonar screen. "Ahead two knots and engage course-keeping thrusters. Begin active sonar, narrow beam, 100-meter sweep."

I stepped up next to the helmsman, watching the chart plotter as we neared the location where we estimated they'd started dumping. When I glanced over at the sonar man, I noticed he had a small device in his hand with a single button—a counter of some kind. Occasionally, he clicked it.

When we finally passed the last point, the sonar man looked up at the captain. "I suggest a reverse course, sir. Paralleling the original, a hundred yards to the north of it."

"Make it happen, helm," the captain said.

A woman came out of the aft control center. "Sonar readings," she said, handing Armstrong a piece of paper. "Close, but no cigar."

Armstrong looked at the paper and passed it to Deuce. "The red dots are what sonar wants to look at again."

Deuce and I looked at the paper. It was a color rendering of the bottom of the ocean in varying shades of brown. Everything was shown in great detail, what little there was, as if the water had simply been evaporated away. All the red dots were on the right side of the image. The rest was just undulating brown and tan waves, showing the contour of the bottom.

The sonar man continued studying his screen. There was no need to use the clicker. I could see the bottom on his screen, nearly half a mile below us. Every pass of the focused sonar revealed rectangular irregularities in the bottom.

"Must be dozens of them," the sonar man said, not looking up.

When we finished the pass, the woman returned, handing Armstrong another sheet of paper. "I think we covered the whole field, sir."

She smiled at me as she turned toward the control center. My eyes lingered on her back as she returned to her station in the darkened room.

Armstrong showed us the sheet. The bottom was nearly smooth, only the slightest of dips and rises. The barrels stood out in stark relief, scattered haphazardly across the seafloor. I counted at least forty, the concentration of barrels diminishing at both ends before the image showed nothing but the bottom for several hundred yards in both directions.

"The ship must have been dumping barrels for longer than we estimated." I said. "We saw fewer than half that number get pushed overboard."

"Good job finding this," Armstrong said, clutching the paper. "We'll begin clean up operation in the morning, if you want to hang around another day."

Deuce touched a finger to the earwig he wore. "Anyone have anything pressing for the next couple of days?" After a moment he looked at me and Charity, a question in his eyes.

"We can pick up *Wind Dancer* in a day or a week," Charity said.

I nodded my agreement and Deuce turned to Armstrong. "Yes, thanks. But is that it, you just clean up after them?"

Armstrong smiled. "Oh, that's just the beginning." He turned aft and called into the control center. "Comm, contact Captain Wilson. Have him depart for Bimini immediately. We'll need him in the morning to pilot the submersible."

"Submersible?" I asked.

Armstrong smiled broadly. "It has room for two. I think you'll like Captain Wilson."

CHAPTER NINETEEN

We returned to the *Revenge* and spent the night anchored on the edge of the shelf in 40 feet of water. *Ambrosia* lay at anchor just half a mile away. Before sunset, she'd put a tender in the water, and Armstrong, Stockwell, Bremmer, and Knox had motored over to the *Revenge*.

I had to admit, the man was organized. He'd outlined a detailed plan to take the submersible to the bottom and see if it was feasible to bring the barrels back up. If he could get the right assets together, that is. His pilot was away, but he told us that John Wilson would arrive before first light.

The four men had stayed aboard with us just long enough to lay out Armstrong's timetable. As his new head of security, Stockwell returned to *Ambrosia* with them.

Before sunrise, with *Ambrosia*'s work deck awash in lights, I stepped over onto it with Deuce. Andrew moved the *Revenge* a couple hundred yards away.

"John will be here in less than half an hour," Armstrong told us. "Have you eaten?"

"Yeah," I replied, looking over the small submersible on the side of the deck. "How deep can this thing go?"

Armstrong joined me. "It's rated to 15,000 feet, with a crush depth of 30. We've never had this one past 6,500."

I looked up at him from where I knelt beside the strange-looking vessel. "Almost 200 atmospheres of pressure?"

"And it has performed flawlessly for over 200 dives," he assured me. "Captain Wilson has piloted similar submersibles into some of the deepest Atlantic trenches, including the Puerto Rico Trench. After his first year of college, he was part of the *Trieste* surface team when she dove Challenger Deep."

"There's John now," Bremmer said, pointing astern.

To the stern, the navigation lights of a boat could be seen slowly approaching the port side of the platform. When the boat materialized in the circle of light, I recognized it as the old Seaton I'd seen among the many registries of boats owned by or contracted by Armstrong Research.

The old steel-hulled trawler came alongside, a gray-haired man standing outside the pilothouse hatch. The windows were dark, so I couldn't see the pilot, but under the bright lights, the boat looked immaculate, as if brand new. Yet she had been built the year I'd turned seven. The forward-leaning pilothouse windows bespoke a no-nonsense, sea-going heritage. The throaty rumble of the old military surplus engine was a far cry from the screaming supercharged engines of the *Revenge*, or the high whine of *Ambrosia's* turbines. She was a more sedate vessel than either, stately and proud.

John Wilson was an older man, probably in his late sixties. But he carried himself with practiced ease as he dropped the three feet to the platform. He pushed some buttons on a small tablet he carried, and the boat moved away from *Ambrosia*. The name on the stern was *Floridablanca*. I smiled. It was the name of José Gaspar's last ship.

Introductions were made, and Wilson turned to look at his boat, now chugging away from us about 100 yards distant. He tapped the screen of his tablet, then put it away.

"That sends messages to your mate?" I asked.

"Not exactly," Wilson replied. "I sail solo."

"Remote control?" I asked, amazed.

"It runs one of several preset programs through the autopilot, GPS, and radar systems. Right now, it's in station-keeping mode, at a safe distance from *Ambrosia*. If we move, *Floridablanca* will follow. You're going down with me?"

His accent sounded Texan, or maybe he was from New Mexico.

"Yeah," I replied, jerking a thumb toward my boat. "I'm on *Gaspar's Revenge*." I definitely wanted to learn more about his computerized antique trawler.

"I take it you're from Southwest Florida?" he asked, looking toward the *Revenge*.

I somehow got the impression that he already knew that, and probably much more. He and Armstrong seemed to share a familiarity.

"Yes," I said. "Fort Myers."

The old man smiled, showing perfect white teeth. "Manasota Key," he said, extending a hand.

I shook it. "We might have swallowed some of the same swamp water."

As *Ambrosia* got underway, Wilson's boat remained alongside, powering up to maintain the same distance off the starboard rail, as if she was tethered. The *Revenge* escorted us on the port side. I spent the next two hours going over all the systems and controls of the small sub. It was a thick glass sphere, partially encased in a metal frame, with small propellers fixed inside tubes that could be rotated countless ways. The whole thing was painted bright yellow and resembled a tear drop on its side.

With the sun halfway up the morning sky, we arrived at the dump site, I climbed nervously into the cramped confines of the glass bubble and moved to the left side. The controls were in front of the right-hand seat.

Wilson climbed in, settling into the pilot's seat as if it were made for him. My own felt more than a little cramped and he noticed. "Try to relax, Jesse. This is a shallow dive, as far as this sub is concerned. It'll be ten or fifteen minutes before they button us up. Sara usually co-pilots. Sorry, she's a bit smaller than you."

"Sara?"

"Sara Patrick," he replied. "If you visited *Ambrosia's* bridge, you might have met her."

"Attractive, blond lady? About thirty-five?"

"Forty in two months," he replied. He must have read the puzzled look on my face. He shrugged. "She's my kid."

"Your daughter?"

"She accepted a job offer from Jack, just after Greg— he was my son-in-law—after Greg was killed in Afghanistan a little over two years ago."

Greg Patrick, I thought. The name was familiar from long ago. I searched my memory for a moment, and then it came to me. "Greg Patrick? Played defense for Riverdale Raiders?"

John looked over at me surprised. "You knew him?"

"He was a couple of years behind me in high school, if it's the same Greg Patrick. I was a wide receiver for Fort Myers High."

He laughed. "You were a *Greenie?*"

I'd hated our school name. Whoever had come up with *Green Wave* obviously didn't know anything about football. Teams should be called names like the Tigers, Eagles, or Raiders. But the Green Wave had only had ten losing seasons in the 60 years before I'd played there.

"Sorry about your loss," I said. "So, you take your daughter down in this bubble?"

"She's Captain Hansen's first mate," he said. "Cool under pressure."

I smiled at his diving reference. Armstrong had been right—I immediately felt relaxed and at ease with this man, and we certainly had a lot in common.

He handed me a pair of earphones and put another set on his own head. When I put mine on, I could hear several people talking, all running through a check list. Wilson switched the submersible's systems on as someone above us closed the hatch. He reached up and turned a single dogging mechanism to keep it closed. The pressure would keep it tightly sealed after just a few feet of descent.

He turned toward me and put a hand over the mic boom in front of his mouth. "This'll be a piece-a-cake, Jesse. Just keep your eyes open as we get near the bottom."

"Pilot?" said the female voice running through the check list.

John uncovered the mic. "Roger, all systems on and reading nominal."

"Boom?" the woman said.

Another voice replied that he was ready.

"On Captain Wilson's command," the woman said. She sounded like the one who worked in the control center, John's daughter.

"Whenever you're ready, Tommy," John said.

"Good luck, Dad," Sara Patrick said over my earphones. "You too, Captain McDermitt."

The tiny submersible lurched slightly as a crane lifted us from the cradle. I grabbed at the frame of my seat. Slowly, we were swung out over the water. A couple hundred yards away, I could see the *Revenge*. Everyone was on the bridge, watching.

The water came up to meet us, and then we were under. It was so clear, I could make out the entire length of *Ambrosia's* hull. To the right, the hull of the *Revenge* looked closer than it had on the surface, a typical illusion created by the water. Looking up, I could still see above the surface through the upper part of the glass bubble. Several people were looking down at us from *Ambrosia's* decks. A man in a wetsuit, with a mask and fins on, stepped off the platform and swam out to us. There was a clanking noise and then he swam back to the platform. I watched as the derrick swung all the way out. An electrical umbilical was now attached to the steel cable, unwinding from a large spool on the deck.

"Shore power on," John said. "Batteries are fully charged and offline." He turned a valve and said, "Blowing air."

There was a whirring sound, like a small pump would make. Then air bubbles rose, and we began to descend.

"Might as well get comfortable," John said. "Our descent rate will be 100 feet per minute. It's gonna be nearly half an hour before we reach the bottom."

"I appreciate you letting me tag along."

"You've done a submersible dive before?"

"No," I replied. "Went down in a submarine once."

"Same, same," he said. "Except a sub doesn't need a line to the surface. We can detach and move about autonomously, but the batteries only carry enough charge to run things for 30 minutes."

Darkness quickly enveloped us. At 300 feet, there was only a faint blue glow above.

"Lights on," John said, flipping several switches.

The blue glow above us was washed out by the bright lights mounted all around the hull. The water was mostly clear, so the lights didn't illuminate much of anything other than the submersible itself. Now and then, the occasional speck of something floated by, well-lit by the bright lights. I leaned forward, looking down into the abyss.

"You won't see anything down there for a while," John said, pointing to our depth gauge. It was approaching 500 feet. "It's still more than 300 fathoms below us."

"This is officially the deepest I've ever been," I said, watching a large moon jellyfish undulate past us in the light.

"Thought you said you served on a sub."

"Rode on one," I corrected him. "Night insertion from the Persian Gulf."

He looked over, regarding me carefully. "SEAL?"

"Marine Recon," I said. "Desert Shield."

He waited a moment, then asked, "But not Desert Storm?"

I shrugged. I didn't know the guy, and others were listening in. But I'd started it, and none of it was classified. "I entered Kuwait a few days before Christmas and a month before the invasion." I grinned. "Four weeks later, Desert Storm kinda ran right past me."

Wilson stared at me a moment in the light of the gauges. Then he chuckled. "You spent a month in the desert alone? You're a real-life, honest-to-God snake-eater, son."

I shrugged again. "Just doing what Uncle Sam told me to do."

"I was Air Force," he said. "Retired in '91—30 years."

I knew he was being humble. Chyrel had said that the Seaton's owner was a retired Air Force spec-ops guy. And Armstrong had said he'd somehow, at no more than nineteen or twenty, been a crew member of the only bathyscaphe to ever reach the deepest part of the ocean, Challenger Deep in the Mariana Trench.

"Had I stayed for 30," I said, "I'd have retired last year. I took the twenty."

"So, you missed this latest dustup, huh? That's a good thing."

"Yeah," I replied.

I'd missed it. I'd been retired for only a couple of years when the Twin Towers fell. I'd tried to reenlist but was politely told to *leave this one to the younger guys.* Kind of a blow to a man's ego, especially one who wasn't even 40 yet.

In the dim red glow inside the bubble, John studied me a moment longer. "Not for lack of want, I'm guessing."

We descended in silence, the depth meter counting a little faster than seconds on a clock. We were nearing 2000 feet, ten times my greatest mixed gas dive. At 300 times the pressure on the surface, if the glass bubble were compressible, the weight of the water all around us would crush it to the size of a ping-pong ball.

Something moving caught my eye. A huge shark, of a species I'd never seen before, moved slowly past, disappearing above us. Its eyes were larger and set further forward on the head than most sharks I'd seen, and it had a very long upper tail.

"I've never seen a shark like that," I said, looking up where it had disappeared.

"Coming up on 2000," Sara said over the headphones.

"Roger that," John replied, looking over the console. "Everything looks good." Then he turned to me. "Sharks are attracted to any kind of electromagnetic source, like our umbilical. That one was a bigeyed sixgill shark."

"Seriously?" I asked. "That's the name of the species?"

Nodding, he grinned over at me. "I guess all the cool names had been taken before that one was discovered. Or maybe scientists aren't as creative as the fishermen who named the others."

We continued downward with no visible indication of movement. After several minutes, the depth gauge was approaching 2400 feet. The bottom was at 2550.

"Slowing descent," Sara said. "You should see the bottom soon."

She'd no sooner said it than the lights picked up several brightly colored barrels, stark against a neutral seafloor, no more than twenty feet below us. They rested on a stark, brownish-gray seafloor. John moved one of the lights, showing the bottom stretching away from us, other barrels just visible in the distance.

"We see the barrels," John said. "Going neutral on buoyancy."

"Roger that," Sara said. "We're in position over the southeast end of the debris field. There's a trench perhaps 100 yards across and 50 feet below the sea floor, just beyond the debris field."

With a practiced hand, John moved a lever and I could hear a hissing sound; compressed air pushing the water out of the ballast tanks. Using one hand on a small joystick, John turned the submersible. Using his other hand, he directed all the lights forward. Bright yellow barrels extended as far as the light penetrated. Touching several more buttons, a small monitor came to life between us.

"Receiving visual," Sara said. "My God, they're every-where."

"I'm going to get closer to one and see just what's in it," John said. "I don't think it'll be anything more than a time-consuming job to move them into a lift."

Moving the joystick, John piloted the sub closer to the bottom, approaching one of the barrels.

"Hydrogen chloride," he said, reading the label just a foot in front of the glass. "These assholes need to be drawn and quartered. Put that shit in a steel drum and let it rust in the ocean—real soon you'll have a toxic dump of hydrochloric acid. With no current to speak of, it'll just lie here on the bottom and kill anything that comes near it."

Armstrong's voice came over my headphones. "How long do you think it'll take, John?"

"Wait one," he replied, as he moved the joystick. The small submersible flew slowly across the debris field as John scanned from side to side, surveying the area. I noticed that a few of the barrels were covered in rust, which I hadn't detected through the rooftop camera on the *Revenge*.

"At least two long days, Jack," John replied, after assessing all he'd seen. "Sonar showed 47 barrels. That'll be 24 lifts."

"You can't take more than two at a time?" I asked.

"Too much danger of them banging together. Each lift takes an hour. So, two twelve-hour days."

"Why do you think some of those are already rusting?"

John stared out over the mess below us. "I see what you mean," he said, moving the joystick. The sub moved toward one of the rustier barrels. As we got closer, John drew in a sharp breath.

"Oh, hell no! This one's hydrogen *fluoride*."

"Get away from it, Dad," Sara said, her voice on edge.

"What's that?" I asked, feeling woefully inadequate for the circumstances.

"When dissolved in water in any form," Sara said, "it creates hydrofluoric acid. That's the super acid that can eat through glass."

John reversed the sub's thrusters to move the submersible away from the rusty barrel. That slight movement of water was all that it took.

Suddenly, the side of the drum flexed and broke open. I held my breath as brown rust flakes fell slowly to the seafloor.

"This wasn't dropped here today," I said. "That barrel's been here at least a year."

"Get away!" Sara screamed, as a wavy, transparent cloud emanated from the barrel.

John moved the controls quickly, adding a little air to the aft ballast tanks, and reversing the motors. As we started upwards, stern first, I heard three sounds almost simultaneously.

There was a sharp crack, like a small caliber rifle, a high-pitched hiss, and as John dove sideways into me, his agonizing scream.

A tiny jet of water was coming through the seam where the glass met the metal frame of the boarding hatch. That jet of water had hit John in the right side of his head.

"What's going on?" Armstrong asked.

I looked around the interior of the cramped bubble. Water was already pooling at my feet. Not finding what I needed, I ripped the T-shirt from my body, knowing I couldn't get it off in one piece in the now doubly cramped space. I wrapped it tightly around John's head, careful to keep him away from the high-pressure leak.

"John's hurt!" I said. "We have a leak."

"Beginning retrieval. There's an emergency high-pressure water pump, Jesse. The switch is below the joystick, between his knees."

Reaching over, holding John close to me, I found the switch and tripped it. Immediately, I heard the high-pitched whine of the pump. The water was now over my ankles.

The sub lurched to the right as the umbilical cable snatched tight and we began moving horizontally and a little upward. The sub began spiraling, bringing the barrels into and out of view in a gyrating motion. The submersible twisted and twirled like a kite out of control in a high wind. The lights played over the bottom in a dizzying spin. As they rotated away from the barrels, for a second, I thought I saw something in the distance. The trench Sara had mentioned?

Having watched John control the lights, I reached for the servo and turned them into the direction we were spinning. When we came around again, I saw it and tried to move the light with the spin, but only succeeded in seeing it for an instant longer. But I was certain of what I'd seen. An old sailing ship was resting partially on its side on the bottom of the trench. It had only appeared for a second, a vague shape at the edge of the light's reach, almost like an apparition. Its masts were broken, the hull partially buried where it had crashed into the base of the cliff after a half-mile fall.

The sub spun around once more, but I didn't see the old ship again. Had it really been there? We were rising more vertically now, and nothing was visible in the darkness.

Three of the lights popped and went off, one after another, leaving only one spotlight. Apparently, the acid had breached the bulbs, too.

"Jesse, you've got to vent the air out of those ballast tanks," Armstrong said.

He was right. As we rose, the air would expand, and we'd become more buoyant, causing us to rise even faster. An out-of-control ascent could cause stress on the submersible's frame and tear it apart.

Holding John away from the water still hissing through the cracked glass, I found the switch to pump water into the ballast tanks.

The next few minutes became a blur, as Tommy hoisted us as fast as the derrick would manage. John was badly hurt. The water had cut like a laser across his forehead and down through his right eye and cheek, destroying the soft tissue, and laying his face open to the bone. Miraculously, he was still alive, but even with my hasty bandage, he was losing blood fast.

"Depth is 100 feet," Sara said. "Blow all ballast tanks, Jesse."

The stream of water from the crack in the glass had slowed to a trickle now. I reached over John and opened the air valve all the way, inflating the buoyancy tanks.

The surface appeared, and I could see several people waiting on the work platform as the crane lifted us out of the water and started to swing us toward the deck.

Within seconds of the submersible banging onto the cradle, two men climbed up on top of it, while others worked to secure the sub in its cradle.

"Secured," I heard a voice shout from outside. Quickly, the two men on top undogged the hatch and with my help, they pulled John out and lowered him to other men, waiting on the deck with a litter.

As I climbed out of the hatch, Sara was hurrying down the steps built into the former yacht's hull. As soon as she reached her father, she took his hand and began talking to him. Several men helped move the stretcher up to the cockpit, with Sara following alongside.

"What happened, Jesse?" Armstrong asked as I climbed down. "Are you okay?"

"I'm no scientist, Jack," I said. "So, I have no idea what failed." I paused a moment and looked him straight in the eye. "But I *can* see into the future. At least the future of the turd-fondler who ordered that shit dumped."

CHAPTER TWENTY

I n the cockpit, a crewman handed me a towel and a dry shirt. I ignored the towel and pulled the black polo shirt over my head, noticing the gold and silver *M/V Ambrosia* logo on the chest. My pants were still stained with John's blood.

Sara stepped through the hatch from the main part of the ship. She looked distraught and was obviously holding back tears. Armstrong put a hand on her shoulder, a gesture an uncle would make.

"How's John?" Jack asked her.

She looked up at him, and then over at me. "The doctor said his eye is gone."

"I'm really sorry," I said.

She stepped toward me. "He also said your quick action to stop the bleeding probably saved his life."

I didn't know how to respond. I'd kept harm from coming to a few people and accepted their thanks without much thought. They'd have done the same if the situation were reversed. But I couldn't remember one time when their loved one had expressed their gratitude.

It had all happened so fast. I'd only met the guy an hour earlier, but in that short time, I felt as if I'd become reacquainted with an old friend I hadn't seen in years.

Sara took another step and extended her hand. "Thank you."

I took her hand and she melted into my shoulder, sobbing. It was uncomfortable, but I held her in my arms for a moment until the spasms passed. She stepped back and sniffed. I offered her the folded towel.

"He wants to see you both," she said, stepping back, and wiping her eyes. She shook her hair back, composing herself. "Dad does. Before the doctor puts him under to treat the wound."

Sara left for the bridge and a moment later, Jack Armstrong led me into the sick bay on the lower deck. John was on a table, a blanket pulled up over his chest. Two men in scrubs stood next to him.

"He won't let me put him under until he talks to you," one of the men said. I assumed he was the ship's doctor.

"Jack?" John said, his voice cracking a little, in obvious pain.

Armstrong went to his side. "I'm here, John." He motioned me toward him. "Jesse's here, too."

John Wilson lay still on the table, one eye looking straight up, the other covered with what I recognized as a clotting bandage.

"I'm too old for this shit," John croaked, steeling himself against the pain.

Armstrong looked over at the doctor, his eyes questioning. The doctor shook his head. "I need to go in and clean the eye socket out. But he needs a better facility than we have here."

"Don't talk crazy," Armstrong said, patting John's shoulder. "We'll fit you with a glass eye, or a pirate patch, whatever you want. You'll be back to work in no time."

John's chest heaved, and he grunted in obvious pain with any movement.

"Ha," he said through gritted teeth. "I'm almost seventy, Jack. You need a younger man to be doing my job." He raised his hand and Armstrong took it. "And I want you to sell *Floridablanca* for me."

"Sell your boat?" I asked, without thinking.

"You in the market, son?"

Armstrong looked up at the doctor. "Is he thinking clearly?"

The doctor nodded somberly. "He's in intense pain, but he's completely responsive and lucid."

Armstrong put a hand on the man's arm, leaning over his face to make eye contact. "I'll take care of it, John. If you're sure that's what you really want to do."

"My decision is final," John said.

Armstrong nodded at the doctor. "No pain meds?"

The doctor shook his head again. I looked at John's face. The lines in his forehead and around the jaw muscles were deep. He was focusing to stay conscious. I couldn't imagine the pain he was enduring.

Armstrong turned toward the hatch. "Come with me, Jesse."

I followed him out of the small sick bay. He crossed one arm, his right hand going to his chin, deep in thought.

Finally, he turned to face me. "John just resigned."

"Resigned?" I asked.

"At any time, any person in my employ, or anyone contracted to me or my company, is free to leave or cancel the contract, no questions asked. They just have to say that their decision is final."

"What exactly did John do for you?"

"Forward scout and submersible operator. *Floridablanca* is capable of great range on her single main engine. John sometimes finds things for us to do. And he's taken that boat to a lot of places."

"But his boat can't carry a submersible."

"No," he replied thoughtfully. "But *Ambrosia* can get to where he is pretty fast, as you've seen."

"And *Floridablanca* can get to you in a hurry, too."

A crewman hurried past, Armstrong stepping out of his way. "There isn't any way you could know that."

"Just a guess," I said. "You don't have the only high-tech snoop. A scout needs to blend in but also has to be able to move fast if necessary. I researched all the boats in your fleet and those you've contracted. All are capable of either great speed or great distance. Some, like John's

Seaton, were designed for both. But his had only a single, underpowered, antique diesel. I figure you paid to have it refitted with a couple of bigger engines."

Armstrong smiled. "You did your homework. Yes, *Floridablanca* has a pair of supercharged Mercedes diesels, driving a single, heavier shaft. The engine room is enormous. She can idle on the main engine for thousands of miles without refueling or disengage it and cruise at 30 knots all day, stopping for fuel at sunset after covering 400 miles. He wants me to sell her to you."

"You don't know that."

"I've known John a long time. Sara and my son went to the same preschool. He's like the wise old uncle I never had."

That's when the connection hit me. "You should meet one of my guys. He lost his wife and son on that same day. Same daycare maybe."

His eyes came up to mine, searching. "What do you mean?"

"Over on my boat is a retired Coast Guardsman named Andrew Bourke. He lost his wife and son, too. They were at a daycare facility in Tower One."

"I'd like to meet him," Armstrong said. "But to answer your question, I know John wants you to take his place."

"I was right there with you," I said. "John asked you to sell his boat, neither of you—wait, this was decided before the accident?"

Armstrong's smile looked weary. "Yes. We've gone to great lengths to find you and bring you here. Jack's been planning to retire for a while. We just haven't found a suitable replacement. Until now."

"I don't know how to operate a submersible."

"He and Sara can teach you, or we'll hire someone else for that," he said. "They aren't the only sub pilots we have. No, John wants you to take his place as the forward eyes for our expeditionary division. That's what *Floridablanca* was built for. You have an amphibious plane, right?"

Nothing he knew surprised me anymore. "Yeah, near where my house is in the Middle Florida Keys."

"And two large cruising vessels?" he asked, turning toward the ladderwell.

"The *Revenge* is hardly a cruiser," I replied, following him. "What is it you're getting at?"

"With three boats in three areas, and a plane that can get you to any of them, you'd be a very valuable asset."

We emerged onto the large cockpit and Armstrong looked over at *Floridablanca*. I stood next to him, admiring the lines of John's old boat. She was big and beefy, solid steel hull and decks. But in my mind, I could see her riding on top of the water at a speed most owners of fiberglass boats her size could only dream of. The vision in my mind was a complete juxtaposition to the sedate-looking beauty I saw with my eyes. Still, it was another boat, an asset for its job, but really just another thing.

I turned and faced him. "Material objects don't mean a lot to me."

"That's one of the reasons we choose the operators we do. What's at issue is your independent streak. Like I said earlier, when we need you, we'll call. You'll get all the details of the op, nothing hidden. Any and all costs are covered, including hiring others. Then you decide if you want it."

Deuce had been right. This was all too familiar.

I walked to the rail and looked down into the water. "What about those barrels down there?"

"The hydrogen fluoride is just too dangerous to move in the degraded condition of those older barrels. I'll have another submersible on the way by morning. We'll use explosives to detonate them in place, after retrieving whatever other barrels we can. The hydrogen released in a chemical combustion will make for a massive blast, neutralizing the acid before it can form."

I chuckled softly. "I was serious what I said when y'all first pulled us out of that glass bubble. I'm no scientist. I'm just an old door-kicker."

Armstrong smiled broadly. "That's almost word-for-word what John said to me nearly twenty years ago." He pointed down at the ocean's surface. "You don't need to be a scientist, Jesse. We have those. The stuff in those rusted barrels is hydrogen fluoride, a liquid when stored below 67 degrees Fahrenheit. The sea floor temperature here is well below that, about 40 degrees, so the hydrogen fluoride remained a liquid as the barrels slowly rusted. When that one broke open and the hydrogen fluoride mixed with the surrounding water, a chemical reaction took place, creating hydrofluoric acid, which can slowly dissolve glass. Enough of it came into contact with the submersible to compromise the glass, causing a small fracture."

I looked over at Armstrong and grinned. "There's another guy on my boat that might be able to help with the blowing up part."

Armstrong looked over at me as Sara approached. "You and Mister Livingston do have some unique associates."

"The doctor has him sedated and the wound dressed, Mister Armstrong," Sara said. "Captain Hansen is awaiting orders."

"Make for Miami," he said. "We need to get your dad to a hospital. How is he, Sara?"

"He'll be okay," she said, back to her usual *cool under pressure* manner.

"And you?"

"I'm fine, sir. It just got a little scary there for a minute." She turned toward me. "Will you be staying aboard?"

"What's happening in Miami?" I asked Armstrong.

"We'll put together a team to come back out here," he replied. "And find a way to bring down whoever was responsible."

"I'll stay with you," I said. "For now. You'll need someone to pilot John's boat."

"Why don't you do it?" Sara said. "You have someone who can pilot your own?"

"I'm not familiar with your dad's boat," I protested.

"I'll go with you," she replied.

It was decided. A satellite phone was produced, and I called Deuce. He told me that Captain Hansen had kept them abreast of the dive and everything that had happened. "How's Captain Wilson?" he asked.

"We're taking him to Miami," I told him. "I'll be on his boat."

"We'll follow along," Deuce said. "Chyrel has some information Armstrong might like to have."

"What's that?" I asked.

Deuce paused, then said, "The name of the person who ordered the barrels dumped. He's a mid-level waste management official at one of the commercial warehouses on Dodge Island. It looks like he's been skimming money that was meant to be used to ship and properly dispose of hazardous waste for years, then apparently just dumping it. Next load's in ten days."

"I'll relay it," I said and ended the call.

I turned to Armstrong and Sara, who was tapping at the screen of John's tablet. "Does John's boat have a laptop aboard? With Wi-Fi?"

"Yes," Sara said. "And encrypted ship-to-ship communication and direct satellite access."

I turned to Armstrong. "Let's get underway. Have your tech people contact Deuce. He'll patch in our tech team for a video conference. Our analyst knows who's responsible for the dumping."

Floridablanca moved slowly toward the stern of *Ambrosia*. Sara and I went down to the work deck, and when the boat moved close enough, I stepped over onto her swim platform and opened the transom door. I saw no ladder to the fly bridge as I scanned the covered cockpit.

"Follow me," Sara said, as she moved forward along the starboard side.

The side deck was wide and also covered. The flybridge above extended to full beam width, providing some shelter from the elements. We went up a short ladderwell to a Portuguese bridge, then entered the pilot house.

They say first impressions are important. My first impression of *Floridablanca* was that she was a stalwart old beauty, built tough to take on any seas. But my initial thoughts were contradicted once I laid eyes on the pilot house. The bridge was beautifully appointed with traditional dark brown woodwork. The helm was classical in design, but modern in function, housing the same sort of expensive electronics, as I'd seen on *Ambrosia*. They were mounted perfectly in an antique wooden dash, which surrounded the stock engine gauges and switches. The radar and chart plotter were active, and an identical pair in an overhead compartment were turned off, as were a pair of sonar screens.

The wheel and helm were centerline, with matching desks to port and starboard. The desk on the starboard side had a large computer monitor mounted to it, and a keyboard in front of that. The port desk looked to be more for writing, or physical chart-reading.

Aft the helm was a narrow table at bar height, which could be folded out to double its size. Behind it was a raised couch that could seat three comfortably. The table could be lowered to create a double bunk.

On the port bulkhead, accessible to the end seat on the couch, was the comm center, complete with several radios, ship-to-shore telephone, and weather fax. Aft the couch was a small watch berth, raised above the couch. In every way, the bridge was comfortable-looking, well laid-out, and functionally efficient.

"Take the helm," Sara said, as she settled in front of the computer. "I'll turn off the autopilot and lay in a course for Miami."

Doing as I was told, I took the wheel and turned it away from *Ambrosia*, heading roughly west. Looking through the forward-leaning windshield, I knew the outer radar beacon, marking the entrance to the Miami shipping channel, would be visible in just a few miles.

The trawler felt like a large ship and the view reinforced that. The foredeck had steel rails to thigh height, a separate raised companionway to the forward part of the boat, and a huge hoist that could also double as a mast for a steading sail, to heel the boat slightly in rough seas.

I gave Sara the name of the website to connect her dad's computer to the secure server in Deuce's office.

"It's asking for login information."

"User name is JSM," I told her, then gave her my password.

"Now it's telling me to download an encrypted file," she said.

"That's for the video feed," I explained. "It just means the connection is already in use and you'll need permission to patch in. Accept it and install the software. I'm told it's a small file and automatically erases itself when you sign off. I've gotta do the same thing every time."

A few clicks later, three screens opened on the monitor. Chyrel was at her desk at Deuce's office, while Deuce was in the salon of the *Revenge*, using my laptop. The other quadrant was empty.

"Hey, Jesse," Chyrel said. "I just got off the landline with a guy named Pete Jacobs on *Ambrosia*. They should be up in a second."

Looking over at the monitor, I could see the image of John's bridge in the third quadrant, me standing at the helm. The camera gave an elevated view laterally across the bridge. I looked along the overhead by the starboard hatch and found the camera. The tiny red dot under the lens told me it was probably infrared-capable.

"Hey, Chyrel," I said, looking toward the camera. "This is Sara Patrick, *Ambrosia's* first mate. Her dad owns the boat we're on now, *Floridablanca*. He's been hurt and we're heading to Miami to get him to a hospital."

The fourth quadrant came up. Armstrong's face filled most of the frame. Behind him, it was mostly dark, but there were other people sitting at consoles. He was in the control center aboard his ship and Deuce made the introduction for him.

Armstrong smiled. "You're a tough woman to find, Miss Koshinski."

CHAPTER TWENTY-ONE

The doctor on *Ambrosia* knew John's eye wasn't savable, so he'd done his best to stabilize him and stop the bleeding. The high-pressure stream of water that came through the glass bubble of the submersible had passed across his eye as he'd involuntarily jerked his head up and to the left. The skin and muscle were no match for the tremendous pressure stream of water. Only the bones of his forehead and cheek had stopped the jet. The doctors at University of Miami Hospital had performed a series of surgeries to reconnect muscle and tendon, in the hope of restoring function to the facial muscles.

During the following days, as he recuperated, I'd visited him daily. We'd talked about southwest Florida, the sea, the places we'd been, and what his duties and allegiances were to Jack Armstrong.

"You know he lost his wife and son in the Trade Center attack," John told me the day before he left the hospital. "She was pregnant; they were gonna have a daughter. He went deep for several months and nobody saw him. Then he started liquidating assets, building a pile of cash. He was going to hire mercenaries to go after bin Laden and any of his thugs that popped up. That got him on the radar of the CIA, and they started funneling money to his companies. The war dragged on, and Armstrong started taking out other villains. Our SEALS only beat Armstrong and his mercs by about 30 minutes.

"He was there?" I'd asked.

"First one off the chopper, just a few minutes after our guys left with the body."

When it came time for John to be discharged, I continued to visit him at his modest home in Coconut Grove—one of several homes he owned, but the only one in the United States.

"You're sure about this, son?" John asked.

We were sitting in a den, or what had probably once been the second bedroom of a very old little house. The room was done in dark wood and leather, with bookcases to the ceiling on two walls. The only light in the space was a lamp with a tan shade, which gave a warm glow to the rich wood paneling.

"Yeah, John, I'm sure. They're not expecting trouble. Hell, they have no idea that anyone is on to them."

"Still," he said, fixing me with his one eye, "he's gonna have people around him. And what you've got planned isn't the way Armstrong usually operates."

"I'm not worried about a few dock workers. And you and I both know there are some people who are just not going to respond to Armstrong's usual tactics. I'm just going to add a little emphasis."

Sitting in an overstuffed leather recliner, John looked older, smaller. He had indeed opted for a black patch, rather than get fitted with a glass eye. Under the patch was a flesh-colored bandage, to keep contaminants out while the eye socket healed and grew skin. The patch's strap paralleled the gash across his face, the stitches still in place. The wound was healing, and would leave a white scar, with visible stitch marks. John hadn't mentioned plastic surgery to hide the scar.

"I'd go with you," he said. "You know I would."

I smiled at him. His passion for the sea knew no bounds, except for the physical constraints caused by the trauma and multiple surgeries. Where Jack always had an axe to grind for any sort of terrorist, John focused on maritime concerns and environmental terrorists.

"I know you would," I told him, and meant it.

Lifting a bottle from the table next to his chair, he uncorked it and poured two fingers of dark liquid into a pair of highball glasses. "This is from Panama. Ever been there?"

"Yeah," I replied, reaching over, and accepting the glass. "But I wasn't carrying a passport."

His face came up and he winked. Or maybe it was just a blink; no way to tell. "Good people, the Panamanians. Hard-working."

John raised his glass. "To the ship that goes, the wind that blows, and the lass who loves a sailor."

I clinked his glass with my own, then took a healthy swallow of spiced rum. "Are you sure you were ever in the Air Force? Armstrong said you were part of the Trieste crew."

"It was a year of decision for me," he said. "I was all set. My first year of college started and I'd been chosen to be a part of the crew. I had to take three months off my studies right after Christmas of '59. But it was worth it. I got a bunch of offers for oceanography and engineering scholarships. Chance of a lifetime. Then I met a girl and the president."

"Kennedy?"

John settled back in his recliner and looked off toward the bare beams of the rafters. "I was sitting in the bleachers at a football field," he said, taking a small sip of rum. "I'd just started my second year of college at Rice. I remember it was bright and warm that day, hardly a cloud in the sky. It was a Wednesday afternoon, but the stands were filled to capacity. It wasn't for a football game, though. The president had come to Rice to talk about the moon. I was there because a girl I'd met was going to be there."

John's eye drifted upward as he turned thoughtful again. Then he waved his hand, holding the glass, as if pushing past an invisible web. "Long story short—I married the girl and Kennedy's words on that day prompted me to join the Air Force Reserve. I was determined to be an astronaut."

"An astronaut?" I asked incredulously. This man had been there for the dawn of the space race. It'd only been a year since Shepherd had become the first American in space and suddenly the president was talking about a man on the moon within eight years.

"Then Vietnam came along," John said. "Selection to the astronaut corps was mostly from test pilots, but now combat pilots were getting called on. I graduated and accepted a commission as a second lieutenant."

"Wait," I said. "I thought you retired as an enlisted man."

"I did," John replied, taking another sip from his rum glass. "After flight school, I flew escort missions during Nixon's carpet-bombing campaign. That left a nasty taste in my mouth, the indiscriminate killing of anything and everything. It was barbaric. I resigned my commission and enlisted as a private, finally working my way into special operations. One man, one target. It was about then that I rediscovered sailing. Been a steward of the sea ever since."

Classic French doors behind him opened to a neat patio and tropical garden. The shadows from palm trees on the west side were getting long.

"I need to shove off, John."

We both tossed back the last of our rum and stood.

"Meant to ask you," John said. "You gonna keep the name?"

"*Floridablanca?*" I asked, remembering what Jimmy had once told me years ago about renaming a boat. "She's nearly half a century old, John. No telling where her name might be written. I don't wanna piss off Neptune."

"She fits you, son," John said, leading me to the door. "Hope she takes you as far as she has me, and always brings you back safely."

At the door he stopped. "Have you seen Sara since last week?"

"No. Why?"

"She was asking about you. *Ambrosia's* back over in Bimini. The new shipyard is nearly finished."

"Tell her I said hi," I said, as he reached for the door.

"She told me to have you call her," John said, handing me a card.

I looked down at it. There was only a phone number in block letters.

"That's her personal cell phone number. You should call her. Tomorrow."

I took the card and put it in my pocket, wondering what it was she wanted. "I'll do that," I said, shaking his hand.

"You be careful, son."

An hour later, I was back aboard *Floridablanca*. Under the cover of darkness, I motored the old girl toward the channel going to the commercial docks on Dodge Island. Half a mile from the bustling terminal, I turned into Norris Cut and dropped anchor. I allowed the incoming current to carry *Floridablanca* backward until a blue and red crab trap float neared the stern. There, I engaged the windlass brake and backed down hard.

From my vantage point on the fly bridge, I could look across to the long row of warehouses that lined the south shore of Dodge Island. Built on a concrete sea wall that now covered the entire island, the island rose vertically several floors above the water in many places. My target was the warehouse on the southeast corner, half a mile away.

Switching on my earwig, I inserted it, and adjusted the bone mic around my ear. "Comm check."

"I'm here," Deuce said. "Two blocks west of the warehouse and one block over."

Tony, Chyrel, and Andrew responded, the two men giving me their locations near the warehouse. Chyrel was in the office.

"We can be on you in seconds," Deuce said. "But it'll go much better if we don't have to."

"Roger that," I said, slipping into my thin wetsuit.

I pulled my rebreather on and strapped everything up. The big port lights around the salon were tinted and the cockpit darkened. Within minutes, I was in the water, uncoiling the tether for the antenna that would trail behind me.

Though breaking into a warehouse where dock workers were engaged in illegal activities had its own level of danger, crossing a busy shipping channel at night under water wasn't without risk either. Tony was in a position where he could see me all the way across and warn me of boat traffic. If I had to, I'd simply dive deep and pull my tether down with me.

Following the crab trap line down from the float, I found the bright yellow barrel floating just off the bottom at fifteen feet. It had been one of the ones Armstrong's second submersible pilot had recovered, before blowing the more dangerous ones. At my request, Armstrong had this one placed here by one of his divers. I'd told him that I'd get it over to the warehouse and make sure the report of the discrepancy between the manifest and cargo was sent to the Environmental Protection Agency, so they would inspect the shipment more closely before the *Argosy* sailed. That was *his* plan, not mine.

I was planning to secure the warehouse, by whatever means, then find a way to get the barrel up onto the dock. I intended to locate the documentation saying it was properly disposed of and plant the video evidence to the contrary. And if anyone got in my way, they'd be removed.

"I still think you're nuts doing it this way," Deuce said.

Silently, I unclipped the crab float, attaching the clip to a weight resting by the barrel. I then unclipped the barrel from the anchor and attached my horse-collar tether to it. I checked my compass and began to kick.

There was no way to count kicks. I'd never done it while pulling a buoyed drum of dangerous toxic chemicals. So, I had no reference as to how many kicks it would take to cover the distance. Tony would keep me apprised of my progress on the surface. The miniature floating antenna had an infrared flashing light. It was only enough to be seen using night vision and knowing where to look.

"You weren't there, Deuce," I finally said. "Cramped inside a glass bubble with more than 1000 pounds of water pressing in on every square inch of it."

"Hey, I said I was behind you, didn't I?" Deuce's voice came over the comm. "I just don't agree with the need for vengeance."

"Pay back and vengeance are two different things."

"Um," Andrew's deep voice came over the comm. "Not to get off track, but pay back is sort of the definition of vengeance, isn't it?"

"Not in my book," I said. "It's what's due, not the act of doing it." I grinned inside the mask. "I'm just a tool."

I continued swimming. I had my power fins on, large, rigid blades—shorter than the ones I use for free diving, but much broader. They gave the thighs a hell of a workout.

The listing harness and inflatable buoy attached to the drum kept its weight neutral and the horse-collar yoke slung around my head and shoulder did all the pulling. That left both hands free. I wasn't setting any speed records, but I was moving. I concentrated on a steady, rhythmic pace, to keep my respiration rate down.

I could hear boat traffic. It was coming from everywhere, and from many sources. I trusted that Tony was watching out for me and continued kicking. Halfway across, he warned me of a pleasure boat coming toward me. I dove a few feet deeper and hauled the tether down. Once it passed, I rose again to ten feet.

"You're about 100 yards out," Tony finally said, "and a little off course, due to the current. Turn right about five degrees."

Watching the compass bezel in front of my face, I made the course correction and continued kicking.

The pull of the weight around my shoulder was constant. It felt as if I was carrying 50 pounds. I knew it was only the resistance of the unwieldy barrel trailing behind and below me. If I stopped kicking, the perceived weight would disappear.

"Ten yards," Tony said. "The sea wall is just ahead. You have 30 feet of water there and the ladder is slightly to your left. I don't see anyone near that part of the dock. Three men are just standing around at the opposite end. You can surface there and not be seen by anyone on the dock."

Finally, I stopped kicking. Pulling the horse-collar over my head, I released the barrel, but kept a grip on the twenty-foot heavy dock line tied to it. The barrel sank slowly for a few feet, then settled below me. I rose until just the top of my head was above water and looked around.

The freighter we'd seen, *Argosy*, was tied up at the wharf, just twenty feet away. In front of me was a concrete seawall, rising eight feet straight up out of the water. It had steps sticking out of it that looked like pieces of bent rebar, inserted as the concrete was poured.

I tied the dock line off to one of the steps and shrugged out of the rebreather. Using the bitter end of the dock line, I hung my mask, fins, and rebreather to the ladder as well.

"I'm going up," I said quietly.

"This late, there will only be a few men on duty inside the warehouse," Deuce said. "And you know that you're going to have to fight your way through those guys on the dock as soon as you get to the top of that ladder."

"Counting on it," I said, reaching the top, and peeking over to where the men stood. "With any luck, it'll be the same guys who pushed the barrels off."

I knew I was walking into a fight—something I rarely do. If a fight was brought to me, I'd take it, and react with even greater violence. But intentionally going out of my way to hurt people wasn't what I did.

At least, not very often.

Stepping up the last few rungs, I stood on the wharf and pushed my hair back, wringing the water from it. There were three men standing together around a barrel, smoking. I took a deep breath and strode straight toward them. I didn't run, nor did I meander. My walk had purpose.

"Hey!" one of the men shouted. "Where'd you come from?"

With the element of surprise intact, I continued toward them, my eyes moving from one to the other, assessing each man by nothing more than physical attributes. I was armed, but none of the three dock workers appeared threatening enough to warrant it.

The other two men turned, and seeing me coming toward them, they spread out. The one who'd first spotted me was Latino, another was white, and the third was a big black man with a shaved head and dark black goatee. He was about six feet tall and close to 200 pounds.

"Manuel asked you a question," the bigger man said.

In my experience, the first to speak once everyone was aware of an intruder or threat was usually the leader. Take out the leader and you diminish the will to fight in the others. Still five feet away, I took one more step and planted my right foot, spinning around to my right. My left leg whipped out as I went low, my foot and calf striking the backs of the leader's knees at great speed.

His legs went out from under him with enough force to carry his whole lower body with them. He landed hard on the concrete, the back of his head taking most of the impact.

Without stopping my spin, I came up from the crouch, swinging a long, left hand that clobbered Manuel on the side of his head, where his lower jaw hinged.

The third man turned, as if to run, before Manuel had even fallen to the deck. I went up onto the balls of my feet and caught him in two strides. Running is difficult with your pants sagging off your butt. I snatched the white guy by the collar and pinwheeled him, head first, into a stack of 55-gallon drums. The drums were apparently full and didn't give an inch.

I looked around the dock. Nobody else was in sight and none of the three men were moving.

"Three tangos down," I said, calmly walking toward the door to the shipping office.

The outer door creaked open, revealing a short hallway. There were three doors on the left-hand side, the exterior wall on the right. At the end, the hallway opened into a huge warehouse. The warehouse was completely dark.

The first door was obviously the bathroom. There was no knob, just a rectangular brass plate to push against. I tried the second door and it was locked.

Hearing voices, I approached the third door cautiously. I could hear two men talking. I couldn't tell what was being said, but the tone suggested they were finishing their conversation. I flattened myself against the wall next to the door and waited.

A moment later, the door opened, and light spilled into the hall. Without hesitation, I turned and grabbed the man coming out by the front of his shirt and yanked him through the door. Stepping back as the man started to fall forward, I slung him forcefully into the opposite wall. His face left a deep imprint in the drywall as he crumbled to the deck.

Drawing my Sig, I let the barrel lead the way as I stepped inside and closed the door. I leveled the gun at the middle of a man's fat belly. He was balding, pale, and out of shape. There was nobody else in the room.

"Don't do anything stupid," I said.

The man sat perfectly still, both hands on the desk. But he didn't seem afraid. "And now for the latest on *Dumb Crook News*," he said in a mocking tone. "Ya know, there ain't no money in any of these offices."

"I'm not here for money, Ryan Gower. Now, here's what you need to do. Real slowly, I want you to stand and move out from behind that desk."

The look of surprise on his face was evident. Chyrel had checked his background. Aside from a few traffic tickets and being more than a year behind on his child support payments, he didn't show up on any database listings.

Slowly, Gower stood and side-stepped around the desk. Too late, I noticed a spear gun beside a file cabinet. Gower lunged for it, bringing it up quickly. It was already loaded with a shaft and the bands pulled taut. I didn't want to kill him and fortunately, he fired without aiming. I ducked under the spear easily.

Moving the Sig to my left hand, I came up with a hard, overhand right to Gower's midsection. He gasped, but no air entered his lungs.

I stepped back and roared at him. "What part of *don't do anything stupid* did you find confusing, Gower?"

He went to one knee, his elbow resting on the desk. Before he could collapse, I grabbed his other arm and pulled him down onto his belly, twisting his right arm up behind his back. I grasped his other hand and quickly put a pair of flex cuffs on his wrists.

Leaving him on the deck, I slipped on a pair of latex gloves and went to the file cabinet. I found the shipping manifests in the second drawer, sorted by date. The turd-fondler made it too easy. Everything was right there. I took the shipping manifest listing the number corresponding with the one on the barrel that now floated beside the dock and put it in a manila file.

"On your feet," I ordered him.

The man only groaned. I nudged him forcefully with my foot. "I said get up."

"I can't," he wheezed.

Grabbing his shirt collar, I lifted with all my strength until he was able to get his knees under him. Then I helped him get up onto his feet.

"Out to the dock," I said, opening the door.

After Gower obediently filed past the downed man in the hall, I bent and quickly put flex cuffs on his hands and feet as well. Once we reached the dock, I did the same with the three men there.

"What the hell are you doing?" Gower asked.

"Shut up," I said, spotting a forklift in the shadows.

I forced Gower down on the concrete in the middle of the dock area. There was no way he could stand on his own. It would probably have been a struggle even if his hands were free. Then I hopped into the forklift. The keys were in the ignition.

Starting it, I raised the forks a few inches and drove the lift over to where I'd climbed up, parking with the forks out over the water. It only took a minute to retrieve my gear and tie the dock line to the forks. The other end was tied securely around the barrel, rigged for lifting.

Once I had the barrel on the dock, I got Gower to his feet and duck-walked him over to it. There, I forced him to bend over the barrel and I used two more flex ties to secure his hands and knees to the barrel.

Now he was afraid. He began babbling incoherently. I'm sure thoughts from the movie *Deliverance* were playing through his mind.

I went back to the office and made copies of the documents, then returned with the copies and a stapler. The originals were in a water-tight bag inside my wetsuit. I also dragged the unconscious man from the hallway out onto the dock.

With no remorse at all, I flipped the stapler open and positioned the file on Gower's back. He screamed in pain with each of the four staples. I knew they wouldn't even get halfway through the thick layer of fat on his back, and he was in no danger of blood loss. I'm sure the pain was far less than he let on.

It was nothing compared to the pain of a high-pressure water jet slicing through your eye.

"Make the call," I said into the bone mic, as I returned to the ladder.

Gower screamed for me to let him go.

In minutes, I was in the water. Chyrel called the local office of the Environmental Protection Agency first and reported an emergency situation. She arranged for the call to look as if it came from Gower's own landline.

Knowing that it would take them far longer to respond than the police, she waited until Deuce heard the approaching fire trucks before she called the police to report a burglary in progress at the chemical shipping dock.

Climbing out of the water, I could hear the approaching sirens and see the flashing red and blue lights on the Port Boulevard bridge. "I'm back aboard," I said, stepping through the transom door. "Thanks for the help, everyone."

"You mules head for the barn," Deuce said. "Good job."

"I'll see you guys at the *Anchor* tomorrow," I said, then removed the earwig and turned it off.

Perhaps Armstrong would have wanted it done differently, but the desired result was achieved, the perpetrator made a fool of, and nobody was killed. I rubbed the knuckles of my left hand, where I'd punched Manuel. Mission accomplished.

In the darkness, I watched the flashing lights converge on the warehouse just across the water as I stripped out of my wetsuit. I quickly rinsed everything, opened a deck hatch, and carried it down the ladder into the lazarette, hanging it all to dry.

In the galley, I poured nearly three fingers of rum from a bottle of fifteen-year-old Pusser's, grabbed a card from the breakfast bar, and then carried both through the port hatch and up four steps to the small fly bridge. I parked myself in the captain's chair, flipping the card endways on my knee. Finally, I stretched my legs out, resting my feet on the table.

After opening a cabinet, I withdrew a pair of binoculars and focused over toward the warehouse. Cops were moving cautiously toward the men lying on the deck. One was approaching Gower, still bent over the barrel.

"I shoulda yanked his pants down," I said to Finn, who'd followed me up.

Finn loved *Floridablanca*; like *Salty Dog*, no part of the boat required going up or down a ladder. And access to and from the water was a lot easier. There were wide steps up and down from all parts of the boat, except the forward hatch to the v-berth. There, you had to use a ladder mounted to the back of the berth's hatch. But the forward compartment was also accessible from the master stateroom below the pilothouse. John had told me that the v-berth had once been the crew quarters. Finn's tail thumped the low steel bulkhead around the fly bridge. The whole boat was steel, with wood interior decks and trim. No fiberglass anywhere.

Taking a sip of rum, I turned the card over and over between my fingers. Finally, I set the rum aside and picked up my phone, punched in the numbers and waited. Sara sounded half asleep when she finally answered.

"Hey, it's Jesse. Sorry if I woke you."

CHAPTER TWENTY-TWO

*F*loridablanca eased her way slowly up the canal to the *Rusty Anchor*. The mid-day sun was hot, the air heavy with moisture.

"Is that your plane?" Sara asked, as we passed my little amphibian, *Island Hopper*. Her red wings created a shady roost for a pair of pelicans and a few gulls.

"Yeah," I replied, looking longingly at the plane. I hadn't been up in her in four months. "She's a De Havilland Beaver, built in'53."

"Can we take it up?"

I glanced over at Sara. Her bare feet were propped on the dash, toenails painted red, and she'd pulled her knees up almost to her chest, stretching the fabric of her jeans, which fit her amazingly well, and ended just above shapely, tanned ankles. The loose-fitting, ruffled blue top she wore did little to hide the curves beneath. Her face and what I could see of her feet, shoulders, and chest were lightly tanned and smooth. She wore her blond hair at shoulder length, but had it covered with a blue *Ambrosia* ball cap. All in all, a very attractive package.

"Yeah, but my younger daughter will want to be the one to fly her."

"I feel weird meeting your friends and family," she said. "I hardly know you, and I'm sure I won't know anyone here."

"I get the feeling that you're more than just Captain Hansen's first mate," I said. "And I know your dad's ties to Armstrong are far more than just an employer-employee relationship."

"You'll learn it soon enough," she said. "Suffice it to say, yeah my dad and I sometimes worked very deep for the company."

Spook talk, I thought. Or submersible? I knew nothing of Sara's background, other than what John had told me, and the few details she'd filled in during the trip over from Bimini.

I looked over at her and smiled. "I'm assuming you probably know *who* some of the guests will be, and maybe their backgrounds. I don't know if you'll know any of them personally, though."

I'd left Norris Cut well before dawn, after just a three-hour nap. Sara was waiting at the dock when I arrived back on Bimini an hour after daybreak. We'd talked last night for nearly an hour—a long time for me. She was an easy person to talk to, and before I knew it, I'd invited her to go with me to Rusty's wedding, and she'd accepted.

I'd brought both engines online after the sun had risen, and they pushed the heavy steel boat amazingly well, so long as the helm stayed straight. She wasn't a sportscar, more like a high-speed M-1 Abrams tank. Sara and I ran them again for half of the trip to Marathon. She reminded me to try not to let anyone see *Floridablanca* at high speed. It tended to invite suspicion. The old steel boat covered 200 miles in less than ten hours, without a single hitch. Not bad for an old trawler approaching the half-century mark. Amazingly, she burned less than 200 gallons of fuel.

Seeing no boat moored next to Rusty's old, flat-bottomed barge at the end of the turning basin, I decided to tie up there. Nobody had ever complained of maneuvering room when I docked the *Revenge* there.

Back against the wall and a clear view of all exit points. In this case, just the canal.

Reversing the engine, I toggled the bow thruster to push the bow to port, and even though the rudder was mostly useless in reverse, I spun the wheel to the left to help ease the stern around. As the boat slowed and started to slide sideways, I spun the wheel back to starboard.

Sara had already put the fenders out and now went down the steps to the Portuguese bridge and around the front of the house to the starboard side.

Moving up on the foredeck, she took a big, orange ball fender from its holder and dropped it down off the bow. I hadn't timed things right. Even with the thruster, we'd bump the barge at an angle. Sara moved the fender about halfway back on the curving bow and we gently bounced off the barge.

I spun the wheel to port and put the single diesel in forward for a second to swing the stern in closer, and Sara jumped lightly to the barge deck, two dock lines in hand. I killed the engine and quickly joined her. Together we tied the boat off.

"You'll get the hang of a single screw," Sara said, grinning.

"You knew I was late, didn't you?"

She shrugged. "*Floridablanca* is all steel. Momentum is hard to judge. It's completely dependent on weight. You're just used to fragile, plastic boats, that's all."

"*Floridablanca*?" Rusty said, stepping over onto the barge with his fiancée, Sidney behind him. "I know that name. Gaspar's last ship, and Gasparilla's first."

"Good to see you, Rusty," I said, leaning in for a back-slapping man-hug before turning to Sara. "This is Sara Patrick. Her dad once owned *Floridablanca*." I turned to Sara. "Meet Rusty Thurman and his fiancée, Sidney Carter."

The two women shook hands, then Rusty lifted Sara off her feet with a big bear hug.

"I was beginning to worry you wouldn't make it," Rusty said, putting Sara back down and turning to me. "Then Deuce and Julie arrived a coupla hours ago and said you were on the way. So, you bought another boat, huh?"

"Yeah," I replied. "It just sorta called—"

"She called your name," he finished. "Yeah, I don't think I ever heard ya say that before." He turned to Sara. "This old boy tell you how many boats he already has?"

Sara looked over at me. "You're a boat collector?"

"This is the third one that's over 40 feet," Rusty said, looking Sara over slightly. "And five more under 40."

"That's not true," I said. "I gave one of the Mavericks to Kim."

He looked over and winked his approval. "But it's still there, under your house, ain't it?"

The four of us stepped up to the dock and walked across the yard to the bar. Off to the side, I could see rows of seats and a white altar covered in white flowers.

I'd seen this same setup at the *Rusty Anchor* three times before. Rusty's first marriage to Julie's mother, Juliet, had taken place here. I'd been Rusty's best man. I remember it being a great time, with terrific guests. The other two weddings I'd attended here had been marred by violence. I'd married Alex DuBois in this same place, and she'd been murdered later that night. Deuce had married Julie here, too. But a bomb had been placed in a van at their wedding and a young man Charity was becoming involved with gave his life to save a bunch of others by driving the van into the sea as it exploded.

"Rusty's like a brother to me," I said, letting them walk ahead of us a bit. "Sorry, I forgot to warn you he was a hugger."

"He's sweet," Sara said, walking along beside me.

"There will be a few others here who are like family," I said. Rusty and Sidney had already disappeared inside. I reached for the door and opened it. A rush of cold air and noise nearly knocked us over.

We walked in and waited a moment for our eyes to adjust. The bar was packed and through the back door, I could see that the deck was full as well. But it was cool inside, and all the windows were closed.

Had Rusty finally installed air conditioning?

I spotted my youngest daughter, Kim, and our eyes met across the room. She rose, and then Eve, who was sitting across from Kim with her back to me, turned around.

Both of my daughters came across the floor and I held them in a tight hug for a moment. Then I stepped back and introduced them to Sara. Eve was polite, as always. But I could see something in Kim's eyes.

I returned with them to their table. Nick and Alfredo Maggio rose, and I shook hands with them. The father-and-son law firm had once tried to kill me and my friends. But they were now two of our most trusted legal advisers. It was called *turning* an asset. I introduced Sara and asked where Fred was.

"He's out back playing with some other kids," Nick said. "Our nanny is with them."

Kim pulled me aside. "Is she another sailing bimbo?" The look on her face told me that she was disappointed.

"No," I said. "She's first mate on a 200-foot research vessel, and only a few years younger than me."

"Bull crap, Dad. She's barely older than Eve. I know all about what you've been doing this past year."

I grinned. "Never judge a book by its cover. She'll be forty in two months."

Kim turned and reassessed Sara. "Are you sure?"

"Pretty sure," I replied. "I don't think her dad would lie to me."

"You planning to stay around this time?" she asked. "Eve doesn't know. She thinks you've just been digging around in your garden on the island for the last year."

I took Kim's shoulders in my hands and held her at arm's length. I'd missed her. I missed all of them. But I missed Kim more. She was a lot like me in many ways. "No," I replied. "Charity and I are flying out on Monday."

"Where?"

"California," I said with a smile. "To bring her boat back here."

"*Here*, here?" she asked, excitedly. "At the *Rusty Anchor*?"

I nodded. "But there is one thing."

"What?"

"She, Deuce, and I are starting new jobs, and I may have to go away for a while, every now and then."

"Will it be dangerous?" she asked, her face showing her concern.

"I don't think so." I knew this question was coming. I didn't want to lie to my daughter, but sometimes the truth could be a little scary. So, I told her what I knew to be true. "Probably no more so than cruising around on the ocean. I'll be a scout of sorts. For a company that does a lot of ocean research, oil exploration, environmental concerns, mostly stuff like that."

"And you'll be back on your island the rest of the time?"

"Yes," I replied.

"Did she have anything to do with that decision?" Kim asked, nodding toward Sara.

"Not directly, no. She and I may work together from time to time."

"And if you told me what all y'all are gonna be doing, you'd have to kill me, right?"

"Not that secret," I replied. "Our work will mostly involve ocean research and conservation."

"Cool!" she exclaimed. "Then I'm happy you met her."

Finding Deuce and Julie, I introduced Sara to them and their little boy, Trey, along with Charity, Tony, and Andrew, all sitting together in a corner. They'd all driven down in the big van.

"Yes, I know who they are," she said to my unasked question, as we left the table and headed for the deck. "And their backgrounds."

Finally, we made it outside, where I introduced Sara to Jimmy, Angie, Rufus, and Dink, one of our local guides. A singer I didn't recognize was getting set up on the stage. My eyes searched the yard until I saw my grandson playing with some other kids under the watchful eye of a middle-aged woman.

"There's someone I want you to meet," I told Sara, taking her elbow, and guiding her away from the local fishing report. Normally, I'd have pulled up a chair to hear what Dink thought was going to happen in the coming months.

"Pappy!" Fred cried out, when he saw me approaching.

"Hi," I said, waving a hand to the nanny. "I'm Jesse, Fred's grandfather."

She nodded but watched closely. I knelt on one knee as Fred jumped up to get his arms around my neck. "Mom said you'd be here, Pappy."

With him hanging on tight, I stood and turned to Sara. "Fred, I want you to meet someone. This is my friend Sara."

I smiled at her. "Sara, meet Alfredo Jesiah Maggio, my grandson."

EPILOGUE

The evening Rusty married Sidney, the yard had been packed. Sol, orange and enormous, had dropped below the tree line, its dappled light filtering through the mangroves across the canal and sending beams of golden light to dance across people's faces. All our friends, from Key West to Key Largo, were there and nothing marred the occasion.

Rusty had married the former Playboy bunny that he'd lusted after as a nineteen-year-old. Sidney and Rusty made for quite the couple. Both were outgoing to the point of gregariousness. I sensed that she also shared Rusty's passion for life and for helping others. Rusty was always giving out-of-work fisherman tasks to do around the bar and marina—things that really didn't need to be done, or that needed to be undone from the previous temporary worker.

Chyrel was delayed in arriving, as she was compiling a report, but she made it in time for the nuptials. During the festivities after the ceremony, she told Deuce and me what she'd learned.

Gower had been arrested at the scene and charged with conducting an ongoing toxic waste dumping scheme in violation of international law. Somehow, the EPA had clear shots and video footage of barrels marked with hazardous material stickers being intentionally dumped from *Argosy*, the ship Gower owned. Some of the images were clear enough to identify three other men who were also arrested at the scene. Also discovered were documents showing toxic waste being received, payments for proper disposal being paid, and same-day transfers of large sums of money from Gower's business account to his personal account. The EPA had no idea where the information had come from. Computer technicians determined that the calls and files found on the flash drive all came directly from Gower's own phone and computer.

His attorney, who was meeting with Gower when the arrests took place, was treated for facial injuries, and released from the hospital. He had no comment about what had happened at the warehouse.

The following morning, Kim and I took Sara flying. Kim was already an accomplished pilot and didn't need me, so I gave the co-pilot seat up and rode in the back. As it turned out, Sara was also a pilot, and Kim let her take the yoke for a while. They seemed to get along well.

Charity and I left from Marathon Airport early the following Monday, crossed four time zones and landed in Los Angeles in the early afternoon. The return trip to Marathon took much longer. She and I spent almost three months sailing her antique sloop back to Florida, under sail almost constantly. We stopped in Panama City and Cozumel, laying over for a few days' rest and resupplying the boat, and also enjoyed a couple of quiet anchorages where nobody was around.

Charity was getting better. I think all the time she'd spent alone at *Wind Dancer's* helm had allowed her to come to grips with her past. At least she seemed happier. We talked a lot while we were underway. Charity was a good sounding board for me, and I guess I was for her, too.

When we got *Wind Dancer* safely tucked in at Rusty's marina, I went down to *Floridablanca*, still tied up to the barge, and made a few phone calls.

I talked to Armstrong about the sunken ship I'd seen in the trench. He said that since I'd discovered it, we should wait until a time when I felt comfortable going down in the submersible again. It would be a huge undertaking to penetrate the wreck at that depth, and if there was no treasure aboard, all for naught. Identifying it would be our first step.

After another call, arrangements were made and a week later, I found myself on Andros Island, thinking about the channels I'd dived at Dead Man's Cay and the dolphin I'd met swimming along the edge.

It was still a few days before the summer solstice. I'd aged a quarter year more. The months and years were flying at me now. Henry had helped me get *Salty Dog* ready, and *Floridablanca* secured. I was planning to take a couple of weeks and dive those canyons again. While I was gone, Henry and one of his guides were going to install a new air compressor in *Floridablanca's* lazarette.

On a Monday afternoon in early July, Henry let me borrow his truck and I drove to the dock. I was waiting for a boat to come in before setting sail for the Eleuthera Islands.

Sara had said she would be taking two weeks off while *Ambrosia* was at the new shipyard for maintenance. If the mailboat wasn't running late, I was expecting her to be arriving from Bimini just about any time now.

The End

If you'd like to receive my monthly newsletter for specials, book recommendations, and updates on coming books, please sign up on my website:

WWW.WAYNESTINNETT.COM

Charity Styles Series
Merciless Charity
Ruthless Charity
Reckless Charity
Enduring Charity

Jesse McDermitt Series
Fallen Out
Fallen Palm
Fallen Hunter
Fallen Pride
Fallen Mangrove
Fallen King
Fallen Honor
Fallen Tide
Fallen Angel
Fallen Hero
Rising Storm
Rising Fury
Rising Force

ABOUT THE AUTHOR

Wayne Stinnett is an American novelist and Veteran of the United States Marine Corps. After serving he worked as a deckhand, commercial fisherman, Divemaster, taxi driver, construction manager, and commercial truck driver. He currently lives in the South Carolina Lowcountry on one of the sea islands, with his wife and youngest daughter. They have three other children, four grandchildren, three dogs and a whole flock of parakeets. He's the founder of the Marine Corps League detachment in Greenville, South Carolina, where he met his wife, and rides with the Patriot Guard Riders. He grew up in Melbourne, Florida and has also lived in the fabulous Florida Keys, Andros Island in the Bahamas, Dominica in the Windward Islands, and Cozumel, Mexico.

Wayne began writing in 1988, penning three short stories before setting it aside to deal with life as a new father. He took it up again at the urging of his third wife and youngest daughter, who love to listen to his *sea stories*. Those original short stories formed the basis of his first novel, Fallen Palm. After a year of working on it, he published it in October 2013.

Since then, he's written more novels and now this prequel in the Jesse McDermitt Caribbean Adventure Series and the spinoff Charity Styles Caribbean Thriller Series. These days, he can usually be found in his office above Lady's Island Marina, where he also keeps his boat, working on the next book.

Made in the USA
Coppell, TX
03 July 2020